PRAISE FOR *IGNITE THE SUN*

"How do you ignite the sun in a world teeming with darkness? Howard explores the answer in this lyrical fairy tale that feels at once familiar and fresh. Her innovative world is filled with fascinating characters that will stick in your heart long after you turn the final page. A vivid story, beautifully told."

JOANNA RUTH MEYER, AUTHOR OF *ECHO NORTH, BENEATH THE HAUNTING SEA,* AND *BEYOND THE SHADOWED EARTH*

IGNITE THE SUN

HANNA C. HOWARD

BLINK®

DEDICATION:

To Jerry Howard, whose belief in my writing was unwavering, and without whose encouragement this book would not exist. Miss you always, Dad.

BLINK

Ignite the Sun

Copyright © 2020 by Hanna Hutchinson

Requests for information should be addressed to:
Blink, *3900 Sparks Dr. SE, Grand Rapids, Michigan 49546*

Hardcover ISBN 978-0-310-76973-6
Ebook ISBN 978-0-310-76975-0

Scripture quotations are taken from the Holy Bible, New International Version®, NIV®. Copyright © 1973, 1978, 1984, 2011 by Biblica, Inc.® Used by permission of Zondervan. All rights reserved worldwide. www.Zondervan.com. The "NIV" and "New International Version" are trademarks registered in the United States Patent and Trademark Office by Biblica, Inc.®

Cover direction: Cindy Davis
Interior design: Denise Froehlich

Printed in the United States of America

20 21 22 23 24 / LSC / 10 9 8 7 6 5 4 3 2 1

PART ONE

"Maybe you have to know the darkness before you can appreciate the light."

MADELEINE L'ENGLE, *A RING OF ENDLESS LIGHT*

PROLOGUE

Yarrow, tell me about the sun."

"Eh?" He looked up from his lap, the unwound strings of his fiddle sprawling like insect antennae into the air. "What for?"

"I want to hear about the way things used to be," I said. "Before the Darkness."

The old man returned to stringing the instrument, brows furrowed. I glanced across the small cabin, warm and smoke-scented from the fire in the hearth, to where Linden Hatch, Yarrow's grandson and my best friend since I was six years old, sat mending socks. He waved me on with an enthusiastic nod.

I stood up, forgetting the feathers I had been sorting into piles for arrow fletching, causing them to flutter down around me in a whirling cloud. I laughed and spun away from them, toward Yarrow.

"*Once upon a time, there was something called the sun,*" I prompted, staggering to a halt in front of his rocking chair.

Yarrow pressed his lips together, but his stone-colored eyes had gone warm and sparkling. He scratched his bald head and wrinkled his brow, making his bushy, gray eyebrows look so much like caterpillars I half expected them to crawl right off his face. "You start at Gildenbrook next week, Siria. Don't you think you might do better to go home and get to bed?"

My shoulders sagged. Gildenbrook: stiff lace gowns and tedious lessons for the next six years of my life.

"I wish I could learn to be a gardener instead," I said wistfully. "You and Linden could teach me."

Yarrow snorted. "What would your mother and father do with a gardener for a daughter? They want you to become a proper young lady, not a hired hand."

He didn't point out the obvious: that my tramping around the dark grounds of our manor with him and Linden every day practically made me a hired hand already. I looked around the old cabin: at the scrubbed wooden table, the mismatched curtains I had helped sew, the floor-to-ceiling piles of firewood beside the hearth—more home to me than Nightingale Manor had ever been—and wilted slightly. Yarrow was right: my parents didn't want a gardener for a daughter.

But one more week couldn't hurt.

I leaned forward and put my hands over the wiry strings of Yarrow's fiddle. "Tell me about the way things used to be," I pleaded. "Tell me about how the sun would light up the whole world, and about the trees being green and leafy, and about grass, and blue sky, and sunlight, and birds, and magic—"

His laughter rolled out in an infectious rumble, making his rocking chair lurch backward and sending me toppling sideways. "I think you already know it all, Weedy."

"Not the way you do!"

Linden had abandoned his darning and was now dragging a fat sack of grain across the floor to the woven rug in front of the rocking chair. We plopped back against it and gazed expectantly up at Yarrow, who sighed. Linden grinned at me, messy brown hair everywhere, the dimple winking in his right cheek.

Setting aside his half-strung fiddle, Yarrow reached for his pipe and began packing it. I sniffed to catch the spicy, loamy scent—the smell of stories—and waited with my feet tapping while he went to light a taper in the fireplace and ignite the tobacco.

"Once upon a time," he said, turning back to us as the bowl glowed orange and a trickle of smoke crept from the corner of his mouth, "there was something called the sun."

1

CHAPTER

FOUR YEARS LATER

The day had been dark, even for us. In early evening, the Darkness was denser than tar, and it made the sweeping drive before Gildenbrook School for Girls look like a black river that glistened in the light of many windows as it curved downhill to meet the road. I gazed at it from my tower dormitory. In just a few hours, its current would carry me away, perhaps forever, to the Royal City of Umbraz.

Upon meeting my eyes in the reflection of the darkened window, I released a breath—fogging the chill glass. An impulse seized me quicker than thinking, and in a swift motion of my index finger I swirled a circle over the misty surface and sketched a half dozen lines branching out from it, just like Yarrow had once showed me. A sun.

I stared at it for a moment, surprised and slightly ashamed. Nearly sixteen years old, and I was still drawing mythic totems to ward off the Darkness? I would deserve it if the queen didn't choose me tomorrow.

"A message for you, Miss Nightingale."

I jumped. Smearing my palm across the window,

I whirled to find a slight, plain woman standing in my doorway. She wore the shapeless black tunic issued to all Gildenbrook's servants, as well as the gleaming obsidian band the queen herself had fixed around the upper right arms of every nymph who surrendered to her after the rebellion. The band blocked magic, and without it, this nymph—a naiad, or water nymph, by the look of her lank hair, blue-tinged skin, and enormous aqua eyes—would be able to perform unspeakable horrors with her elemental powers.

She held out an envelope. "It just arrived from Umbraz with the post." Her voice was throaty, heavily accented, and carried the merest trace of mockery within its polite neutrality.

I didn't know her name, but I certainly recognized her. She had been at Gildenbrook almost exactly as long as me, and in the course of those years—for reasons best known to herself—had never once failed to treat me with subtle disdain.

I scowled at her and took the parchment envelope. It was addressed to me in my mother's swirling penmanship, and the wax seal was the sigil of our house: a songbird in flight. The paper was thick, so finely made it looked as if flecks of silver had been worked into the fibers. Which, I reminded myself, they probably had.

Dear Siria,

I'm sorry your father and I could not attend the banquet at Gildenbrook last week. We were simply too busy at court. We will look for you at the Choosing Ball, however, and trust you will conduct yourself in a manner befitting your family's status and rank. Please do honor

to your education and upbringing, and we will be proud
to introduce you to Her Highness, the queen.

Sincerely,

Milla Nightingale

I admired the looping letters that were so much prettier
than my own hurried scrawl, and then my eyes fell upon
the valediction. *Sincerely.*

My heart contracted, and a sudden, fierce spike of
determination shot through me. They would be proud to
introduce me to the queen if I behaved well, my mother
said. *Proud.* I held her letter tight, willing her to sense
across the distance how desperately I wanted that approval.
Perhaps if she knew, she might make it easier.

The nymph servant had departed as soundlessly as she
arrived, so I gently kicked the door shut and drifted back
to the window, scooping another scrap of parchment off my
bed as I did. This note was much shorter, much sloppier,
and scribbled on the back of an old seed inventory list.

Weedy—Come to the cabin after dinner? Y and I
need to talk to you. Urgent. I'll wait by the back step.

—L

Linden Hatch had given me the parchment just before
breakfast, callused hand slipping in and out of mine as
he brushed past me in the entryway. He had worked as a
groundskeeper at Gildenbrook for nearly four years, leaving my parents' employ to follow me shortly after I began
school, and for a while I couldn't imagine a better situation
for him. But things had changed between us, and my childhood best friend was now someone I almost dreaded to see.

Almost.

I rubbed the skin where his hand had brushed mine this morning, wishing I couldn't still feel his touch. Wishing the mere memory of his fingertips against my palm didn't make heat flood my stomach like a swallow of hot tea.

I leaned my forehead against the cold windowpane. "He's a servant," I mumbled. "That hardly qualifies as 'befitting your family's status and rank.'"

The heat from my breath had once more spread fog across the glass, and beneath the smears my fingers had left a few moments ago, I could still make out the faint outline of my sun.

Closing my eyes to rub them, I said, "The Light was dangerous and destructive. Thank Her Highness the queen, the Darkness protects us now."

Our school mantra. It was the first thing I learned when I came to Gildenbrook, and it was what I would remember if I wanted the queen to choose me for her court tomorrow. I could not risk leaving the school at all tonight, much less gamble a trip across the dark moor to visit Linden and Yarrow Ash in their cabin at Nightingale Manor.

I opened my eyes again, and they fell on the dark shape of a carriage far below that had not been on the drive a few moments ago. I squinted down at it, trying to make out the crest on the side, but it was too dark. A messenger for the headmistress, I supposed.

Putting the carriage, my mother, and Linden firmly from my mind, I crossed to my bed, stuffed both notes beneath my pillow, and picked up my lantern. A good step toward success tomorrow would be arriving on time for dinner tonight.

2

CHAPTER

Though I was the only pupil without the queen's favored dark hair, and definitely the only one who spent her childhood trailing after a gardener, I had come a long way in my four years at Gildenbrook. Ridicule and scorn taught me the value of mimicry, and I had finally learned how to walk through a room without drawing stares. The rising popularity of black lace hair cauls helped too, as it allowed me to pile my deep red hair into a netted snood that disguised its odd color, tricking my peers into forgetting my most obvious oddity.

When I joined the queue of rustling skirts and carpet-muffled footsteps leading into the cavernous dining room, though, I realized my usual camouflage habits might be unnecessary. Dinner was typically a restrained affair of idle gossip and practiced elegance; but of course eating on the eve of a Choosing Ball was not *typical*.

Chattering voices echoed off the buttressed stone columns, and everywhere heads bent together, laughter rang out, and girls gestured animatedly from their seats. The teachers had patently given up trying to maintain order. I joined some fellow fourth-years at a long ebony table—set as usual with silver candlesticks, green glass goblets, and pearl-handled silver cutlery—and found my theory was correct: no one even looked up when I sat.

"I would be the perfect choice," a petite girl named Rinna teased the others. Like the rest of us, she was dressed in a tight-bodice, black lace gown, complete with whalebone corset, heeled leather boots, and black pearls. It was an uncomfortable uniform, but Gildenbrook followed the queen in all things, and the queen valued aesthetics far beyond practicality.

"I love dancing," Rinna went on, raising a fawn-colored hand to tick off fingers as she listed. "I adore our queen's taste. And who could possibly enjoy the society of all those young men at court more than me?"

A few girls laughed, but most rolled their eyes and began to argue with her. We had been training for the Choosing Ball our whole time at Gildenbrook, and tomorrow would decide who would move to the Royal City, Umbraz, to adorn the queen's courts—and who would return to the ranks of lesser nobles vying for her favor.

The thought made my fingers tremble around my fork. Though moving to Umbraz would mean leaving Linden and Yarrow forever, gaining the queen's favor would secure the approval of the two people who had always found reasons to withhold it from me: my mother and father.

Someone giggled, and I followed a half dozen turning heads to see a tall figure with tousled, nut-brown hair striding along a far wall, heading for the concealed door to the kitchen. My stomach lurched. Linden Hatch—all lean lines, two-day stubble, and shocking green eyes against dusty-brown skin—threw a quick glance in our direction before pushing aside the tapestry over the door. His homespun shirt and deerskin trousers, which I had watched him sew, were dirt-smeared and sweaty, but somehow that worked decidedly in his favor. It was getting more and more difficult to picture the gangling, scrappy boy I had grown up with whenever I looked at him.

"He's a servant, Tira," I heard another girl say in a lofty voice. "Surely you don't fancy a *servant*."

I looked up in time to see Tira shrug, tossing her perfect sheet of silky black hair. She never wore a netted caul, and I didn't blame her. "So? He's brutally handsome."

No one seemed able to contradict her on this point, and in another minute they were all snorting and laughing into their hands, craning to look at the tapestry behind which Linden had disappeared. Its woven depiction of Queen Iyzabel's conquest of the former king and queen of Terra-Volat had stopped rippling, and Linden did not reappear.

Foolish disappointment stirred in my stomach, and again my mind went to Linden's note. If I didn't go to their cabin, I might never see him or Yarrow again. Yet if I made even one mistake tonight, I could lose my chance at the Choosing Ball.

The half-eaten meat pie on my plate suddenly blurred as tears swam into my eyes. *Dolt*, I thought, blinking them away before anyone noticed. *Get a grip, Siria. You're a Nightingale, and it's blighting well time you acted like one. Gardener's urchins do not get chosen for the queen's court.*

"I saw Nightingale talking to him last week," said Rinna, jolting me back to the present. Her voice had a sly, cruel edge to it, and dread seeped into my stomach. "Maybe she'll arrange a rendezvous for you, Tira."

"H-he worked at our manor when I was young," I stammered, wishing I could melt into my chair and disappear. "Last week, he had news of my parents. That's all."

Rinna looked disappointed, but Tira leaned forward with bright eyes. "Introduce me!" she demanded to panicked whispers of alarm and shock from the others, and I felt my face flame with embarrassment.

"Nightingale's bright as a sunchild," Rinna observed slyly. "Maybe the redhead likes servants too. Though I don't know if even a servant would go for someone so . . . bony."

A good strategy might have been to force a careless laugh, to try and deflect their attention, but mortification had frozen my brain. What was more, Rinna's reference to sunchildren had made it impossible to stop thinking about Linden. So many of the fairy tales Yarrow told us growing up had featured them, and though I now knew his versions had been a far cry from truth, making heroes out of monsters that were now, luckily, extinct, I remembered many afternoons playing Sunchild with Linden out in the dying woods, pretending to light up the world with just our hands.

"Dark night, she's getting redder," Rinna said with a mix of glee and disgust.

Heat radiated from every inch of my skin, and the more I tried to think of something to say, the blanker my mind became. Before this table of raven-haired beauties, whose courtly poise and careless disdain came to them without effort, I suddenly felt as if I belonged to a lesser species. My hair seemed garish atop my head, my arms felt gangling and awkward at my sides, and my clothes, though tailored to my ramrod frame, seemed to sag in all the wrong places, like the upholstery of an old armchair. The thought that had haunted me from the moment I'd arrived at Gildenbrook and seen how different I was from everyone else returned: *It's no wonder my parents find me a disappointment.*

Tears burned hot in my eyes once again, then—

"Watch out!" someone hissed down the table, voice slicing through the laughter. "It's the Head!"

I jerked up alongside everyone else, shoulders back and etiquette recalled as silence enveloped all the tables around us. The clipping heels marched closer, and I heard them stop a few paces behind me. I swallowed and tried not to move.

The headmistress's stern voice rang out, transforming my burning skin to ice: "Miss Nightingale? Come with us, please."

3

CHAPTER

I turned mechanically, as if I were made of rusted metal, and found Gildenbrook's headmistress standing alongside a tall woman in fine black silks. The newcomer had kohl-painted eyes, and they glittered like jewels in deep water as she gazed down at me.

"Today, Nightingale, not next week," the headmistress snapped, and I scrambled out of my chair, clattering a spoon onto the floor in my haste. The headmistress's nostrils flared as she watched it fall, but she merely jerked her chin and set a sharp pace back across the dining hall.

My mind groped for explanations as I trotted after her, and guilt over imaginary crimes turned my hands clammy. Did she somehow know I was considering a visit to Linden and Yarrow's cabin that night? Had someone seen me draw that sun on the window? Perhaps I had talked in my sleep about how much I hated the Darkness, and my roommate overheard . . .

We stopped in the black-and-white-tiled entryway of the school, and the stranger strode forward to face me with a rustle of skirts. "Hello, Miss Nightingale," she said, her voice low, with a slight Umbraz accent. "I am Madam Corbin Pearl, court advisor to Her Majesty, Queen Iyzabel."

I fumbled an awkward curtsy, heart throbbing. "It's an honor to meet you."

She smiled. "What would you say if I told you that you've been selected for something rather special at tomorrow's Choosing Ball? A privilege that gives you greater prominence among the contestants?"

Greater prominence? I gaped at her, uncomprehending. "Me?"

She laughed. "Of course, you!" She reached out and hooked an index finger into the netted caul just above my ear, pulling forward a long strand of auburn hair and laying it over my shoulder. "You'll be among a few girls who are pampered and dressed before the ball, by the queen's own handmaids. How does that sound?"

My whole chest filled with something light and buoyant as a wonderful thought occurred to me, extinguishing my worries: Could my parents have arranged this? Had they, perhaps, hoped I would be chosen so much that they'd decided to give me a little extra help? "That sounds . . . amazing!" I breathed.

"Excellent," said Madam Pearl. "Then please gather anything you might need for the journey and meet me at the top of the drive in five minutes. The Choosing Ball begins at dawn, so we must leave at once."

I blinked at her in shock before turning for the stairs. The rest of the school was leaving at midnight, so I'd believed I had hours to prepare, to plan . . . to say some kind of goodbye to Linden and Yarrow. A shadow fell across the bright feeling in my chest.

Would I ever see them again?

I hurried up four flights of stairs, repressing the thought as well as I could. This was an opportunity I could not waste, could not afford to jeopardize with any trace of regret. When I reached my room, I pulled on my black, fur-lined traveling cloak and quickly stepped to my bed, where I had hidden the two notes beneath my pillow. My mother's went into my pocket, but Linden's I squeezed tight in my fist as I crossed to the low-burning fire in the grate.

I stood for a moment, irresolute and trembling as I fought back a thousand gilded memories of a childhood spent with two people who were not my family. Then I dropped the scrap of parchment onto the glowing embers, where it began to curl and smoke. Biting my lip hard against the urge to cry, I gripped my mother's note inside my pocket and hurried back down the stairs.

These were the fierce, desperate last days of winter, and I shivered as I strode across the flagstones outside into the fathomless dark, lantern lit and boots clacking as I made my way toward the small black coach in the drive. It stood behind a pair of snorting and stamping horses, whose breath looked like clouds of silver in the gloom as each puff caught the lamps' refracted light. A footman held the door open for me as I climbed inside. Madam Pearl was already seated by the far window, smoothing her silk skirts, and we rumbled into motion almost as soon as the door clicked shut behind me.

"Try and get some sleep, if you can," Madam Pearl said, gesturing to the cushioned walls and armrests. "Preparations will take all night, and you don't want to be drowsy when you meet the queen."

I nodded, feeling awkward. Much as I knew she was right, I doubted I would be able to sleep on this journey.

Though would she expect more conversation if I stayed awake? To my relief, Madam Pearl seemed prepared to take her own advice, and as she settled herself back against the plush green brocade, I pushed aside the lace curtain to peer through the window.

Gildenbrook sat on a broad hilltop in the middle of a bleak, boggy landscape that stretched to the north and south like an ocean into the void. According to Yarrow, prior to the Darkness this moor had been a rolling green stretch of countryside that bordered the east bank of the Elderwind River on one side and the western edge of the Forest of Eli on the other. But fifteen years without the sun had reduced it to scrubby heath, and it blurred by like smudged charcoal as we raced alongside it on the road. Gildenbrook was an hour's walk to Nightingale Manor and the split-wood cabin that Linden and Yarrow called home, but I saw their lights glittering in the darkness after only fifteen minutes inside the coach.

My stomach twisted. How long would it be until Linden realized I was not going to meet him on the step? And how much longer until he figured out I had left—perhaps forever—without saying goodbye?

But I could not think about that; not now, when things were going well for the first time since I had arrived at school with my oddball looks, social ignorance, and tendency to befriend servants.

It was only about an hour's journey to Umbraz, but it seemed like no time at all before the first distant glow of green told me we had arrived in the royal city. I had felt the Darkness's potency increase with every clop of the horses' hooves, but that was nothing new. My anxious sensitivity to changes in the Darkness—like an ever-tightening and loosening corset around my ribs—seemed as unique to me as my hair. Even Linden and Yarrow, who hated the Darkness, didn't experience this kind of reaction, and I never mentioned it to my peers for fear of their ridicule. I tried not to think about how challenging it would be to *live* in Umbraz; I would deal with that if and when the time came.

Madam Pearl awoke as the emerald-paned streetlamps grew larger outside the windows. She sat up straight and inhaled deeply through her nose as though she knew Umbraz by smell alone. As the carriage clattered over a narrow canal bridge and onto one of the main thorough-fares, the city grew up out of the darkness, great silver spires gleaming like vertical swords in the mist. Slate rooftops hulked between steeples, bell towers, and chimney stacks, their colors muted in the green glow, and the dark stone streets reflected the lamplight almost as vividly as the water. In fact, the whole city was misty green, as if we traveled beneath the canals instead of above them.

And then as we turned down another street, the inten-sity of the royal city's Darkness seemed to peak, settling over me like a stifling, weighted cloak. I was expecting it, having been there twice before, but I still ground my teeth in frus-tration at its baffling strength. Queen Iyzabel's enchantment began within her seat of power, of course, and from there spread out over the kingdom like spilled ink, but that did nothing to explain why no one else reacted to it like I did. While Madam Pearl checked her reflection in a handheld mirror, I took long, steadying breaths, trying to loosen the pressure constricting like a band around my chest.

"Ah," she said as the carriage began to slow. "Here we are."

I looked up, and the sight was almost enough to make

me forget my discomfort. My parents always left me with a nanny when they came to the Black Castle, and a distant view of its spires was all the experience I had. The sight of the structure through the window now stilled my breath. I had never seen a mountain, but I supposed this castle was on the same scale: bigger than comprehension allowed, stunning, majestic. And unlike every other building I had ever seen, this palace was not made of stone or brick, but of some gleaming black substance, flawless and smooth and rising in organic spikes and spirals toward the black sky as if it had been grown, not built. It reminded me of a raw cluster of crystal I had once held in my hand. There were no windows.

A guard opened the carriage door, and a gust of humid, clammy-cool air swirled inside, a full season warmer than it was even at Gildenbrook. For that effect of the Darkness, at least, I could give thanks: the closer you got to Umbraz, the warmer the temperature became. In winter here, the air was still chilly enough to require a cloak, but in summer it was warm as a subterranean cave. Rumor whispered that temperature and loyalty to the queen were linked, which was why the far north suffered from such dangerous weather. Or so people said. I didn't know anyone who had ever been farther than the southernmost edge of the Battlement Mountains. No one with any sense would dare such a journey.

Madam Pearl gathered up her skirts. "Come along, Miss Nightingale," she said with a smile. "Let us start your transformation."

4

CHAPTER

A butler bowed us through the towering front doors of the castle, and Madam Pearl led me down a wide corridor with a brocade runner rug, its black walls gleaming in the light of many bracketed green candles. I gazed around in wonder. Countless silver-framed paintings—some depicting the queen herself, others scenes of her triumph over the madness of the House of Luminor, and still others sensual images from mythology—seemed to watch us as we passed, the painted eyes gazing back from every angle. The walls themselves were made of the same seamless rock as the exterior, yet they formed hallways as even and precise as the corridors at Gildenbrook.

We turned another corner, and I saw two guards at the end of the passageway, standing before a set of short steps leading to an open door. Nervous anticipation seized me, and I began to tremble. *Surely* my parents would be waiting inside this room, though Madam Pearl's expression gave nothing away. I hurried up the steps, ready to fly into the first proper hug my mother would ever give me—and then I caught sight of the people inside.

Freezing in the doorway, I passed disappointment in the briefest of flashes and landed squarely in dumbfounded shock. My parents were nowhere to be seen. Instead, there were seven girls about my own age. While their skin ranged from the usual pallid gray to ash-tinged coal, each one was as unlike my Gildenbrook classmates as myself: Burning ochre, sandy straw, orange-peach, and vivid, shining gold gleamed on their heads in the lamplight, dazzling in bright variety. Every hair in the room was bold with a pigment artists had been banned from using for fifteen years.

I suddenly felt faint. Never before had I seen another redhead, and only once, many years ago, had I seen a blond. Not even my parents had hair like mine.

Before I could do more than gawk once around the parlor, Madam Pearl buffeted me inside and clapped her hands in an unnecessary call for silence. Several women seated on plush velvet settees rose and walked to her side, their satiny black skirts rustling like the wings of many large birds.

"Girls, choose a seat." Madam Pearl gestured us toward the ring of mirrored vanities lining the deep-green tapestried walls. "You have been selected as probable favorites of the queen and are to be dressed here, with special attention, for the Choosing Ball. I do not need to remind you that there is no greater honor than to be chosen for this court. And now—" She crossed the room and pulled a bell chain hanging from the ceiling. A curtain rippled at the back of the parlor, and a line of she-faun servants trotted through it, each one cradling an enormous, finely made gown in her bare arms as if it were a giant, floppy baby. "Let us begin!"

I still felt dizzy as the women of the court dispersed, each attaching herself to a bright-haired girl. *No greater honor*, Madam Pearl had said. I tried to focus on that assurance instead of my bewilderment as a plump woman made her way toward me. She smiled through lilac lips.

"Hello, my darling," she said in the low, seductive tone people in Umbraz considered fashionable. "Let's get you ready for the ball, shall we?"

I nodded. After this, I told myself, my parents would be eager to see me, to spend time with me, to induct me into the life they had always led apart from me.

It took six long hours, including breaks, for my attendant to declare herself satisfied with my appearance, by which time the other red- and gold-haired girls had undergone similar transformations. They all wore voluminous gowns in vivid shades of green, blue, and purple, and had such blackened eyes and pigmented lips they might have been painted porcelain dolls. I was no exception. My skin—as faded and lifeless as any other sunless Volatian's—looked almost transparent beside my bold eyes and lips; and the turquoise gown I wore, heavy with peacock feathers, silver filigree, and sapphires, was large enough to conceal the whole of my canopy bed at Gildenbrook. My school-issued heeled boots had been swapped for a tight pair of satin slippers. But my hair had taken the most time and attention. It had been woven and braided into an intricate beehive coif atop my head, and I struggled to hold my neck up as the drowsiness Madam Pearl had predicted stole through me. To complete the ensemble, I was to wear a peacock feather mask until I was officially announced.

"You girls will be the only ones wearing colored gowns," my attendant said with an impressive nod, straightening a sapphire. "We want *you* to stand out."

As if we wouldn't already with our unusual hair colors. But if it improved my odds, I thought, I wasn't about to complain.

An interminable period of tweaking and sitting and yawning ensued. I started pinching my thigh through the silk of my dress every few minutes to keep myself awake. Eventually someone whispered that the other guests had arrived but were delayed by myriad precautionary checks because the queen's security was so high. She was worried about mages, one of the attendants said. Mages?

Mages!

The word spread about the room in fearful murmurs, shaking us into wakefulness, and I felt a chill trip down my spine as the sharp voice of Gildenbrook's history mistress rang through my memory.

"Mages are more powerful than any other magical species, girls, and more dangerous. Never forget that it was mages who brainwashed the nymphs into rebellion against our blessed queen fourteen years ago, and their evil influence that threatened our kingdom's very existence. Magic cannot go unchecked. If history teaches you nothing else, let it teach you that."

I shuddered. Mages were not allowed the option of an obsidian band like the nymphs; they were universally slain.

Madam Pearl burst back into our parlor, startling me so badly I nearly fell off my chair. "It is time!"

The women of the court jumped into action, arranging us into a line, then swooping around like excited magpies, tucking a bustle here, polishing an amethyst there. I untied my mask and used it to fan myself. The bulk of so much fabric was stifling, and unsettling thoughts about mages had increased the pressure around my chest. I took a few deep breaths, trying to loosen it.

"Ladies, let us go!" called Madam Pearl.

I shook myself. Soon my parents would see me. Soon they might even see Queen Iyzabel choose me for her court.

I could let nothing distract me.

5

CHAPTER

One torch-lit corridor led into another, and gradually the strains of an orchestra drifted toward us as we walked in our jewel-bright line. I could hear the low murmur of voices, the faint strain of a soprano's aria. A flush of anticipation swept through me.

"Stay together please, girls," called Madam Pearl. "Once we are inside the ballroom, I will lead you onto a platform where you will be announced to the queen."

The corridor opened into a green-tiled foyer where four sets of carved double doors stood open before our long-awaited destination. The floor inside was some combination of silver and glittering black stone, polished to liquid perfection and inlaid in a vast spiraling pattern. The walls were hung with plum velvet, and green light fell over everything—though there were so many people crowding the doors, they obscured most of the details. And the people were distracting enough in their own right. All of them were staggeringly beautiful, and in spite of my finery, I felt clownish and plain among them.

We progressed into the teeming crowd, Madam Pearl leading our line at a determined pace, and as we did, another wave of heat rippled through me. It was more powerful than the first time, and I wished I could take off my mask and fan myself again. Sweat trickled down my back.

All around, masked faces turned to watch us file into the ballroom, and now I could see the whole room— buttressed and columned and ringed by a mezzanine level packed to brimming. Dapper young men in tail coats and top hats flashed smiles at us as we passed, and dark-haired girls raised sculpted eyebrows. A tall, tousle-haired youth slipped through the crowd just ahead of me—

My heart cartwheeled, and I wrenched my neck to try and catch a better look. Surely that wasn't . . . ?

I wanted to kick myself for even thinking it. Of course it wasn't Linden, and in any case, he was the absolute *last* person I needed to be thinking about.

A bead of sweat slipped out from my hair and down the back of my neck, and I swatted at it as our procession wound toward a raised platform. It was an island amid the gleaming sea of black ball gowns, and it faced a dais upon which sat a woman I had heard about my entire life but never seen before.

As I looked up at her, I forgot everything else.

Queen Iyzabel was tall, and paler than anyone else in the ballroom, with skin like misty quartz. Her figure was a perfect hourglass, and her raven hair was piled high atop her head, woven with green jewels that glinted like dragon scales in the lamplight. She was beautiful—by far the most beautiful woman I had ever seen—and her black gown swirled and eddied about her like a garment of living shadows. Like her eyelids, her lips had been painted emerald green, and they were curved into a slight smile. Beside her was a small table, on which she rested one arm, curled loosely around a gleaming black urn.

Her presence was mysterious, with an aura of seductive power, and for the first time I truly understood why my parents preferred to spend their time in her court rather than at home with me. I had come here out of a desire to please them, but as I looked at the queen, I felt an equal, blooming yearning to please *her.*

Someone nudged me in the back, and I realized I had stopped walking. Our procession was now filing up a set of short wooden steps onto the platform, and I followed the golden-haired girl ahead of me, wondering whether she was sweating as much as I was. I couldn't remember ever being so hot in my life. But then, neither could I remember ever being so excited.

On the dais opposite us, Queen Iyzabel rose and raised her arms to the crowd. The orchestra and opera singer fell silent, and a hush rippled through the ballroom until the silence echoed. She smiled brilliantly. I looked out over the crowd—and my excitement tripled. My parents were there, just *there*, two rows back from the platform, close enough I could see the silver paisley embroidery on my father's black tail coat. They were not looking at me yet, but I knew they would be soon. I clenched my fists to stop them from trembling.

"My guests." The queen's voice was the low purr of a cat. "Thank you for coming to this Choosing Ball. To all who have traveled great distances across my kingdom, I thank you for being here. And to you," she said, turning to us on the platform, "I thank you most of all, my radiant creatures, for being so cooperative. You are my guests of honor."

I beamed, anticipating my parents' pride, but then had to bite my lip as another wave of heat—much more intense than the two before—crashed through me from scalp to toes. I swayed as it passed, and realized with a jolt of panic that my vision had gone slightly blurry. Was my corset too tight? I spaced my feet farther apart and jiggled my knees, trying to steady myself. It would be disastrous to faint.

"Hear me, my court, my schools, my subjects!" Queen Iyzabel cried, her voice strong and commanding as it rang among the buttresses of the vaulted ceiling. "Nearly six-teen years ago, I overthrew the Light-loving government of Luminor and established the Darkness. I blotted out that destructive inferno in the sky that parched and burned the land, threatening all life."

A murmur of approval ran through the crowd. With a rush of shame I remembered the sun I had sketched on my window mere hours before. From now on, I resolved, I would love the Darkness with all my heart. I would never daydream about Light again.

"And though it nearly cost me my life," the queen con-tinued, "I purged this kingdom of the creatures that loved the accursed sun most: those light-haired, spotted beasts known as sunchildren."

I nodded along with everyone else, feeling suddenly that I had been deeply remiss to let Yarrow talk about sunchildren as if they were good, or even harmless. Sunchildren—fire nymphs, with their flamelike hair and leopard-spotted skin—were widely acknowledged to be sec-ond only to mages as the embodiment of evil. But in typical contrary fashion, *he* persisted in making them the heroes of his fairy tales. I ought to have corrected him.

"But I did not succeed entirely," the queen said, and the already quiet ballroom became perfectly still. "Though few knew it, I failed to eliminate the last sunchild born in

Terra-Volat, and she was lost to me among other infants, not to come into her barbaric powers until the first moment of her sixteenth birthday, like all her wretched kind."

Her dark eyes blazed, and I again felt that intense desire to serve her, but stronger this time: I was almost giddy with longing to help her find this lost sunchild. And though the desire competed with the bizarre heat still passing in waves through my body, it also made me care less about the sweat coursing down my back. If Iyzabel chose me to serve her, my own needs wouldn't matter. I would be the luckiest girl in Terra-Volat. And my parents would love me. I didn't even mind the Darkness anymore.

"But my loyal subjects," Queen Iyzabel continued in a ringing voice, "I have taken great pains to isolate her identity, and I can assure you that she is here today! I therefore give you the evening's entertainment!"

I was so consumed by my hope that when, breast heaving, Queen Iyzabel flung a forefinger toward our platform, I knew a moment of searing joy. I was sure she was pointing at me, choosing *me*. My longing to join her court was all-encompassing, delirious . . . But the heat inside me was growing profound too. My mind tumbled in the wake of reality, and as I slowly understood the queen was pointing in accusation, the heat surged alarmingly. Had I caught fire? I looked down to see if my skirt was flaming.

Flaming?

No, it wasn't my skirt. It was my insides.

They were being boiled.

Am I dying?

My head felt very dim. I tore off my mask and fanned myself again. A moment too late, I realized the queen would surely disapprove, and I tried, shaking, to retie it. But my fingers were clumsy, and the mask slipped and landed at my feet with a soft *flump*.

Queen Iyzabel now gazed directly at me, a strange smile on her face. "The fugitive sunchild," she said, "was born sixteen years ago today, at the precise moment of dawn. The moment approaches. Today she attains her birthright. Today is the day she transforms, and today I shall know at last who among these girls is a wolf in sheep's clothing." She paused, and her next sentence came out in an icy whisper that held us all in frozen thrall. "Today I shall know at last who is the beast I must kill to ensure the everlasting glory of this kingdom of Darkness."

My parents had finally turned to face me. But far from looking proud or adoring, or even worried, their expressions showed revulsion and mortification. It was this sight, more than the heat or the faintness or the notion I might be in danger, that forced the breath from me, and with it a small, wounded sound. My mother heard it and averted her eyes.

It was as if I had been punctured, and I could no longer keep enough air in my lungs to hold myself upright. I slumped, bracing my hands on my thighs. Then a tidal wave of heat seemed to rise, almost visibly, above me.

Beyond it, I could just see Queen Iyzabel, eyes riveted to my face in hungry triumph.

Then the tower of heat broke over me in a blistering swell. I forgot I was on a stage before my queen and my parents and an entire ballroom. I forgot everything except the fire and the burning.

I fell forward onto the hard platform with a crash.

And then—

It was unendurably bright. An orb of roaring fire, its

light all-consuming and radiating heat, raged over me, filling me up until my whole being had caught flame. I writhed against it, but it poured through every inch of my body—from my toenails to the ends of my hair—burning away all that I knew and replacing it with light. I tried to cry out, but when I opened my mouth, I inhaled flame. The heat swelled to an impossible pitch—I couldn't endure, wouldn't survive—and then, quite suddenly, it was gone.

Somewhere nearby, someone screamed.

6

CHAPTER

I was on my hands and knees, blinking down at the wooden platform.

My hair had sprung free of its coif, and I could feel it tumbling down my back and over my shoulders, its weight strangely hot through the silk of my gown. My fingers were splayed, and I gazed at them in confusion. Both they and my arms—indeed, all of the skin that was visible to me— were covered in a multitude of tiny brown dots, as if I had broken out in some kind of rash.

The feverish heat had entirely left me, and I felt so strong and well by comparison that I wondered if I had entered a new kind of illusion. I raised my head and found myself looking directly into a stream of blinding, golden light, flooding in from the ceiling through the labyrinth of ornate buttresses. Dust motes swirled through its beam like a cloud of insects. The light fell directly upon me, deliciously warm, and I realized with amazement that the terrible pressure around my chest had gone. I squinted, searching higher for the source.

Another scream ripped through the ballroom then, sounding both real and near, and the light vanished. Like a band springing back into place, the pressure around my chest returned.

I blinked and sat up as real flames—blindingly bright, as tall as a man—exploded into being in front of me. The fire shot around the platform's perimeter, encasing it like a great fence, and the other girls' screams mingled with more distant cries from the crowd. I fell backward onto my hands, and my heart seemed to fail.

A tall, masked person had hurled himself through the flames over the front of the stage and leapt directly at me. Before I could so much as cry out, his shoulder slammed into my chest and I was flat on my back beneath him, a blinding pain in my head. Then, with a crushing grip, the stranger pinned me to him and rolled sideways, through the raging fire and over the edge of the platform.

For a moment, we were in free fall; then, with a thump that knocked the air from my lungs, we landed in a smoking tangle on the floor, half-covered by the skirted lip of the stage. The ballroom was in a state of advanced mayhem, but Queen Iyzabel's voice screamed above the din: "DO NOT LET HER ESCAPE!"

The stranger scrambled to his knees, yanked off one of the two black cloaks he wore, and flung it around my head and shoulders even as I struggled to rise. Hoodless now, his wild, dark hair stood up in all directions.

"*Lind—*"

Linden Hatch clapped a hand over my mouth and hauled me up, both of us now camouflaged amid the churning sea of black. He slipped a mask over my face with a deft movement, then tugged his hood back up. Behind his own mask, his green eyes were blazing, and I could see in them all I needed to know: We had to get out, quickly.

But how had he known? I thought of his note: *Y and I need to talk to you. Urgent.* Had this been what he meant?

Over the clamor, Iyzabel's voice rang out, somehow even louder than before: "FIND HER—FIND HER! STOP HER! KILL HER!"

Without speaking, Linden took my hand and pulled me into the crowd. I tripped after him, but a shrill cry came from behind and I glanced back. Several tall, armored figures had barreled onto the burning platform, swords glinting in their hands as they prepared to round up the other girls. Icy fear shot through me: in a moment they would know I was the one who escaped. But what would they do to the remaining girls? Kill them?

I tried to pull my hand out of Linden's, but he tightened his grip, and then my eyes snagged somewhere else. Two familiar figures had appeared through a gap in the crowd, standing with their heads together.

My parents!

A mad desire to go to them seized me, and once again, I tried to pull free of Linden's grasp.

"Siria," he hissed, jerking me hard toward him, "you're going to get us both killed!"

At that moment, my mother lifted her head and looked straight at me, as if an invisible thread had linked us. Her dark eyes widened as they darted over my mouth and chin—likely only partially shadowed below the mask and hood—and I saw her throw her head back and shout, "There!" Her finger flew up to point at me.

No one took any notice of her, but I felt as if I had fallen headfirst into an abyss. I couldn't breathe for the searing in my throat, and my stomach churned. Linden's hand felt hard and cold around mine.

My mother had pointed at me. She knew what they would do, and she had still tried to turn me in.

She wanted me to die.

Did it matter what happened next?

A resounding bang sounded ahead of us, and the floor shuddered. All four sets of the thick, ebony ballroom doors had slammed shut in unison. I looked around and saw, on the dais at the back of the ballroom, the queen on her feet with her hands raised above her head, teeth bared. At a flick of her wrist, her eyes glowed silver and a trail of flame retreated from one of the tapestries and shot along the wall toward the doors.

Linden jerked me into a flat sprint toward the blocked exits. I could see his free hand raised, palm extended toward one of the closed wooden doors, which suddenly gave a thunderous groan and opened a crack, widening until two people could just pass through. I stared at it, uncomprehending. Gnarled roots had grown out of its base, puncturing the floor tiles with deafening snaps as they anchored it open.

We pelted into the corridor beyond as the door slammed shut again with a cracking of tree roots and tile, cutting off the queen's terrible, hair-raising shriek—the hunting cry of a predatory beast.

7

CHAPTER

The corridor was not empty.

Eight guards—two for each door—charged toward us, and Linden bent to scoop up one of the broken roots that had skidded across the floor. I watched in dizzy, stupefied shock as a pattern of deep brown whorls, like tree bark, flashed over the surface of his pallid, taupe skin, and his eyes glowed bright and iridescent green as if lit from inside. The root in his hands thrashed and expanded at incredible speed, and he threw it at the nearest guard, who gave a shout and tried to swat it away. The root twisted around the man like a rope and shot after the other seven before their swords were halfway unsheathed.

I could not understand. It was impossible.

Linden could *not* be a nymph.

For the third time, I tried to wrench out of his grasp, and this time I succeeded.

He whirled around. "Siria, listen—"

I shook my head frantically, lurching away. "You're a wood nymph? An elf! All this time, and you never told—"

"Later!" he insisted, snatching for my hand again.

I darted out of his reach, hysteria rising. "I can't go with a nymph!"

A hard determination came into his eyes—now back to normal, along with his skin—and he closed the distance between us in two strides. "*You* are a nymph, Siria," he said harshly. "And when those doors open, the people on the other side will kill you."

He pulled me on, and I stumbled after him, his words banging off the walls of my mind and utterly failing to gain traction. Perhaps I am dreaming, I thought hopefully. But dreams did not usually feel this physical . . .

"We have to get to the kitchens," Linden grunted. "Don't stop running!"

Down a sloping hall we ran, around several corners, up a short flight of wooden steps. A vaulted kitchen of rough stone opened before us, warm and noisy and full of Iyzabel's servants. Satyrs, she-fauns, and nymphs of all kinds flattened themselves against the walls as we burst in.

All kinds except one.

Linden pulled me to the back door and threw himself against it, but it didn't open. "This should be unlocked!" he bellowed, whirling to face the wide-eyed servants. "Quickly—I need the key!"

Once standing still, I could feel myself trembling, starting to go cold with shock.

"We were told . . ." began one of the satyrs, "ah, to keep all doors locked, sir." He and all the rest were ogling me, mouths hanging wide. "Queen's orders. I'm sorry."

"Damn the queen to the blighted Chasm!" bellowed Linden, and then he closed his eyes and took a breath. His eyes glowed when he opened them, and the dark brown lines swirled across his skin again for a fleeting instant. "If

Iyzabel kills her, your hope for freedom dies too." Shouting echoed down the corridor beyond the kitchen door. "Please. She's the sunchild."

The entire kitchen became motionless, staring at us, and I felt outside my own body as Linden's words penetrated the fog in my mind. I croaked, "Sunchild," as if saying the word would compel it to make more sense, and then raised one of my newly speckled arms to inspect it. Several pairs of eyes followed the movement.

I suddenly remembered what Iyzabel had cried to the ballroom just before I collapsed: *Today is the day she transforms, and today I shall know at last who among these girls is a wolf in sheep's clothing.*

One of the nymphs ran forward to Linden, holding out something small and shining in her palm. Linden snatched the key and jammed it into the lock.

"Thank you!" he said, tossing it back to her as he pulled me into the dark street outside.

The air hit me in a blast, far colder than it had been when I'd arrived in Umbraz. Gasping, I hugged my cloak tight and trotted after him. Shouting rose above the ordinary bustle of the city as somewhere nearby the chaos in the castle began to spill into the cobbled streets.

"Linden, I don't—"

A clatter of wheels and hooves drowned out my voice. A black, one-horse brougham careened around a bend in the road toward us, a man in city clothes on the driver's bench. I flinched back, but Linden jumped toward it. "Come on!"

The driver jerked so sharply on the reins that the horse nearly stumbled. The carriage skidded to a halt, and someone inside flung open the door. Linden and I clambered into a plush, candlelit cabin where two other people were already seated: Yarrow, looking drawn and tense in his usual rough tunic and trousers, and a woman with stringy brown hair and enormous aqua blue eyes, wearing a bizarre patchwork dress composed of what appeared to be strips of seaweed.

It was unmistakably the naiad servant from Gildenbrook. The one who hated me.

"You?" I gasped, but Yarrow held up a hand for silence, his gray, lined face distant with concentration as the carriage jerked and rumbled forward again. He muttered something, and my eyes caught on the oblong, flattish disc in the palm of his hand, a single rune carved into its center, glowing all over with silver light.

A Runepiece.

The traditional weapon of the mages.

8

CHAPTER

Blackness crowded the edges of my vision. Before I knew what I was doing, I was fumbling with the latch on the carriage door, trying to get out. Someone hauled me back, prying my fingers loose, and I shrieked with terror, flinging out my elbows and lurching for the window instead. I heard Linden grunt as my elbow connected with his chest, but his arms were unyielding as they pulled me down again.

Everything, everyone I knew and trusted and loved. A lie.

I sagged onto the seat in listless despair. Where could I go? The whole of Umbraz would be searching for me now, to help Queen Iyzabel kill me. Even my own parents.

Maybe I deserved it.

"Siria, look at me."

Yarrow's voice. Something in his composure faltered as I met his eyes, and for a fleeting moment I saw such a range of emotions on his weathered old face that I almost expected him to start crying. My impulse was to trust him, to throw myself into his familiar care and protection, but rationality told me I couldn't; that as a mage, he was the most danger-ous person I had ever met. Not to mention a liar.

"It's still me," he said, as though reading my mind. Maybe mages *could* read minds. "I haven't changed. We wanted to tell you last night, but they came for you early. I should have expected something like that, but we were so focused on how to get you away from Gildenbrook that I didn't stop to think about what *she'd* be planning."

I stared at him for a long, incredulous moment. "*Last night?*" I gave a wild laugh. "I've known you a decade! And you've been a mage the entire time?" I looked at Linden, sitting across from me. "And you, a wood nymph?"

They both started to answer, but I squeezed my eyes shut and shook my head to silence them. Furious though I was at their deception, my anger was like a mild windstorm in the face of a rising hurricane.

Slowly, carefully, I lifted one dappled arm and held it, trembling, before Yarrow's bespectacled face. In the dim carriage lamplight, the brown dots were less pronounced than before, but still quite visible.

"What is this?" I said in a low voice.

He was silent a long moment, during which the clacking of the carriage wheels grew louder. Then he said quietly, "What do you think it is?"

I made a jerky gesture. "A disease? The pox? Some freakish enchantment?"

"It's not a disease," he said, still in that quiet voice. "You might call it an enchantment, but no one cast it."

Dread was spinning up a maelstrom inside me, throwing around words I had heard in the ballroom: *transformation, birthright, sunchild.* Deep down, I knew the truth already—had, perhaps, known it since I fell to my knees on that platform—but I'd be damned if I accepted it without a fight.

"Fix me," I said. "If you're a mage, use your thrice-blighted magic to fix me."

A sad, twisted smile lifted his leathery cheek. "There's nothing to fix, my girl. This is who you are. Who you've always been."

I winced at the way his words echoed what he'd just said about himself. "Stop it. Those monsters are extinct. I am *not* one of them."

But Yarrow was shaking his head. He wore a look of mingled doom and determination. "We've suspected, Linden and Merrall and I. Suspected for many years. Your hair and age were why we came to you, of course, but then your features, your natural fear of the dark, your obsession with the sun . . . We didn't know, however—couldn't know—for certain until today. And now, Siria, I'm afraid there is no doubting exactly who and what you are."

My head throbbed like someone was knocking on the inside of my skull. Would the betrayal never end?

"You *knew* this would happen?"

"Suspected," Linden murmured.

I rounded on him. "And you just packed that away with all your other secrets, did you? Just decided it was better for simple little Siria not to know, because why should she have the truth about anyone, including herself?"

"No, Siria, that's not—"

"What else have you lied about?" I yelled, interrupting him. "Have you ever told me a single true thing?"

Linden's face was a study in devastation; but before he could reply, the naiad sitting beside him, who I had all but forgotten, slid forward on the carriage seat, seized my chin in firm, spindly fingers, and jerked my face around.

"It is time for you to get over yourself, Princess," she said, her throaty voice thick with an Elderling accent. "You are a spoiled brat, and these two men have put their lives at great risk on your account. I suggest you stop whining and start trying to earn the unmerited titles you bear."

She released me with a look of contempt, and I fell back into my seat, stunned. Yarrow and Linden had both half risen from their seats, but now sank slowly down again, looking tense.

"Siria, I haven't introduced you to Merrall yet," said Yarrow awkwardly. "Though I believe you've met at Gildenbrook. She's a naiad from the Elder Bay, and she's been watching out for you these last years, ready to act should any unforeseen situation present itself."

"Such as this one," said the naiad in an acid voice.

A long and profound silence stretched out between us all, while the noise on the streets grew louder, screams mixing with the general uproar. The carriage swayed as it picked up speed.

After what felt like a long time, Linden said, very quietly, "Without knowing who you were, the truth about us would only have endangered you. But we did try to tell you."

I looked up at him, still angry, but also embarrassed and slightly ashamed of myself. Stronger than all these emotions, though, and growing so powerful I knew it would soon eclipse them, was my horror at the increasingly undeniable truth of what I was.

"Many times, over the years," said Yarrow.

"But we couldn't," Linden said, earnest and irritatingly handsome in a fashionable black suit that contrasted with his wild hair and stubbly jawline. "Literally *couldn't* tell you."

I had vague recollections of moments in the past when Yarrow or Linden would seem to choke on their words, or physically struggle to speak. I looked between them with dawning comprehension. "You mean you *actually* couldn't tell me?"

"Iyzabel cursed the knowledge sometime around your fifth birthday. Until today, it's been physically impossible to communicate to anyone that they're a sunchild."

I closed my eyes at the word. It was the first time anyone had spoken it since I entered the carriage. Almost against my will, I heard myself asking the question I most dreaded the answer to: "How can you be sure that's what I am?"

Something small and heavy landed in my lap, and my eyes flew open. Merrall was sitting back in her seat, and I realized she had tossed an ivory-handled mirror face-down onto the turquoise silk of my skirt.

I gazed for a moment into her pitiless face, and then, fingers trembling, grasped the handle and lifted the mirror.

9

CHAPTER

At first, I could only gape from the face in the glass to the hands gripping its ivory frame, because I recognized neither as my own.

My translucent, light-starved skin had transformed. Like my arms, my face was now a ruddy sand color, and covered almost entirely in the same tiny brown dots, as though someone had stippled every inch of my skin with a miniscule paintbrush. Some of the dots were dark as tree bark, some light as toffee, some like pinpricks and some like ink blots, but they were everywhere: a few even dusted my lips and eyelids. My eyes, so recently an ordinary hazel, had become vivid and strange, mingling sea green with burnished bronze and seeming to burn in the lamplight.

But that wasn't all.

If my auburn hair had been unusual against the brown and black shades of my classmates, it was nothing to what it had become. I now understood why the intricate coiffure had not held. My long, straight locks had metamorphosed into flickering waves that spiraled tightly in some places and fell loose in others, all mingling a thousand shades of red, copper, and gold, and giving the impression that the strands were on fire. I had never seen anything so vivid.

I raised a shaking hand and watched it make contact with the wild strands: they felt soft, and also slightly coarse. My parents had always lamented my hair, so different from their own. I remembered my mother's face in the ballroom, twisted with horror at the sight of me.

Was this why?

Hair like fire. Skin like a leopard. Childhood fairy tale and adolescent nightmare come to life.

Sunchild.

I replaced the mirror in my lap and swallowed the rising mound in my throat.

"You're *not* a monster, Siria," said Linden quietly, and I squeezed my eyes shut again. "And neither am I. The things you learned about magic at Gildenbrook are distortions of the truth, not reality."

"And those dots are called freckles," said Yarrow. "Caused by the sun."

The sun. I almost wanted to laugh. But I knew if I did, I would cry, and then I would probably never be able to stop. I had freckles from a sun I had never even seen, and my parents wanted me dead. Because . . . because I was a sunchild?

All the fight drained out of me. "*The Light was dangerous and destructive*," I recited dully. "*Thank Her Highness the queen, the Darkness protects us now.*"

"And who do you think made that up?" Yarrow said sharply. "Who do you think spread all the horror stories about nymphs and mages, and especially sunchildren?"

I gazed at his face, which swayed with the motion of the coach, but did not answer.

"The Witch Queen who fears them above all else, Siria.

The woman who has hunted them all her life because they're a threat to her magic and her Darkness."

"But sunchildren are extinct," I said wearily. "I can't be one—she killed them all."

"Not all," said Yarrow, and there was a deeper, quieter anger in his voice than I had ever heard before. "Though she damn near succeeded at complete genocide. Siria, why do you think Iyzabel knew you would change today? How do you think she knew the exact date and moment of your birth?"

"Today isn't my birthday," I protested, and with the words came one last feeble thread of hope. Even if what Yarrow said was possible, I knew my parents were far too loyal to Iyzabel to keep a sunchild baby from her. And my birthday wasn't for another two weeks. I sat up a little straighter. "Yarrow, today *isn't* my birthday."

"But it is," Yarrow said. "We know that for certain now. No other girl changed at the moment you did. The Witch Queen held her ball at the pinpoint of dawn—the exact time of your birth sixteen years ago today—in order to see you transform."

I stared hard into Yarrow's face. "How do *you* know?"

His nostrils flared as he sucked in a breath, but his eyes did not leave mine. "Because," he said, "sixteen years ago today, this kingdom celebrated the birth of a special sunchild. And that child escaped the witch's bloody purge because she had parents powerful and clever enough to protect her."

I gaped at Yarrow, my brain floundering like a fish on land. My parents had protected me? I felt a burst of joy—was that the reason they had always been so distant?—but it was quickly extinguished by the memory now burned into my mind, of my mother pointing me out in the ballroom. "Why? Why would they do that? They never really wanted me in the first place." I heard the words fall off my tongue as though someone else had spoken them, yet I knew with sudden certainty they were true.

Yarrow's expression became a messy tangle of sorrow, anger, and determination. Across from me, Linden made a sudden movement, as though he wanted to reach out for me. Merrall sat with her arms and legs tightly folded, chewing on her lip.

"Phipps and Milla Nightingale's greatest secret," said Yarrow, "is that they have no children. They stole you from an orphanage in Umbraz and then spent the next fifteen years weaving elaborate lies to make everyone believe you were theirs. Iyzabel was placing great public stock in the raising of daughters at that time, already starting to look for you, and Phipps came to believe a baby girl would improve their standing at court. But Milla was terrified of the risks associated with pregnancy and childbirth."

I paused to take this in. I knew I was missing something bigger, but all I could think of was the distant, aloof way my parents had treated me my whole life. "Why did they lose interest in me? Did I do something wrong?"

He let out a breath that was half sigh, half groan. "I think they became afraid of how different you were, Weedy. Of your strange hair, your anxiety about the dark, your interest in the past. Whether they ever heard rumors of Iyzabel's search, I don't know, but I think in their very secret hearts they feared what you might be. To their slim credit, they never turned you in—though Iyzabel was keeping a close eye on you anyway."

My head was starting to feel wooly, and the tension

from my creased brow was causing a new ache behind my forehead. It therefore took much longer than it should have for me to fully comprehend Yarrow's disclosure. I dug my fingernails into the velvet-upholstered seat beneath me.

"Then who . . . ?" I began, not sure how to finish the sentence.

"The only sunchild left in Terra-Volat, Weedy," said Yarrow, his voice growing stronger as he looked at me with fierce pride, "is not the child of two spineless courtiers who never deserved her. She is—*you* are—the youngest daughter of King Auben and Queen Elysia of Luminor."

The carriage was turning to something insubstantial beneath me—cotton, perhaps, or mist. Luminor? Luminor was the kingdom of madness, of sun worship. How could my parents be the rulers Queen Iyzabel defeated to bring about peace in the kingdom?

But Iyzabel had brought the Darkness, which I had dreaded my entire life. Whose word could I believe? Iyzabel's or Yarrow's? Until now, I would never have hesitated to say Yarrow, but this was the fourth time in under an hour that I had uncovered knowledge, long kept secret *by Yarrow*, with the power to change my entire life.

Yet hadn't I just heard Iyzabel's voice calling for my death in her ballroom? It was hard to trust a person while they screamed for your blood.

And King Auben and Queen Elysia had been dead for fifteen years. If they were really my parents, that meant I would never be loved by a mother or a father in the way I had always dreamed of . . .

"The reason I have watched over you at Gildenbrook these last four years," said Merrall unexpectedly from across the carriage, "is not because you are some fine pet for the

Imposter Queen. It is because you are the last sunchild in Terra-Volat, and the daughter of *my* king and queen, the true rulers of this kingdom."

"Do you see now?" Linden leaned toward me. "Do you understand why we wanted to take you away last night? Iyzabel wants you dead more than she's ever wanted anything before."

"And," the naiad added, "the Witch Queen has never yet failed to get something she wants."

I stared between the three of them for a long moment, all my anger and resentment building up like bracken clogging a bend in a river. Finally, it broke.

"*Why didn't you just tell me?*" I bellowed, flinging the ivory mirror at Yarrow with all my strength. He flinched, but let it hit him in the shoulder. "All this information that changes everything I always thought was true—why didn't you just *tell* me?"

"Siria, we already explained," began Linden. "Iyzabel cursed the—"

I ripped off my mask and hurled that at Linden, though it only fluttered uselessly to the carriage floor. "So she cursed it!" I shouted. "Are you trying to tell me that in ten years you couldn't think of a single way to communicate any of this, just because she cursed one Chasm-forsaken piece of the puzzle?"

"Without endangering you, ourselves, and the entire mission?" Linden shot back, firing up. "No, actually, we couldn't! Because in case you didn't notice, we weren't the only people you talked to during that time! Even if you'd believed any of it, would you have kept it to yourself? Would you have believed it after your Gildenbrook tutors taught you that nymphs were dangerous and mages were evil? You've been so obsessed with Phipps and Milla's approval lately that you've barely made time for Yarrow and me! So don't pretend—"

At that moment a shout came from right outside the carriage, and the cabin lurched hard to the left, throwing Linden against the window and me into the carriage wall.

"Yarrow," Merrall said, alarmed. "Your enchantment . . ."

But Yarrow had raised his Runepiece, and he closed his eyes as it glowed blue again. "Still in place," he muttered. "We're still disguised. But it flickered. Something was attacking it."

"This magic," the naiad said, her voice tense. "It will allow us to pass out of the city, yes? Even if the soldiers block the gates?"

"Only if it holds." Yarrow's expression was as taut as Merrall's voice.

The word *magic* reminded me of the obsidian band I had seen around Merrall's arm, which I now realized was gone. But before I could ask how she had removed it, the carriage gave an ominous, woody creak and the walls began to shiver as if giant hands were shaking us. Yarrow closed his eyes again, but looked up almost at once, his expression wild.

"What?" Linden demanded, but Yarrow merely shook his head and muttered something under his breath, gripping the Runepiece with white fingers. No light came from it this time.

Merrall sat up.

"Iyzabel's blocking it," snarled Yarrow.

"How?" Linden demanded.

Yarrow shook his head again.

"Without your magic—" Merrall began.

"Don't you think I know that?" Yarrow snapped. He massaged his forehead, making his wiry gray eyebrows stand out in every direction. The wild look in his eyes hardened into something grimmer, and he pushed his spectacles firmly up the bridge of his nose. "Siria," he said, "if we get stopped before the edge of the city, we'll have go on foot. In that case, you'll go with Linden and Merrall, and I'll draw off the soldiers."

Despite all my anger at him, panic bloomed inside me. "Yarrow, no."

"We'll meet outside the city in the Wasteland, in a dead ash grove called the Skeleton Trees. Linden knows—"

"No! Surely there's—"

Just then there was another shout from the street, and our driver bellowed a few incoherent words that sounded like curses. The coach rattled, picking up speed. How close were we to the edge of the city? Would he be able to get us out before—

The carriage swung sickeningly to the right, taking a turn with the speed of a chariot. At the same moment something rammed us hard from the left. Outside, the horse screamed. The blow shuddered through the cabin, shifting our momentum too far into the turn—and I knew what was going to happen before it did. The carriage listed hard to the side, tilting upward onto its two right wheels, where it balanced, suspended, for an endless moment.

And then it began to fall.

11

CHAPTER

We toppled over each other like rag dolls. The sounds of splintering wood and breaking glass reverberated endlessly around the cabin. Something struck the side of my head very hard. When I found myself lying on someone's legs on the overturned side of the coach, I could not immediately remember how I had gotten there.

I pushed myself up, cutting my hand on broken glass from the window, and found that it was Merrall beneath me. The candles had gone out, but there was enough faint green light from the streetlamps to see vague shapes. Linden was cutting a hole in the carriage's canvas roof with his knife, and Yarrow crouched beside him, mumbling something.

Outside, the driver seemed to be arguing with whoever had crashed into us. I'd begun wondering whether the collision had been an accident when a deep voice bellowed, "Passengers, present yourselves, in the name of the queen!"

Yarrow shot me a warning look, and my heart seemed to lodge like a bubble in the back of my throat, full of pleas for him to stay. But I could not risk speaking, and he hitched up his cloak and ducked outside.

My hands shook so badly I had to press them into my

lap to keep them still. I could feel blood pooling inside my left fist, and my pulse throbbed in the cut. The constriction around my chest was so tight I could barely breathe.

"Where's the girl?" the deep voice demanded, and Merrall reached for my wrist in the dark, apparently afraid I might run out and turn myself in. The fact I'd had no such impulse sent shame prickling through me.

"What girl?" came Yarrow's infuriated reply. "You've just wrecked my carriage over some runaway, and you didn't even bother to make sure you were following the right person first? You're lucky I wasn't injured!"

"Enough, old man." The soldier sounded annoyed. "Out of the way while we—" He broke into a roar of surprise as the whisk of metal sounded, followed by a horrible, fleshy thud. Shouts of rage came from the other men.

I gasped and teetered where I crouched, but Merrall redoubled her grip on my wrist and slapped her other hand over my mouth. The clamor outside became indecipherable, but mixed now with ringing clangs of steel, which had to mean Yarrow was alive. I heard a clatter of hooves. More shouts, then the hoofbeats faded out of earshot and one of the men bellowed, "Get after him! I'll check the carriage!"

My heartbeat was deafening and erratic inside my head as footsteps hammered toward us outside the carriage. Linden crouched, still and catlike beside the rent in the canvas that had become our door, and when the footfalls stopped just outside, he jumped up like a tripped spring.

Merrall's palm muffled my scream—she gripped my face and shook it hard, jostling my throbbing skull. I shoved her off in fury, scrambling after Linden. At the same moment he gave a cry outside the cabin. Merrall snatched at my ridiculous ballgown and caught a handful, but there was so much fabric I still had enough slack to reach the canvas and push back the flap.

Linden was grappling with a soldier, holding the man's sword hilt away from himself even as he tried to inch his dagger closer to the guard's neck. His arms were shaking.

"Run!" he barked at me. "Merrall, protect her!"

Pulse raging, I threw myself out of the carriage, tripped over my skirts, recovered, and broke into a sprint with Merrall just behind me. We raced into an alley. I was shaking badly, and my insides felt like they were being boiled inside a kettle. A melee of shouting followed us, and then a sound like crashing water, and I burst out of the alley into the green light of a residential lane, its streetlamps hazy in the mist coming off the canal. The black water cleft a quiet avenue between stone mansions, but the banks were empty of all but private canal boats, which bobbed like sleeping ducks beside their moorings. A man in a silk hat was climbing into one, though he stopped dead at the sight of us.

"Guards!" he cried in a thin, terrified voice, and I realized my hood had fallen back. "Guards!" he shrieked again, leaping into his boat.

I yanked my hood forward as three soldiers pelted into view from the next street, drawing swords and bellowing. At the same moment, Merrall hurtled out of the alleyway, reedy hair and tattered skirts streaming as she sent jets of water from her palms at our pursuers, her skin glowing blue. The soldiers split off, one chasing her, the other two running at me and Linden, who had burst into the lane behind Merrall. For a moment all was chaos as we scattered, but then I heard Linden yell, and I whipped around just as Merrall veered toward me and snatched my wrist. She hauled me toward the canal. "No, Merrall!" I shrieked.

One of the soldiers had caught Linden's arm and spun him around so fast he was pinned with the sharp edge of a blade against his throat before he could even draw his knife.

The world narrowed to a screaming point where cold metal touched soft skin. The heat inside me roared, and a kind of poisoned terror filled my chest and spread, hot and swift, all the way to the ends of my fingers. I jerked away from Merrall, and as I did, the boiling inside my body burst into sudden, raging flame. It tore through me from head to foot, so intense I thought I might actually break apart.

I heard Merrall's intake of breath—heard the guards cry out—as a brilliant golden light exploded out of nowhere, blazing in every part of my vision. The soldier holding Linden faltered, and Linden seized his chance. Twisting away, he sprinted flat out toward me.

Relief shot through my limbs, but I was still so hot and the light was everywhere. I looked wildly around for the source . . . and then I caught sight of my own hand.

The skin—*my* skin—glowed fire-bright, as if lit from within by a hundred minuscule candles. Even beneath the black cloak and hood, I bathed the street in light. My mind reeled, and I registered as if from a great distance the sound of Linden's voice, shouting something as he charged toward me.

He was usually a head taller, but now we were somehow eye to eye—until he hooked me about the waist and pulled me down *through empty space.* Down? With a hard bump, my slippered feet connected with the uneven street cobbles.

My brain wheeled and I flailed, tripping backward over my dress and grasping at Linden's neck for balance.

He grimaced, pulled me hard against him, and threw his weight over the edge of the dock, plunging us both into the icy water of the canal.

12

CHAPTER

My body seized as frozen cold attacked from all sides—yet the heat within me barely flickered. Murky blackness contrasted with the light blazing stubbornly from my skin, and Linden's arms clamped me in an iron grip as we sank like a pair of boulders toward the canal bed. I inhaled a mouthful of water and choked, air leaking out of me quicker than we were sinking. I squeezed my eyes shut.

What had just happened? How had I left the ground?

My lungs cried out for air, and I writhed against Linden. But then I felt small, slender fingertips coming to rest against my temple, and miraculously—inexplicably—oxygen expanded inside my lungs.

I nearly opened my mouth on reflex, ready to suck in another deep breath, before I caught myself. The breath began to burn in my chest, and I let out a small stream of bubbles to relieve it.

Then a voice filled my head—Merrall's voice. And my eyes flew open as I remembered what she was.

We must go lower, she said, her husky tones urgent inside my mind. *They might still see the light from above. Sunchild, can you draw it inside yourself, contain it?*

But I couldn't answer, couldn't even think, because by the light coming off my skin, I could see Merrall well, and underwater she was an entirely different creature than she had been on land. I'd known this in theory; everyone knew naiads changed in water. But seeing it was a different matter.

Merrall's legs had become a tail—a long, violet fishtail of glittering scales—and her hair had turned a shocking, dazzling violet. Her face was no longer plain: every feature, line, curve, and eyelash was stunning in its perfection. Her skin glowed pale blue, though flushes of fuchsia and turquoise showed in her cheeks and lips.

I expelled a cloud of bubbles, and Merrall's touch sent another breath of air through my lungs as my slippers sank into thick mud. Her face, I realized, was not just beautiful; it was also furious.

Contain the light! her voice cried inside my head.

A mess of bewilderment and nerves, I turned all my concentration toward the heat still thrumming inside my body and willed it to become smaller. I imagined it withdrawing from my skin, receding inward like a flame burning to embers. I imagined throwing water to extinguish it altogether.

The heat flickered once or twice, but it did not do as I wished. I started to shake with panic, and Linden's arms tightened around me.

My terror for him had sparked this insane light; what if that was what kept it alive? I told myself we had escaped, that he was safe—we were both safe—beneath the waters of the canal. I even lied to myself that Yarrow was safe, that he was strong and hardy, that he would meet us again and we would all be together.

Repeating these thoughts like a mantra, I tried to compress the heat within my body. It seemed to take hours, my shoes sinking ever lower, but finally I succeeded. The warmth remained fixed deep inside me as if it belonged there, though when I opened my eyes the water was murky and dark.

I groaned, exhausted from the effort.

Merrall sent another breath through my lungs. *We must move from this place*, she said. *We cannot resurface here, so we must swim. I cannot keep the connection between us if I remove my hands, which means every ten strokes, we will stop for air.*

The idea of moving at all was horrible, and swimming blindly through the freezing water of a soldier-patrolled canal was almost the worst thing I could imagine, but Merrall had already removed her hand from my temple and taken me by the shoulders.

Her fingers grazed my face—gentler than I knew I deserved—and I heard her voice once more: *Stay as low as you can. Try to propel yourself downward. Let us go.*

I had never been a good swimmer, and being drained of energy didn't improve my skills. Yarrow taught me before I went to Gildenbrook, although we had only used a cold, shallow forest stream, and I hadn't had much practice.

Lights were popping behind my eyes by the tenth feeble stroke, and just when I thought my lungs would surely burst, Merrall's fingers touched my face once more, and a blessed rush of air filled my chest.

Again! she said. We repeated this process over and over, my limbs growing weaker with every clumsy stroke. The ballgown billowed and tangled around me like a great fishing net, and I longed to shuck it off and leave it in the mud to rot. Eventually, Linden found my hand and pulled me along, probably worried I would drown. I held it tight; I would not soon forget the hideous fear of losing him.

After more oxygen refills than I could count, Merrall said, *I think we can climb out here. We have nearly reached the city's edge, and the canal grates will be shut.*

I didn't care if we'd reached Abyssum. All I wanted was to breathe on my own again.

Give me a moment to check that there are no soldiers.

In less than a minute she was back, and with a last surge of effort I kicked up through the cold water until I felt the surface break and a rush of even colder air burn my face. I sucked in needle-sharp breaths, trembling as I blinked into the green light of streets that now seemed blinding compared to the darkness of the canal.

Merrall already stood on the deserted bank, dripping and sodden, but unlike Linden and me, not shivering at all. Though she had reverted to her above-water appearance, she still looked very much the naiad with her straight hair and seaweed garments pouring water onto the cobblestones. She helped Linden climb out, then they each seized one of my arms and heaved. My waterlogged ballgown tripled my weight, and even with their help, I barely made it out. Merrall looked over her shoulder every few seconds as I struggled to my feet, but the ramshackle street remained empty.

Water rushed from the folds of my gown like rivers down a mountain slope, and the fabric hung, heavy and sopping, pulling at me as I struggled to stay upright. I had never felt so drained in my life. My satin slippers were long gone, lost somewhere in the canal, and my corset sloshed when I moved. I hugged myself, trying to stop the shaking.

I opened my mouth to ask what our next steps would be, but the words didn't come out.

Instead the world pitched, darkness poured over me, and I tumbled into oblivion.

13

CHAPTER

"Child," said Milla's voice from a long way off. "Siria, aren't you ready to go?"

It was the day I was to leave home. The day I was beginning my life at school. And despite the fact Phipps and Milla had come home from court for the occasion, I was not compliant in my departure.

I was twelve.

"Today is a very exciting day," Milla said, peering into my enormous bedroom from the doorway. She rarely came inside. "Today you'll start learning how to be a real lady."

"I don't want to be a real lady," I said into my feather pillow. I was lying face down on my four-poster bed, wearing an old woven shirt I had once borrowed from Linden and never returned. My Gildenbrook uniform hung pressed and untouched inside my wardrobe.

Milla's patience was shorter than her average smile. She clucked her tongue. "Get up, Siria, or I shall call your father."

I wanted my mother to come sit beside me, brush the hair back from my forehead, and tell me some reassuring stories about her time at Gildenbrook. The world had been very different then, of course, but Gildenbrook had still been a girls' school. Any action on her part would help, I'd felt, and perhaps eventually I would be comfortable enough to put on that wretched black dress and leave behind everything familiar.

From the doorway I heard a tsking sound, and Milla's footsteps clipped away, back down the manor hall. When she returned, it was not with my father, but with my current governess.

"Up, Miss Nightingale," snapped the governess in her sharp voice. "Up and into your uniform right now."

In five minutes, she had wrestled me into the dress, a pair of black lace stockings, and some button-up high-heeled boots that made me feel as though my feet had grown horns. Milla watched the whole ordeal from the doorway with her arms crossed.

"Can't you make her look any less . . . feral?" Her face was pinched, as if she'd just been made to drink curdled milk.

"She always looks this way, my lady," said the governess with a sigh. "All bony elbows and knobby knees, and there's no making that hair any better. Even if you plait it, she'll forget and scratch her head, and have it coming down and looking worse than before."

Milla pursed her lips. "Well, I hope they can make something of her at Gildenbrook. Siria, look at me. Promise you won't embarrass me at school. I hate to think what the other women at court will say if their daughters write home and report that Milla Nightingale's child is a barbarian."

"I'm not a barbarian," I said in my toughest voice, hoping it disguised my hurt.

"Well then, act like it. Come on, time to go. We can't be late."

"Can't I say goodbye to Yarrow and Linden?"

Milla's manicured eyebrows shot up. "The gardener and his boy? Why on earth would you do that?"

The governess looked suddenly uncomfortable, and I realized my parents hadn't known how much time I spent with Yarrow and Linden. Afraid of getting them into trouble, I shrugged as if I didn't care.

But Milla had grown suspicious. "I daresay that's why you're turning out so uncivilized. Befriending gardeners? Siria, they are *servants*. Don't humiliate yourself at school by treating the servants like friends, or you'll disgrace your father and me as well as yourself."

I resented her for talking about Yarrow and Linden that way, but I was also afraid my bad habits would prove unforgivable to her. I nodded.

My father was waiting beside the carriage in black gloves and one of his fine tail coats. He barely glanced my way as the footman handed me in after my mother. We didn't speak much during the short trip to Gildenbrook; I often had the impression my parents didn't know what to say to me.

The headmistress welcomed us when we arrived, greeting my mother like an old friend and leading us into the grand entrance hall with a sweep of her lace-swathed arm. Phipps and Milla became even loftier in her presence, and when it was time for them to leave, they each gave me a sugary smile and patted my shoulder. Milla hugged me briefly, her fleeting embrace like birds' wings, and as she released me, I threw my arms impulsively around Phipps.

I realized my stupidity at once. I had wanted a hug from Yarrow, whose hugs were strong and tight and made me feel brave. Yarrow, who always approved of me, no matter what I did or how I looked.

Phipps flinched when I seized him around the middle, and then pried my arms loose with his gloved hands as if I might soil his clothes. "Now, don't embarrass me, child," he said with his false smile, smoothing wrinkles from his doublet. He chucked me under the chin, and then they were gone.

"Siria?"

I looked up at the headmistress, who had spoken with Linden's voice.

"Siria, wake up!"

CHAPTER

Someone shook me, and with a groan I opened my eyes to a dark Umbraz alley. I was not twelve, I was not at Gildenbrook, and Phipps and Milla Nightingale were not my parents.

"She is weak," sneered a throaty female voice.

"She just used her powers for the first time *without access to their source*," Linden's voice snapped. "Personally, I'd call that strength. Could you do that without passing out, Merrall?"

Merrall snorted, and Linden shifted me in his arms so I could sit up.

"Do you think you can walk, Weedy?" His voice was gentle. "We need to keep moving."

I nodded, though my head felt like a boulder. "How long was I unconscious?"

"Just a few minutes. We'll rest as soon as we can, I promise." Linden's usually wild hair was plastered all over his face, streaming water into his eyes as he peered down at me. He was so cold I could see the veins beneath his skin, with bluish lips and purple shadows standing out beneath his green eyes. I was sure it was getting colder, but why?

"H-how?" I said through chattering teeth. "How d-did I access my powers? If Yarrow's m-magic is b-blocked?"

"It's a different kind, like Merrall's and mine." Linden still looked worried as he helped me stand, and he grabbed fistfuls of my skirt to wring out some water. "Elemental nymph magic. Not conducted magic like Yarrow's."

I didn't know any of this, of course, and I didn't *want* to know it. It made me feel like I had become everything I'd ever been taught to fear. I massaged my temples, trying to hide some of my misery until I knew what to do with it.

"Why is it so m-much c-colder now than it was b-before? Is it b-because of my disloyalty?"

Linden gave me a bewildered look. "I expect she's thickening the Darkness, trying to hem you in. That means less power for her heat-filtration system. Good riddance, in my opinion. Her version of warmth is like sweaty palms."

I didn't know what he meant, and I didn't have the energy to try and work it out right now. We started off again, and I held on to Linden's arm for support.

"Does anyone live out here?" I whispered through numb lips as we crept into the shadow of an ancient-looking stone wall that was beginning to crack and fracture in places. We had reached the edge of the city.

"Vagrants," muttered Linden. "And people doomed to actually earn their own living."

The cynicism in his voice was pronounced, and it filled me with guilt. In my sixteen years, I had believed there were only three kinds of people: rich ones like my parents and me and everyone at Gildenbrook, vocational servants like Yarrow and Linden, and nymph servants like Merrall. And if I was honest, some deep, unacknowledged part of me had believed the second two types existed to help people like me.

Shame nagged at me. Everyone at Gildenbrook thought that way too, but when had I decided that everyone at Gildenbrook was right? There had been a time when I believed just the opposite, when I didn't even want to go to boarding school.

"The Skeleton Trees aren't far," said Linden, rubbing his wet arms. "Just through that break in the wall, and then a quick sprint northeast. Let's hurry."

As silently as we could, we made our way through the gap in the crumbling city wall and into the Wasteland—which let in no light, green or otherwise. The Darkness pressed against my eyes, and when I shut them, there was no difference. We moved through the void like waders through a bog—all three clutching hands—and I expected to hear a chink of armor in the gloom, or a slither of iron as a sword was drawn. But the Wasteland remained silent.

After what seemed hours, Linden pulled us to a stop, though I had no idea how he knew where we were. He lifted my hand to something solid and scratchy, and I released him to run my fingers over the unmistakable roughness of a tree trunk. We had reached the Skeleton Trees.

Yarrow had not arrived, so I clung to the tree, sagging against the bark. Frozen, damp, and exhausted, I slid down the trunk and curled against it on the ground, ignoring the bracken and small rocks pressing into the side of my face as I shivered. A small fragment of the light in my chest remained, but the Darkness continued to push against me. And worry for Yarrow seared like an open wound.

A thousand horrible fates paraded like ghastly mari-onettes through my imagination, and I felt equally sure, by degrees, that each one had befallen him. I thought of the insults and accusations I had shouted at him in the carriage today; he had left before I could tell him I still loved him.

Eventually I pulled myself off the ground and felt my way through the trees to peer in the direction I thought the city walls must be. There was only uninterrupted blackness, everywhere, and Linden and Merrall's quiet breathing was all the indication I had of where they stood.

The minutes slipped by and stacked into piles. I was shaking harder than before, though from worry or cold or exhaustion, I couldn't tell. No one spoke. I wondered how soon they would tell me we had to leave.

Please, I thought desperately. *Please let Yarrow be alive.*

And then there was a trembling beneath my feet. The ground of the Wasteland shuddered like the crawling skin of a massive beast, and the fortress war horn of the Black Castle gave a deep, echoing moan. It rolled through the city and into the Wasteland, shaking the very trees around us. Somewhere nearby, a limb snapped and crashed to the ground. The second time the sound was even louder, vibrating with such depth that I could feel it inside me, rattling my bones. A chorus of smaller horns echoed the sound within the city like fighters taking up a commander's battle cry, and I knew they were for us.

For me.

I don't want this, I thought, cold dread making me clammy. *I don't want any of it.*

Suddenly a shower of silver mist appeared directly in front of me, and Linden's hand snatched mine up as if he had known just where it would be.

"Those aren't party horns, you know!" growled Yarrow Ash as he appeared out of the mist, just visible in its dissipating glow. "They're coming—the whole lot of them. Get moving!"

CHAPTER

15

I didn't think I had the strength for any more outright running, so I was relieved when Yarrow set the pace at a brisk walk, holding his faintly glowing Runepiece aloft for us to follow. But when he veered off at a sharp angle toward the sounds of rushing water, I began to feel worried again. If running was hard, swimming would be impossible.

As we approached the riverbank, however, I realized that only Merrall would be equipped to cross it without drowning. The Elderwind was a massive, churning force, far too wide and powerful for even Linden to swim. How, then . . . ?

But before I could ask for an explanation, Yarrow bent to place his Runepiece on the ground, where it expanded and broadened, ever darkening in color. A moment later, the pale disc had become a long, narrow glimmer on the riverbank.

A boat.

For a moment I stood in sluggish confusion, weariness dulling my wits. While I could tell the action was nothing extraordinary to Yarrow, I also knew that *crafting boats* would never have made it onto a Gildenbrook list of things mages did with their magic. And suddenly I found myself wondering what other things Yarrow might do with the Runepiece I had deemed so evil.

Remove a nymph's obsidian band, perhaps? I thought, thinking of how Merrall's powers had already saved my life twice.

"Merrall, please guide us to the east bank near Beq's," Yarrow said, nudging me into the boat as he pushed it down the bank.

The naiad's shadowy form disappeared in the direction of the river, and I clambered after Linden as he sloshed into a hull that was wide enough for three or four people to lie down inside.

Which, I realized, was exactly its purpose.

"Lie flat, you two," said Yarrow, following me. "Cloaks over you completely. The Darkness should help us for once, but I'm not taking any chances."

My turquoise gown was the brightest fabric between us, and I had to take my sodden cloak off and drape it fully over myself in order to cover it all. When I pulled the hood up to hide my face, I felt like a corpse being sealed into a shroud.

But I didn't contemplate the idea long. Lying down was all the encouragement my body needed to sleep, and next thing I knew Yarrow's voice was jarring me awake, telling me to sit up and get out of the boat because we had reached the shore.

A crunching sound came from beneath us as the boat rumbled into the shallows, and Linden splashed out to help Merrall guide us closer to the bank.

"We're still dangerously close to the city, and she'll have trackers after us," Yarrow said once we were all standing on the bank and his Runepiece had returned to a disc inside his pocket. "Don't leave any footprints. Hoods up. Let's go."

The bank's rocky slope gave way to a sweep of short, brittle weeds that might once have indicated the beginning of a field. This quickly progressed into the kind of moor country I had grown up exploring: spongy bog disrupted by tough tangles of thicket, patches of hard dirt, and spikes of resilient weed. I could see none of this with my eyes, of course; I recognized it all by sound and feel, familiar as I was with the uneven squelch of peat underfoot.

It had to be nearly midday, I guessed, but Iyzabel's Darkness was outdoing itself in honor of my escape. We lit no lanterns. Even so, Yarrow seemed to have some way of discerning our route: his footsteps plodded steadily on, never swerving or hesitating.

As he had once explained it, the Darkness was like a long swathe of fabric covering our island kingdom. It was thickest above Umbraz—much like a new, tightly woven wool blanket—but as it stretched out toward the coasts, and especially as it spread north, its density thinned. Eventually it became like a shirt you'd worn so much and washed so many times that the weave loosened and thinned, and could be looked straight through. But even in those places the sun could not be fully seen; its light was allowed through only for the sake of the crops, which could not be grown without it. Iyzabel had made certain there was no place in her kingdom the sun might shine its naked face.

Gildenbrook told a different story. According to my teachers, the Darkness had been a necessary measure to save us all from the increasing power of the sun, which had swelled over the centuries due to the sunchildren's reckless magic. Queen Iyzabel had come as the much-needed savior, and her Darkness now shielded the kingdom while the rest of the world burned. But its power weakened with disloyalty, which was why the temperate climate dissipated in the north, and also why those who lived in that part of the kingdom had been made to work as farmers for the kingdom. Left to their own devices, they would have formed rebel groups to plague the true followers of the Darkness, whose fealty kept the Light at bay.

Because the Light was "dangerous and destructive." Or so I had thought.

After fifteen years, there were many people who had never seen the sun at all. Even though I had been a year old when the Darkness arrived, I had no memories from that time. Everything I thought I knew was a mishmash of conflicting information from Yarrow and Gildenbrook, and I was beginning to understand just how much work I would have to do to sort one from the other. I scowled. Even though I was beginning to see the truth now—about Queen Iyzabel as well as myself, Linden, and Yarrow—I still felt the old longing to belong in her world, like the sensation of a phantom arm. I barely even knew what sunchildren were, and everything I had experienced since the ball felt like playacting at best and a nightmare at worst. It certainly didn't feel like me.

But what *did* feel like me? "Me" was a person I barely knew anymore.

We walked for more than two hours before Yarrow's footsteps turned off toward even denser darkness.

"Watch your step," he warned from just ahead. "Once we're in the trees, we'll have to use a little light or we'll never find the place. Siria, grab hold of my cloak, please. And you two. I'm going to feel my way forward and I don't want us getting separated."

Light flared a short while later and I flinched away from it. As soon as I could look again, I saw Yarrow shining his Runepiece over the bracken-covered forest floor. Tree trunks rose around us like shadowy pillars, but the light illuminated only a small patch of forest; the rest was black and featureless.

"Here," said Yarrow.

I saw his figure crouch. There was a rumbling sound, like logs being shifted, and then he peered straight down at the ground and beckoned us forward. A second light shone now, faintly illuminating his face. He extinguished his Runepiece.

By the time I reached him, Yarrow appeared to have sunk halfway into the ground. But then I saw a flight of steep, earthen steps and a warm golden glow drifting up from below. We had arrived at someone's home, and Yarrow had been relocating whatever served as the door.

The stairs were short, and at the bottom I found myself blinking into the main room of a wide, lamp-lit burrow, full of aromas that made me dizzy with hunger. A squat wooden table set for four was in the middle of the room, and many pots sat steaming on a range that vented straight up through the packed dirt ceiling.

"Oh, Yarrow! I've been so worried. I thought you wouldn't come!" A plump, long-haired dwarf woman bustled through a door from an adjoining chamber, wearing an apron and wringing her hands. "I expected you hours ago! I've kept the food hot just in case—oh, I hope nothing's happened!"

Yarrow stepped off the stairs behind me and propped his Runepiece—which had become a cane to aid his descent—against the wall. "Our plans went slightly awry," he said. "Thank you, Beq. And thank you for taking us in on short notice."

"Not at all!" Beq waved away his thanks. "Sit down. I'll put the kettle on and have the food out in two shakes. Please rest! You're all faded as old parchment. Well." She stopped suddenly. "Most of you."

Beq's eyes had fallen on me, and she looked slightly dazzled as she took in my hair and face. I felt my cheeks growing hot.

"I saw a sunchild once before. Before the overthrow, you know. And I remember thinking then that it wouldn't matter if I had one holed up in my house to look at every day, I'd never be used to the sight. You're like a living flame, child."

I could think of absolutely no reply to this. Yarrow cleared his throat as if there was something lodged in it, and I had the sudden strange impression he was trying not to look at me.

"Where's your boy, Beq?" he asked, squeezing into one of the small wooden chairs at the table. "I thought he'd be here."

The dwarf woman turned away and started bustling with the teapot and ladling food into tureens. "He wanted to be but couldn't make it. Called away. Urgent family business."

Yarrow massaged his neck. "I'm sorry to hear that."

Merrall joined Yarrow at the table, and I turned to follow. But as I caught sight of Linden in the first decent light we had been in since the carriage, I stopped dead.

A livid burn that had certainly not been there a few hours ago spanned the left side of his neck and lower part of his jaw. Though broken in places, the mottled, blistered mahogany patch was several inches across at its widest, with five thin, branching burns spreading out from it across his wan brown skin. The shape was familiar, though in my shock I couldn't immediately say what it reminded me of.

"Linden!" I gasped, and he spun to the sound of my voice. "What happened to you? Your neck!"

His alarm vanished, and he darted a look at Yarrow as if for help. There was hesitation and guilt in his expression, and then I saw his eyes flicker down, as if by reflex, to his hands. Before he could hide them behind his back, I glimpsed the palms: blistered raw, just like his neck.

Hands. That was what the burn on Linden's neck reminded me of: a handprint. For a moment I felt dizzy and violently ill, though I did not know why—

And then I remembered the canal: Linden running at me, pushing me back into the water as I hung in the air like a burning torch; and me, scrabbling for a grip on anything that would keep me steady, including Linden himself.

I had left the mark on Linden's neck.

16

CHAPTER

I swayed and reached out for the earthen wall.

I was a monster.

It was almost the only thought I had room for, it seemed so big and unwieldy. *I am a monster.* That was why I was intrinsically different from the other girls at Gildenbrook, and why Phipps and Milla never really cared for me. Perhaps they hadn't known exactly what I was, but they could clearly sense my monstrosity in abstract ways, which was the reason I always failed to meet their expectations.

Linden and Yarrow have always known, though, whispered a small voice.

But now that they saw what I was capable of, I thought, they would surely leave me. How could they not?

I felt hands on my shoulders and looked wildly up. Linden had crossed the room and taken hold of me, looking down into my face with a fierce expression.

"It's not your fault," he said, dark brows drawn sharply together. "Weedy, listen to me, it's not your fault. It's *my* fault, not yours."

His eyes sought mine, but all I could see was the charred handprint across his neck, the spidery lines of crusted skin where my fingers had burned him. I started to shake with deep, uncontrollable tremors. He tried to hug me, but I shoved him away and slid down the wall, folding my arms over my head.

"Don't touch me," I said, gasping for breath with lungs that seemed to be shrinking. "I'll just burn you again. No one can touch me. Back away, Linden, I'm a monster."

"Siria—"

"No!" My voice was a ragged shriek, and I scrabbled back along the wall as he reached once more for my shoulders. The absurd gown caught at my feet, and I fell sideways onto my elbow. I curled myself into a ball on the floor before Linden could try and pull me up again.

It was too much. All of it together was more than I knew how to hold inside my mind, more than I knew how to make sense of. Yesterday I had been an ordinary student at Gildenbrook School for Girls, preparing for a ball that might win me my parents' favor and a life at court. Today I was a terrible being with no parents at all, on the run from the most powerful woman in the kingdom. And I was . . .

I was the last sunchild in Terra-Volat.

The giant truth finally solidified in my mind.

And like a watch that keeps ticking simply because it has been wound, my brain plodded on with the information I had been given, even though I longed for it to stop.

Iyzabel wanted me dead because she hated sunchildren . . . but surely that couldn't be all. If she and her Darkness were supreme, why should she care if one stray sunchild survived her purge?

Today I shall know at last who is the beast I must kill to ensure the everlasting glory of my kingdom of Darkness.

Ensure the glory of the Darkness?

Ensure?

I knew now that I was a beast—Iyzabel had been right about that—but what was I capable of, and what did Yarrow and Linden and Merrall expect me to do? How much would they ask from me?

With a slight shock, I realized there was a hand resting on my shoulder. Keeping as calm and controlled as I could so as not to release more harmful light, I raised my head again.

It was Yarrow's hand. He sat cross-legged on the floor beside me, deep grooves in his pale forehead, his eyes a soft, cloudy gray. Linden crouched behind him looking tortured, and Merrall watched from one of the small chairs at the table.

"You haven't told me everything," I said with a conviction that surprised even me. At the table, Merrall's thin eyebrows lifted.

Yarrow peered at me for a long moment. "No," he said at last, withdrawing his hand and shifting his legs with a grimace. "Not even close."

I nodded, glad he wasn't trying to deny it. "You said Iyzabel wants me dead because I'm a threat to her magic. What exactly does everyone think I'm going to do?"

Yarrow's eyes narrowed behind his spectacles, and his chin wrinkled as he pressed his lips together. I could feel Linden's gaze too, but I did not look at him. I didn't want to be distracted from Yarrow's answer.

"We think," he said slowly, "that you can bring back the sun. That you can overcome the Darkness. That you might reinstate the kingdom of Luminor."

I stared at him. When, after a few seconds, the information had not sent me into hysterics, I said, "I see," though I didn't. "And where are you taking me?"

Yarrow eyed me warily, but to my surprise, he answered, "North. There's a resistance group there. Has been since the overthrow. It's past the mountains in the Northern Wilds, and in addition to its people being loyal to Luminor, there's a place where the sun is sometimes truly visible. The Darkness tapers off significantly there—doesn't even extend over the ocean. We think if we can get you there by the vernal equinox . . . well, we might stand a chance against Iyzabel. Your transformation won't be complete until you're exposed to direct sunlight."

I didn't understand at all, but I wanted as much information as he would give me. I felt like a puppeteer trying to see how many strings she could hold without dropping them all. "And what's a vernal equinox?"

Again, though he was watching me like he might an unpredictable wild animal, Yarrow answered. "It's the point in spring when the sun hits directly over the middle of the world, making the day and night equal. Sunchildren have old magic associated with that day. We think if you're exposed to the light of the sun at midday, the burst of energy might make you more powerful than the Darkness."

I smiled, a wide, empty smile.

Behind Yarrow, Linden was gripping his knees so hard that the tendons of his hands stood out like tree roots. Merrall had folded her arms on the table and buried her face in them, and her lank hair and the seaweed-like strips of her brown-and-green dress made her look like she was melting down the chair to the floor.

The ridiculous image was what finally made me fumble all the strings, and a moment later my smile cracked into a howl of laughter that doubled me up on the dirt floor of the kitchen. I lay there, tears streaming in rivulets from my eyes as I cackled and hooted and crowed, until the hiccups of my laughter became the hiccups of sobs and I couldn't breathe for crying.

Yarrow and Linden both tried to gather me off the floor, but I flailed them away, terrified of burning them. "I don't want— I can't *be* this!" I choked, trying to yell, but thwarted by my own ragged weeping. "I don't want to do any of these things! I'm not a hero or a leader. I'm not even brave! I'm a freak, Yarrow—even my parents think so. How do you expect me to—to—?" I broke off, exhausted by the attempt to translate my untamed, half-formed thoughts into words.

"The only thing I expect you to do right now," said Yarrow, very gently, "is to change out of that horrible wet dress, get some hot food in you, and have a good sleep. We can deal with the rest later."

My sobs shuddered gradually to a halt, and I glared at him through puffy, burning eyes. Slowly, I nodded. My anger with Yarrow was, after all, nothing compared with the disgust and horror I felt at myself, at what I could do.

He helped me up, then explained there was a rucksack in the spare room, which he had packed for me. Folded on top of it I would find the thickest of my old woolen dresses, some stockings, and a pair of deer hide boots that had once been Linden's.

"Merrall?"

The naiad raised her head and looked heavily at Yarrow.

"Please help Siria out of this gown, and make sure she puts those things on. Beq?"

I had completely forgotten the dwarf woman. She was standing beside the range, looking fretful.

"You're sure we're secure here for the rest of the day? And you have our horses?"

Beq nodded and scooped up a platter of tea things. "They're tethered just inside the forest."

"Thank you," said Yarrow. "We'll sleep a few hours, then, and be on our way."

Merrall led me into a side chamber, which turned out to be a modest bedroom with a very short bed, a small desk, and a blazing fire. The bare walls were earthen and curved here as well.

"Turn around," said Merrall, her voice hoarse with exhaustion. I heard a metallic flick, a slicing sound, and the corset strings binding my bodice slackened and fell away with the bulk of the gown, leaving me in my damp linen shift.

I struggled out of the wet silk, disentangling myself from layers of petticoats as Merrall gripped my arm to keep me from falling. A clean, dry shift went on first, then Merrall jerked the thick, brown wool dress over my head and pulled my arms through the sleeves as though I were a child. The stockings and boots I did myself before draping my black fur-lined cloak over a chair before the fire to dry. I felt hypnotically warm, and comfortable for the first time since I had dressed to go to Umbraz.

Merrall frowned at my shuddering yawn.

Tea was steaming from four clay cups when we returned to the table, and Linden and Yarrow were spreading sassafras jam over lumpy biscuits. I sank into the empty chair beside Linden and pulled a mug toward me as Beq slid platters and tureens onto the table. The smell of smoked ham was so intoxicating it made me dizzy.

Yarrow was talking again, but the words were directed at Linden now, to my relief. I listened without really hearing.

"With any luck we'll reach the pass by the middle of

Second Month, and then we'll have a good three or four weeks with the resistance before the equinox. Plenty of time, I think."

"If there's any chance of missing it, though—any chance at all—we'll have to find a quicker way. Are the eastern ports all guarded too?"

"Of course they are, lad. There hasn't been an unguarded port in this country since the overthrow, and even if there were, it would be just as slow. The quickest way to the pass is straight up the Queen's Road, but that'd be suicide. The equinox is almost two months away. I don't think we have anything to worry about."

"I hope you're right."

I looked up. "A month? We'll be traveling on horseback for a *month*?" I had never traveled by horse for any real length of time before. There was no need when your family had a half dozen carriages.

Linden gave me an encouraging smile and started to reply, but at that moment something sounded from the direction of the stairs. A shout, then a loud crack. I jerked around.

The dwarf woman was standing in the doorway with a crossbow, which she raised with trembling hands and pointed at me.

"If any of you moves so much as a hair," she said quietly, "I swear I'll kill the sunchild."

PART TWO

"All the darkness in the world cannot extinguish the light of a single candle."

St. Francis of Assisi,
The Little Flowers of Saint Francis of Assisi

17

CHAPTER

Another crack came from the door—this one louder than the last. Whoever was outside would smash their way into Beq's house within moments.

"Beq . . ." Yarrow began. His Runepiece was still a cane, leaning against the wall across the room.

"They took my son," Beq said, eyes darting between Yarrow and me. "I'm sorry, Yarrow, but they took him. They knew you'd been here, somehow. Knew you'd be back with the girl . . ." Her voice broke, and a tear glittered in the soft, golden light as it slipped down her cheek. "They said they would kill him. I'm sorry, but I have no choice." She swallowed.

No one moved, but I could see Beq's hand quivering on the crossbow. I wondered if she might fire by accident, and tried to calculate whether I would have time to dive out of the way if so.

Below the table, Linden's hand found mine. His touch was like a stimulant, and my blood bounded at the sensation, jolting me as he squeezed my fingers. Almost inaudibly, I heard him whisper, "Duck." Then, with a movement so quick it startled me, he leapt up, his chair crashing backward as he propelled himself over the table. At the same moment I hurled myself below it and heard a heavy *thunk* above me. Beq's arrow shuddered as it stuck in the wall, directly behind the place my head had been.

And now the room was in pandemonium. I clambered up to find Linden wresting the crossbow out of Beq's hands, and Yarrow running toward her with his Runepiece raised. Merrall took the crossbow from Linden, who sprinted to the doorway and laid his palms flat against one of the walls, which immediately began to sprout pale, wormlike roots that wove together to form a dense barrier over the doorway.

"Through the back room!" Yarrow bellowed, but Merrall had already dashed past Beq—who Yarrow seemed to be putting into some kind of enchanted sleep—into the bedroom where I had changed clothes.

"Sunchild!" she yelled. "Now!"

I followed at a run, scooping up my new rucksack and my damp cloak.

Yarrow, who had dashed in with both his and Linden's packs, stopped to face the far wall with his Runepiece raised. As I watched, a small hole began to grow in the packed earth. "Linden!" he roared.

"Half a minute!" Linden shouted from the front room. "Just one more layer!"

"*Now,* boy!"

There was a sudden burst of green from the Runepiece, and the hole expanded before us like a tear in fabric, soil crumbling in great clumps to the floor. Merrall seized an unlit lantern from the desk, clambered into the hole, and began to crawl up the tunnel that had appeared beyond it.

"In, Siria," said Yarrow, who likewise had snatched a

lantern from Beq's house, though he blew it out as he gestured at me.

I hesitated, but a moment later Linden skidded into the room, and Yarrow shoved him after me. I hiked up my skirt, clambered into the narrow hole, and began to crawl. After what seemed miles, I saw Merrall's hands reaching through an opening, waiting to pull me out into the fresh, cold air.

On my feet, I brushed clumps of dirt from my dress and peered around at the forest, which was darker than ever after the light in Beq's burrow. I wondered how much distance separated us from her front door, and whether the soldiers outside it had yet made their way in. A moment later Linden climbed out of the tunnel, and then Yarrow, who sealed the hole at once.

"What will happen to Beq?" I asked Yarrow.

He grunted, and I bit my lip. She had betrayed us, but would I have done any different in her place?

Merrall had already started into the blackness at a brisk jog. We caught up with her where the vague shapes of trees seemed to become denser, and I could just make out her figure turning in circles as she swore under her breath.

"No horses?" guessed Yarrow. "Iyzabel's men probably took them when they came for Beq's son. We'll have to go on foot, then."

"On foot?" Linden repeated with a hollow laugh. "We'll be lucky to get there by the *autumnal* equinox, Yarrow."

"Pessimism's never been a problem-solver, my boy. Hurry, you three—we'd best be hidden by the time those soldiers come out again. Linden, our tracks, please."

"The entire length of the kingdom *on foot*?" I said in disbelief. A month on horseback was bad enough; walking would take at least twice as long, and probably kill us all in the process. My voice grew shriller with every word. "Yarrow, we can't possibly walk all the way to the Northern Wilds. Even if we don't get murdered by soldiers or eaten by wild animals, we'll freeze or starve to death, or—"

With an abrupt movement, Merrall dropped her rucksack, marched toward me, and slapped me hard across the face.

It was the first time anyone had ever deliberately hit me, and I was shocked at what it did to me. Instead of making me feel cowed or hurt, sending me sprawling or making me cry, it was as if someone had dumped oil on the smoldering ember of my internal flame. Blinding red rage tore through me from my belly up to my eyes, and I reeled back from the slap with another explosive blaze of gold light.

Surprise registered on the naiad's face, but her anger was equal to mine—if not stronger—and she flung a watery shield between us with one sweep of her hand, her skin blushing blue.

"You do not want to find out what happens if you attack me, sunchild." She hadn't yet called any of us by name, I realized.

"What the *hell* is the matter with you two?" Yarrow cried, looking incredulous.

"She is the matter!" said Merrall, growing angrier by the moment. My fury was fading with the pain in my cheek, and I crossed my arms to glare at her. Though I tried not to show it, I was horrified by the intensity of my reaction.

The naiad retracted her water shield, and it flew back into the skin of her palm even as the blue glow dissipated. But she pointed at me as her eyebrows met above flashing aqua eyes. "She is a pampered princess who has known nothing but privilege and excess! All she has done since we left the city is whine and cry and feel sorry for herself. Never once has she stopped to consider that she might not be the only one here whose life is impacted by this mess. Never once has she considered that there are more important things at stake than her *feelings*."

"I am *not* a—" I began, outraged, but Linden was quicker.

"Hold your tongue, siren," he snarled.

Yarrow held up his hands, furiously glaring furiously around at all of us. "Siria, put that light out. Anyone in these woods will see us a mile off."

As I had done on the bed of the canal, I imagined the light retracting, and this time it obeyed more quickly, though I felt an immediate sag in my energy as I withdrew it. Yarrow's glare fell into shadow.

"Squabbling and yelling?" he said quietly. "Fighting each other? You seem to think we're somehow safer than we were in the city. Let me remind you we're less than a mile from the edge of the forest, and there's a mad queen behind us with an army none of us can fight. Siria, Merrall's right. If you don't get a grip on yourself, you'll put us all at risk. And Merrall? I don't care what you think of Siria. Hit her again and we'll leave you in the next pond we find. Are we clear?"

The dark outline of Merrall's body flushed blue again, but she nodded.

"Good. Now, we've got at least ten miles to go before we can rest. No lanterns yet, so watch your step. Follow me."

As the adrenaline seeped out of me, and the retraction of my new power left weariness in its place, it became impossible to fend off fatigue. I walked in a kind of stupor, my entire body sore and protesting, but committing every ounce of my concentration to the dark forest floor, scanning it for roots and rocks that might trip me. I stumbled twice in spite of this, and at some point was offered a hand to hold, though I pushed it away in fear I might burn it.

We must have stopped and made camp, but I had no memory of doing so, or of lying down to sleep. When Yarrow shook me awake the next morning, I felt like I was reviving from a period of long death. My whole body was stiff and screamed at me when I moved, as though my muscles had been subjected to terrible punishments while I slept. My legs and feet were the worst. I had never walked or run as much in one day as I had since leaving the Black Castle, and at first I was afraid I would not be able to stand at all. But Linden showed me how to stretch the muscles that hurt most, and after some work I could walk without agonizing pain.

We started off again, following Yarrow in dour silence. The morning was as inky black as the previous midnight had been, and while darkness was nothing new to any of us, we were at least used to days that paled enough to give depth and variation to the shadows. This darkness was complete, and it was only by risking help from Yarrow's Runepiece that we made any progress at all. A faint white light shimmered from the disc as we passed among the dying trees, some enchantment of Yarrow's glowing and spreading around us like a mist as it wove into the fabric of the air. I didn't know what exactly he was doing, but I hoped it was making us hard to find.

Our pace was slower the next day, and I knew Yarrow was trying to make things easier for me. We kept as silent as we could, wrapped in the thick traveling cloaks that doubled as our bedding—all except Merrall, who apparently only needed her magic to keep warm; she slept curled inside a swirling orb of water at night and wore no cloak during the day. All the while, Yarrow wove his protection around us with the faint white light.

It was easier to walk without tripping when I could see, but it was also easier to think, which I was loath to do. Instead of letting my mind dwell on my monstrous powers, my treacherous parents, Yarrow and Linden's deception, or my death sentence, however, I deliberately reexamined things I already knew. Things that had gained new meaning since I'd left Umbraz.

It now made sense why the Darkness inspired more dread in me than it did anyone else. I tried to remember what Yarrow had told me during those countless times I had wheedled stories out of him—stories I had tried to forget once I reached Gildenbrook. He had told me plenty about the old days—about the way sunshine looked on the trees, and the glitter of the sea at sunset, and even about sunchildren and the way they used light to make magic— but he always left off long before Iyzabel's ascension and the arrival of the Darkness. I had learned all of that at Gildenbrook.

Had there been clues in those early stories as to what and who I was, and I was simply too dense to see them? Yarrow had said he'd kept the knowledge from me to keep me safe, but I wondered now if all the sunchild stories had been his own small—even subconscious—way of trying to show me the truth.

I frowned at the back of Yarrow's bald head, haloed in white light from his raised Runepiece. In the carriage, he said he, Linden, and Merrall had only come to me in the first place because they believed me to be the sunchild daughter of the king and queen of Luminor. Bitterly, I wondered who had sent them, and how they had known where to find me. And—I wasn't sure if I would ever have the courage to ask this question—did they want to stay with me, or had they been given no choice?

What I knew about Yarrow and Linden now seemed pitifully incomplete. But was that because they had been so good at maintaining their charade, or because I had never bothered to think about the lives they led apart from me? Merrall had called me a selfish brat and a spoiled princess.

Perhaps she was right.

18
CHAPTER

L et's stop here." Yarrow's raspy voice was startling after so many hours of silence. "I've disguised us as well as I'm able, and only time will tell if it's enough. We need to rest in any case."

The light from his Runepiece had changed from a whitish shimmer to a more substantial gold that illuminated the clearing we had stopped in. He bent to place the stone on the ground, where it grew into a pale lamppost that threw light over us all in a wide circle. The forest here was much like everything else we had seen so far: sparse trunks rising into darkness, and the ground blanketed in dead twigs, fallen branches, rotting logs, and the occasional hardy shrub or pale stalk. Above us the sky was a deep, smoky color, bare branches drawing charcoal lines across it like bars.

Merrall announced she was going to find a stream to soak in to refill her magic supply. As Yarrow explained to her how to detect the edges of his enchantment so she wouldn't wander past them, I picked out a broad, flattish boulder and dropped my rucksack beside it. Then I lowered myself gingerly onto it, stretching out my swollen and sore legs.

Linden had found a stump to sit on and was unpacking cooking gear from his rucksack. I caught myself staring at the long, muscular lines of his arms as he rifled through the bag. His woven sleeve strained a little, highlighting the curve of his shoulder, the lean cords of his forearm . . .

I turned away, blushing, even as a sly, unbidden voice piped up in the back of my mind. *But you don't have to worry about Milla Nightingale's approval anymore. You and Linden are both nymphs. You could even marry him now—*

For a moment the idea bloomed in my mind like one of Yarrow's flowers opening its petals in spring. And then I remembered the truth: I couldn't marry *anyone.* I couldn't even touch another person's skin without risking deadly harm to them. Miserable and disgusted with myself, I dug my fingernails into my palms and yanked my thoughts in a different direction. They landed on the subject that had been foremost in my mind all day, and before I could stop myself, I heard words tumbling out of my mouth.

"So what now?" My voice sounded bitter and caustic.

Yarrow looked a bit confused—perhaps he thought I was asking about food or sleep—but I could tell Linden knew exactly what I meant. I wondered if he had been thinking something similar.

"You mean, how can you trust us, now that you know we've been keeping the truth from you for ten years?" Linden had been digging out a small firepit in the dirt with a rock but sat back on his heels to look at me as he spoke.

I nodded, oddly relieved to hear him state it so baldly.

Yarrow was pushing several logs into a circle around Linden's work, and he lowered himself onto one before looking at me. A small crease formed between his wooly brows. "We told you the knowledge was cursed, Siria."

"But that was just one piece of it all," I argued. "You still could have told me the truth about other things, surely."

"Could we?"

Despite my bitterness, I gave this fair consideration. Each scenario I could imagine, in which they told me one of the wild secrets I now knew to be truths, I saw at least a half dozen ways for it to end in disaster. But I also saw one or two ways for it to end well. Would honesty have been worth the risk?

"Even if I understand why you lied," I said slowly, "it still doesn't change the fact I don't know how to trust you now." I thought of my parents, who had never bothered to tell me I was their adopted child, and felt, if possible, even flatter. I wasn't sure I knew how to trust *anyone* now.

Yarrow nodded. "That's fair." He paused a moment, forehead furrowed. "Well then. Do you mind if I tell you a few things? Not massive revelations. Small things."

Apprehension coiled in my stomach, but I shrugged.

"Okay. Here we go." He fixed me with a very serious gaze and said, "From the time he was nine to the day after he turned fourteen, Linden asked me every day—*every single day*—if he could tell you what he was. And every day I wanted to say yes, because the more we grew to love you, the worse it felt to keep such huge secrets. But do you know why I said no? It's the same reason he eventually stopped asking."

I shook my head, chest tight.

"Because I knew—and Linden grew to realize—that we, the only two people in your life who knew the truth, would be taken away if anyone ever found out what we were. And you would eventually be murdered by the queen."

I swallowed.

"A few more things," said Yarrow, leaning onto his knees. "But let's go a shade lighter. To begin with, my favorite food is barley stew. And Linden hates the taste of it more than anything."

The surprised laugh that burst from my mouth startled even me. "I know that."

Yarrow's gray eyes twinkled. "I know you do. I just want you to know that it's true. Here's another one: I think that sun you painted when you were eight is the best work of art that's been done since the overthrow. Other people might disagree, but other people are wrong."

I laughed again, but only briefly; a constriction was growing in my throat.

"Here's another one," said Linden, the dimple creasing his right cheek as he tried to force a grave expression. "Yarrow only plays the fiddle so well because he can't carry a tune in a tin bucket."

Yarrow gave a bark of laughter and tossed a stick at Linden, who grinned at me. I smiled back, but their reassurance was already being crowded out by more doubts and questions. They both seemed to guess it, because Yarrow's smile faded, and Linden cast me a shrewd look before he said, "I know that can't fix it. But we want you to see that our relationship with you was always built far more on the things we did tell you than the things we didn't."

I nodded, trying to believe him. From the shadows behind Yarrow, Merrall reappeared, soaking wet and looking better tempered than she had all day. She sat down on one of the logs and raised a sarcastic eyebrow at me.

"I expected you to be crying by now," she said. "Well done. You are already braver than yesterday."

From Merrall, this was probably a genuine compliment, but it still rankled me back into speech. Even as Yarrow turned a look of exasperation on the naiad and Linden opened his mouth to retort, I said loudly, "There's something else I need to know."

There was a rather startled silence. All three turned to look at me.

"Who sent you to me?"

Blank looks.

"At Nightingale Manor," I said. "When I was six. Who sent you? Was it these rebels in the north?"

Both Yarrow's and Linden's faces showed understanding and a flash of guilt. I braced myself to hear they had never wanted to come at all and, like Phipps and Milla, had been motivated by an agenda rather than love.

For a long time there was silence. "Yes," Yarrow said finally, his gravelly voice weary. "It was the rebels in the north."

I nodded, trying to seem stoic.

"They sent a pair to each of the girls who were with you at the ball yesterday, each of the children we, like Iyzabel, thought might be the missing sunchild. The hope was that we would have someone watching over each of you, who you trusted, ready to help you escape when the time came."

I felt slightly lightheaded again. Even braced for it, the truth was like a slap in the face. "Who we trusted . . ." I repeated faintly. "Would you have let me die on that platform if I wasn't who you thought I—?"

"No, Siria," said Linden, dragging a hand through his hair.

"What happened to all those other girls? Would you have helped one of them instead of me if someone else had transformed? Did their *trustworthy* mages just leave them to die?"

"*Siria.*" Yarrow's voice was a deep rumble.

I stopped talking. Merrall was smirking at me from behind her curtain of wet hair, and I had a sudden urge to strangle her with it.

"I don't know what happened to all of the others," Yarrow said. "I heard several years ago that a mage in Heraldstone had been executed, but whether one of the other girls was his charge, I don't know. It's entirely possible there were others at the ball beside Linden, but what became of them, we may never find out. But think, Siria. What did Linden and I ask you to do the night before the ball?"

The terrible knot in my chest loosened minutely. "You . . . you asked me to come see you."

"To tell you the truth and ask you to leave with us. *Before* you transformed."

I stared at him, looking for hints of deception, though it was clear enough by now that I was terrible at detecting them.

"It's true we came to Nightingale Manor because we were sent there. But we didn't spend time with you because of rebel orders. Linden didn't play with you every day for six years because of rebel orders. I didn't tell you stories or feed you dinners or teach you how to garden because that was some kind of edict from higher up. And we'd have rescued you yesterday whatever you turned out to be."

There was logic in what he said. "How can I believe you, though? You still need me because you think I'm going to defeat the Darkness or Iyzabel. How can I believe you actually care about *me*? *Me*, separate from anything my supposed powers can do, anything you hope I might accomplish?"

I could hear the desperation in my voice, but not even Merrall seemed willing to mock me for it. I didn't think I had ever cared more about the answer to a question in my life.

Yarrow was watching me so closely he appeared unaware his glasses were slipping down the bridge of his nose. "I don't know, Siria. I think only you can answer that. What will it take? What do you need?"

"I—" I broke off on a weary sigh, the answer coming plain and obvious. "Time," I said dully. "It will take time."

Linden looked as if this answer was as unwelcome to him as it was to me. But Yarrow nodded. "Fortunately, time is not something we're lacking. And for my part, I'd like to prove myself trustworthy by continuing to tell you the truth about your life, insofar as I know it. So if you feel up to it, there's one more rather large piece of the puzzle I'd like to give you."

I could tell by the instant flare of resentment and mistrust at these words—there was *more?*—that time was absolutely the only remedy to the deep fracture in my trust.

"Your teachers at Gildenbrook discussed the overthrow, I think?"

I nodded warily.

"Do you remember any of what they said about the royal family of Luminor?"

My family. I shivered. "I . . . I remember they ruled Terra-Volat for a long time. Many centuries."

"But King Auben and Queen Elysia—your parents—do you remember learning anything about them?"

Chills rolled down my arms and legs as I shifted my memories of Gildenbrook history lessons into this new context. I could practically hear the papery voice of our history mistress, crackling like turning pages as she told us about the corrupt, Light-loving family Queen Iyzabel had deposed. Along with King Auben and Queen Elysia, a crown prince and two princesses had died in the overthrow.

But one of the two princesses had not died.

I had not died.

I stared into Yarrow's face while the dark forest appeared to wheel behind him. "I had . . . a brother and a sister," I whispered faintly. "W-what happened to them?"

Yarrow's face was taut. "It was chaos the night Iyzabel raided the palace. No one knows how your mother smuggled you out, or to whom, but by the time Iyzabel followed Elysia out of the city, your father and your older sister Kysia were already dead. We know that Iyzabel killed Elysia on the banks of the Elderwind and then went back to find you and your brother. You were already gone by that time, but the seven-year-old crown prince was nowhere to be found. Iyzabel didn't learn until later that he'd been away on a trip with your uncle at the time."

I clutched at the rock beneath me, trying to keep the world from spinning. Six years older than me. A brother.

"Iyzabel started her search of the kingdom after that, to purge the magical species, which she saw as a threat. But her other purpose was to find your brother, Prince Eamon."

My throat was dry, and my voice came out a croak. "And . . . did she?"

Yarrow shook his head, his expression gentle in the light of the fire. "No. No, she did not." He smiled. "Siria, your brother is alive."

CHAPTER

19

My brother—my older brother—was alive.

I have an older brother.

"The rebel camp formed to protect him," Yarrow continued. "And Iyzabel never found them. Eamon is twenty-two now. He's still there, in the Northern Wilds. From what I've heard since we left, he wants nothing more than to see you safely among the rebels."

Yarrow was still smiling at me. But I didn't smile back. Instead, I looked down into my lap at my freckled hands.

"What is it, Weedy?" Linden's voice.

I raised my eyes, first to him, then to Yarrow.

"I . . . I just don't feel like I fit."

"Fit what?" said Yarrow.

I swallowed. "This wild story, this history. A brother is . . . wonderful. But I don't know how to be sister to a prince any more than I know how to be a sunchild. It feels like we're talking about a stranger. I'm not those things."

I didn't say the rest of what I felt, that despite their hopes for my new powers, I positively dreaded using them. Linden's face was beginning to heal, but he would always have a scar where I had burned him. He would always wear a reminder of the horror I could inflict. And while a flesh and blood brother was more than I had ever dreamed of, he came parceled up with a list of roles I had no desire to inhabit: Long-awaited sun-bringer? Lost princess? Secret weapon of the resistance? It was like a bad dream, in which I only wanted to wake up someplace safe and comfortable while everyone else insisted on charging ever forward into new and more haunted territory.

Yarrow looked sympathetic, but there was a familiar glint of iron spreading through his gray eyes. It was like watching clouds harden into stone. "Maybe not," he said, "but that doesn't mean you aren't those things. You're just going to have to learn, because no one else can be who you are. And we need you to be who you are, Siria. Terra-Volat needs you to be who you are."

Yarrow shook me out of confusing dreams the next morning and handed me a steaming tin mug of tea. "Rise and shine," he said with grim irony. "We've a lot of ground to cover today."

I groaned.

It was colder than the previous two days—colder, indeed, than anything I had ever experienced in a life lived so close to Umbraz—and my teeth chattered as I slipped out of my bedding to layer on the rest of the warm things in my rucksack: leather trousers over my stockings, a second woolen skirt belted at the waist, a snug deerskin jacket that would help keep in my body heat, and a knitted cowl for my neck. When the cloak went on over it all, I felt bulky but warm.

Though this was only our third day of travel, I felt like we'd been trudging through the dismal, gray forest for half a lifetime. I had never considered myself pampered before, especially compared to the other girls at Gildenbrook, but now I realized that *pampered* was exactly what I had been. Never before had I slept on the ground, or eaten carefully rationed portions, or worn the same mud-stained clothes for days on end. And not since I was a child had I relied only on my own legs to carry me everywhere I needed to go.

I held back my complaints, though. Even Yarrow, more than four times my age, seemed equal to the exertion, and the idea of drawing attention to my weak endurance was mortifying, especially when Merrall was already so keen to notice my defects.

Midway through the morning, Yarrow called me up to walk alongside him in the lead.

"We're in a bit of a predicament, Weedy."

I raised a sardonic eyebrow. "I've noticed."

"I mean with regard to your powers," he said, and my stomach immediately tensed. "It'd be foolish to let you use them much out here where we're so exposed, of course. But at the same time, I think we'd be negligent if we did nothing useful with the time we have."

I said nothing.

"There's plenty of theory I can teach you," he went on, "and some small things you can practice without attracting notice."

When I still made no reply, Yarrow looked curiously into my face. "What's wrong? Don't like the idea?"

I shook my head tersely. "It sounds dangerous."

"What would be dangerous, Weedy, is for you to carry on not knowing what your powers are, or how to use them. Believe me. Learning about them is the quickest way to make them safe."

I bit my lip.

"What you did in Umbraz tells me that without ever being taught—without even accessing your power source—you have strong natural instincts of how it should be used. So everything I teach you will only give you more control, more understanding for the future."

"I don't want to use them in the future. I don't want to use them *ever.*" I clenched my hands into the wool of my skirt and lowered my voice until it was barely more than a whisper. "You saw what I did to Linden, Yarrow. I'm a monster—I'm unsafe to be—"

"You are *not* unsafe to be around." His voice was impatient now. "And if you're a monster, so are Linden and Merrall and I. Would you call a dog a monster just because it has teeth?"

"It's different."

"It's no different at all. So stop using that word. I'll give you a day to get used to the idea, Siria, but starting tomorrow I *will* begin teaching you how to control your power."

Around midday, when I was tired of sulking and beginning to feel oppressed by the silence, I fell into step beside Linden. In ten years, I had rarely seen him wear anything other than the homemade leather trousers, woven shirts, and light boots he worked in at home, but now he had layered on much hardier garments that made him look rather intimidating. There were thick boots, laced up his calves almost to the knee; more than a few sheathed blades tucked in various places, along with his bow and quiver; and beneath his traveling cloak, a belted leather jerkin, with sleeves laced on at the shoulders. He could have been a rebel woodland scout who had spent his life wandering.

"It's a good look for you," I said with an appraising nod.

He grinned, but hesitantly, as if he wasn't sure whether

we were friends again or not. "And you. Much better than those torture devices they made you wear at Gildenbrook."

I laughed my agreement.

"Listen," he said, his voice low so Merrall and Yarrow wouldn't overhear, "I'm sorry we never told you any of that stuff before. About me and Yarrow . . . and about you. I know you feel betrayed, and I would too. But I hope you know . . . well. I'm sorry."

I nodded, looking down at the dim, rocky ground, but found that I wasn't angry at Linden anymore.

"Thanks, Linden."

He gave a real smile this time.

After a few steps I said, quietly, "He's not really your grandfather, is he?" It was just a guess, but one I had been feeling more and more sure of since learning what they were.

Linden looked surprised, but not abashed. "Yarrow? Not by blood, I suppose. But he may as well be in every other respect. I was only seven when I met him. He'd known my father, so when the rebels hatched this scheme to send people to look out for all the girls who might be you, Yarrow asked if he could take me."

For the first time since learning about my birth parents, I remembered Linden was an orphan too. I couldn't believe how little consideration I had spared for this fact in all the time I'd known him. "You always said your parents died in the overthrow . . . somehow I thought that meant they were fighting for Iyzabel."

Linden gave a bitter laugh. "What else would you have thought?" He sighed. "No, they died after Iyzabel killed your parents, when she slaughtered half the nymphs in the king-dom and gave the rest the 'opportunity' of the obsidian band. My family lived in a village that was among her first targets."

I stared at him. "Do you . . . I mean, do you remember . . . ?"

"No, thank the Light. I was too young—only three. My father didn't die then; he managed to escape the massacre with me. We went to the rebels, and lived there until I was seven. When I met Yarrow. My father had just been killed on a scouting mission, and I think Yarrow felt sorry for me."

Linden had been eight when they came to Nightingale Manor. The year after he'd lost his father, the last member of his family he'd had left. He was my best friend, but I had never bothered to ask him any of this. Not only that, I had also spent the last four years trying fit into the society that enslaved, persecuted, and murdered his people.

My people too, I realized with a start. My family.

If they had survived, might his parents have been branded as nymphs and made to serve in disgrace at Gildenbrook or Nightingale Manor? Might Linden? And if so, would I have treated him with contempt, instead of friendship? And how narrowly had I escaped any number of those fates, just by being in the right orphanage at the right time?

"Linden, I'm sorry." My voice sounded small. "For so much. I haven't been a very good friend to you."

He regarded me for a moment, then looped an arm around my shoulders, hugging me to him. "On the contrary, Weedy," he said. "You've been my best friend. You've just been lacking some important pieces of the story."

This was generous, but I was grateful for it. I hugged him back, and felt warmth spread through my body at all the points we touched. A moment later I remembered with a shock of dismay that warmth had become dangerous. Stiffening with the effort to control the fire in my chest, I let my arm fall and casually stepped away.

20

CHAPTER

By the time we made camp that night, I was starting to feel a definite sense of doom about the journey ahead.

"We still have roughly two months until the equinox," Yarrow said, sitting down heavily on one of the sturdier-looking logs in the clearing we had picked. "And while we may be taking the longest route possible to the Northern Wilds, it's also the safest."

"We'll stay in the forest the entire way?" I tried not to sound too appalled, but I could easily visualize the map of our kingdom that hung in the Gildenbrook library. By its depiction, the forest curved around the entire eastern side of our island. It eventually touched the Wilds in the north, but the route was at least three times longer than the Queen's Road, which ran straight from Umbraz.

Yarrow rubbed his forehead, looking just as weary as I felt. "Better to spend twice as long trudging safely through the wilderness than to cut across the kingdom and get murdered along the way."

"I suppose." I crouched beside the crude stone ring we had assembled and began to mimic Linden's fire-building technique, even as he stomped out of the trees with an armful of thick branches. He raised an eyebrow at me but didn't object as I built the little twig-and-leaf pyramid and held out my hand for his flint and knife.

Beneath my palms, a small shower of sparks cascaded off Linden's knife and fell into the pile of dry twigs, smoldering a little. I blew gently and was gratified to see a tiny orange tongue lick up the side of one twig. In another moment the entire pyramid started to burn, and I reached for slightly bigger twigs.

"That's impressive," said Linden as I handed back his flint. "You only had to try twice."

"Maybe I'm a natural," I said, and Yarrow snorted.

Merrall came tramping up to our fire ring then, soaking wet and levitating a gourd-sized, swirling ball of water in front of her, which she carefully directed into the tin pot Linden had just untied from his pack. He nodded his thanks and began adding herbs and pinches of spices from our supplies.

"Yarrow, why did Iyzabel create the Darkness?" I asked, my eyes drawn back to the fire. "The truth would be nice."

He frowned at my jibe, and then considered the question. "She created it," he said at last, "because that's what she needs."

I dusted myself off and crossed back to sit beside him. "Meaning?"

"What do you know about witches?"

I chewed my lip. "I know they're magical, and more powerful than any other being. And extremely rare. They're the blessed ones. Only once every few hundred years is one born, and they are always given rare magic to save and to rule. Queen Iyzabel is the only one in Terra-Volat."

Yarrow leveled his gaze at me.

"What?" I said defensively. "That's what I was—"

"Taught at Gildenbrook?" finished Merrall with a sneer.

"Well, it was," I said, glaring at her. "What's the truth, then, if you're so smart?"

"That you are gullible," said the naiad, rolling her eyes.

Yarrow frowned and turned back to me. "All right, Weedy. I want you to forget what you heard at Gildenbrook. Just chuck it all out, and we'll start over."

I nodded, then angled my body so I couldn't see Merrall in my peripheral vision.

"First of all," he said, "nymphs and mages are all born with their magic, and they can be born to humans or nymphs. Lineage matters more for mages, but for nymphs, it's about birth circumstance. A sunchild is only born at the precise moment of dawn, and elves—wood nymphs—are always born outdoors, under trees. That sort of thing. Their powers don't change, they just develop. You, for instance, were born a sunchild, but your powers stayed dormant until you turned sixteen. Now, for the rest of your life, those powers will continue to develop, but they won't ever change. The same with Linden, except elves come into their power at birth."

"And naiads?" I asked, curious in spite of myself. "When do they get theirs?"

"Age nine," said Merrall, leaning into my line of sight with an irritating smirk. "But naiads are sainted at birth because they are so naturally benevolent and pure and suited to being worshiped."

"Shut up, Merrall," I grumbled.

Yarrow plowed on, ignoring us both. "Wind nymphs—pixies, I mean—grow wings at twelve, but can't begin to truly manipulate the air until they're eighteen. And mages have power from birth, but it takes extensive training and a conductor"—he held up his Runepiece—"to learn to use them."

Yarrow looked critically at the gray disc, then peered at the hard, prickly log beneath him and gave a decisive grunt. He stood up. There was a shimmer of white light, and the Runepiece became a rocking chair identical to the one he'd used at home, except this one was silvery gray. He shifted it onto a patch of ground that was slightly less uneven and sank into it with a groan of relief.

"Nymphs sometimes use a conductor too," he added. "But you don't need it the way I would—nymphs use them only to focus the power they already have, whereas I need my conductor to make the magic occur. And in this respect witches are more like mages, because Iyzabel needs her conductor as much as I do."

"She uses a Runepiece?"

"No, she uses a dagger. In that way alone is she like Linden and Merrall when they use a conductor. Like you would too, if you'd grown up learning your powers. A stone in the hilt connects to the magic, and for Iyzabel, that stone works to pull out the magic inside her and activate it in the world. Whereas for nymphs, it's merely helpful when you want to increase the strength of your power, and is usually a stone whose properties are associated with the element in question. Linden's is agate, which is an earth stone. Merrall's is aquamarine." He nodded at them, and Linden pulled out his short dagger—which I'd seen him use a thousand times—and turn the hilt toward me. Sure enough, there was a swirly, reddish-brown stone set into the top. Merrall looked like she'd rather not humor me, but after a pointed look from Yarrow, reached into her boot and unsheathed a deadly-looking silver stiletto, which she flipped carelessly, causing the watery blue stone to glitter in the firelight.

"Iyzabel uses obsidian," concluded Yarrow.

"Like the obsidian bands that stop nymph magic?"

"That's right."

"So when do witches come into their powers?"

He rocked back, looking ominously through his spectacles at me. "When they take it."

"Take it?"

"Witches are not born with magic. They have to steal it from someone else."

I gaped at him. "How can you steal magic? Magic isn't a pair of shoes you can just take off. Or . . ." I faltered at the look on Yarrow's face. "Or is it?"

A wild hope rose in me, that maybe I could discard my own magic. Then I would be safe to touch, safe to be near. I could meet my brother as an ordinary human, and live an ordinary life—

"You can't take it off, no," he said, squashing my hope flat. "But it can be taken from you, if the thief is desperate enough."

I waited, leaning toward him. But it was not Yarrow who answered me.

"A witch becomes a witch by eating a magical person's heart." Merrall's husky voice was flippant and hard, and as I jerked around to look at her, she raised a challenging eyebrow. "Yarrow, you should not coddle her so much. She has to grow up some time."

Yarrow looked angry, but I was too horrified by the information itself to be troubled by the way it had been delivered. A prickling chill swept down my spine.

"Eating?" I repeated, staring at Yarrow. I imagined the

queen, with her fair skin and perfect features, raising some-one's hot, bloody heart to her face while her hands and mouth dripped with gore. My whole body convulsed. The last traces of desire to belong in her court vanished.

"And . . . and then they get that person's magic?"

"After a fashion," he said, looking every bit as disgusted as I felt. His lips were pursed, and his chin—growing the first stubble I had ever seen on it—was scrunched up. "But a perverted, backward version of it. A witch who had killed an elf would be able to destroy plant life instead of create it, or manipulate dead wood instead of bringing roots back to life. They could set animals to savage others, rather than earn their trust."

"And if," I said slowly, the horrible truth dawning on my mind, "a witch ate the heart of a sunchild . . ." I stared at him, hoping he might contradict me.

He nodded. "Yes," he said. "She would have the power to bring Darkness instead of Light."

21

CHAPTER

For a moment all I could do was sit with my mouth open in silent revulsion. Iyzabel—*Queen Iyzabel*—who everyone worshiped, who even I had fumbled over myself to try and serve, had gotten her powers by eating the heart of a sunchild.

Someone like me.

The questions that occurred to me were dreadful, but I had to know the answers. "Does . . . does she eat the heart of every sunchild she kills? Does her power increase the more she does it?"

A shadow crossed Yarrow's face before he shook his head. "It's only necessary once. A witch cannot steal more than one kind of magic, and she can't gain more by repeating the act. But I believe Iyzabel wanted to kill you *while* you transformed, which was why she waited so long to do it."

"Why, if she already had her power?"

"That I don't know. We know a fair amount about Iyzabel's past, but very little of her plans after she claimed the throne. Her manipulative power became too great with the spread of the Darkness, and she never let anyone close to her until they fell completely under her sway. But I have no doubt she was planning something hideous. If Linden hadn't been there to stop her in those moments when you were so vulnerable—"

"*Linden* stopped her?" I twisted around to find him frozen in the act of stirring the stew.

"You didn't tell her?" Yarrow sounded surprised.

"There was no reason to," Linden muttered, cheeks darkening slightly.

I turned back to Yarrow and found him studying Linden. Finally he looked at me and said, "He set the queen's gown on fire as soon as you started to transform. She was distracted just long enough to miss her moment."

A glance back at Linden showed him bent studiously over the pot, face still flushed.

"Linden," I said, and he looked up at once. "I had no idea. That's why the whole place was on fire, wasn't it?"

He gave a half shrug, half nod.

"Thank you," I said, as sincerely as I could.

He met my eyes and smiled—not his usual teasing grin, but a new, almost bashful one—and inclined his head before bending back over the stew.

I was intrigued by this bout of humility, but a sudden memory drove everything else from my head.

"That urn!"

Yarrow raised an eyebrow.

"She had an urn with her in the ballroom! A black one. Was that meant for me?"

Yarrow shook his head. "I doubt it. She's often seen with it—even in portraits—and I've wondered before if destroying it would weaken her or weaken her Darkness. We've theorized that it holds her twin sister's ashes, the sunchild she killed to become a witch."

I froze, gaping at him. "Her *sister*?"

He nodded grimly. "Sources in Abyssum, where she grew up, told us they were as unlike as two girls could be. The sun-child was loved by their mother, and Iyzabel was loved by a father who was deeply prejudiced against nymphs. In hating her sister, Iyzabel learned to hate and fear the sun, but we also believe she was secretly jealous of the girl's power. When her father died, she left home and learned she could take magic for herself, use it to fight the magic she feared. Another witch with very anti-nymph views took her under his tutelage, and eventually became her lover and co-conspirator. We have reason to believe he suggested she use her own sister as her source. Since the strength of a witch's power is directly correlated to the tie between witch and victim, Iyzabel had a distinct advantage in stealing her magic from a twin."

I couldn't believe I could feel more horrified at Iyzabel than I already did, but this information certainly proved me wrong.

"So why does she need the Darkness?"

Yarrow kneaded his forehead. "She can no longer endure the light of the sun. Someone less powerful would simply become nocturnal, or enchant herself a patch of sky, but for Iyzabel that was never enough. I think she truly believes that sunlight is evil, destructive. When she took the kingdom, she channeled her focus in three directions: First, strengthening and spreading the Darkness, so sunlight couldn't weaken her; second, eliminating all magical opposition to her rule, beginning with sunchildren; and third, using her powers of influence and manipulation to convince people that what she had done was right and necessary and good. An easier task, since she believes it herself. Most sunchildren are magnetic, the power of their warmth both physical and emotional, and we're certain Iyzabel's Darkness channels a perversion of that power. There's almost no one willing to betray her within a hundred miles of Umbraz, where the Darkness is thickest, but if you go into the far north, the spell of her influence is easy to break."

I thought of Iyzabel's court, the instructors at Gildenbrook, and Phipps and Milla—all falling over themselves to do Iyzabel's bidding. And even *me*. With a flush of loathing I remembered the way I had felt at the ball, when I saw her for the first time. Like I would do anything for her.

"Linden said something in Umbraz about the cold." I said, looking across at him. "Something about Iyzabel's warmth being like sweaty hands. What did you mean?"

"You'll see when spring comes in the north," said Linden with a wistful expression. "It's a completely different animal."

"The warmth from sunlight is hard to imagine if you've never felt it," said Yarrow, "but Iyzabel's version in Umbraz is like a crowding into a small, closed room packed with people, as opposed to sitting in front of a nice crackling fire. It's the best she can do to keep from living in a glacier, though, and those who live there with her are so far under her sway that they don't know the difference. And of course she tells them it's her generosity at work." He snorted.

"So it's just magic, then? Not a result of loyalty?"

"More a way of ensuring rather than judging loyalty, I would say. Arctic temperatures have a way of making people grumpy."

We were silent a moment, and then Yarrow said, "Do you see now why she wants so much to kill you—and why we believe you're the best hope for the kingdom?"

I shook off my abstraction. "Because my magic is opposite to hers?"

"Because it channels the very thing that weakens her power. Sunlight is like poison to Iyzabel. Linden and Merrall and I can set our magic against hers, and it might make dents here and there, but it's like trying to fight a swordsman bare-handed. You'd need just the right moment and a lot of luck to bring them down, whereas they only need one good swing."

I started as Linden held a wooden bowl out to me, steaming with a stew that smelled of carrots and thyme. My conviction that magic was monstrous was a habit I didn't know how to break, but I began to understand those beliefs had been born from years at Gildenbrook and in my parents' house, and indirectly, from the sway Iyzabel held over her subjects' minds. I still thought my gift had horrible potential, but Iyzabel had chosen—had *created*—her monstrosity. And I couldn't deny she needed to be stopped.

Yet the idea that *I* had to be the one to stop her . . . surely there was another option.

"Why did she do it?" I asked eventually.

Merrall scoffed. "Because she is the embodiment of evil upon the world."

But Yarrow shook his head. "Things are rarely as simple as that. Apart from fearing the sun, hating her sister, and wanting power—and frankly, people have sold their souls for less incentive than that—I think we must assume that her formative years were . . . not ideal. I blame Iyzabel for much, but I cannot blame her for the circumstances and people that shaped her when she was young." He laid his empty bowl down beside his rocker.

"But she's not young anymore," I said.

Yarrow shook his head, and his face darkened. Merrall made a sound like water hissing over fire.

"No," said the mage. "She is not."

22

CHAPTER

It was colder than usual that night—so cold my many layers gradually became ineffectual and my face started to feel numb in places. Linden banked the fire with some stones he'd carried in from the trees, and when I spread my blankets beside the heat, he tugged my bedding even nearer to the rocks.

"The closer the better," he said. "It's just going to get colder."

I could make out Merrall's bizarre water-bubble den on the other side of the dying fire as a glinting orb, which I supposed kept her warm enough. Yarrow's Runepiece probably afforded him some warmth, and though I suspected I could help myself in a similar way if I was willing to experiment with my powers, it seemed much safer just to shiver.

My blankets and cloak seemed to grow thinner and flatter when my mind wandered to the giant feather bed I had slept on at Gildenbrook. I'd swept the ground for rocks before spreading out my bedroll, but I still felt as though every part of my body was being poked by some root or lump. Shivering, I turned onto one side and faced the fire.

And like the treacherous villain it was, my mind presented me with a most delicious and practical solution to the problem.

Body heat. *Linden's* body heat.

No, I thought, balling my fists so tightly they shook. It was a deadly dangerous idea and would only make me ache more for what I could never have. The thought of what I had done to Linden's face in Umbraz still made me nauseous. If emotion was what made me burn like a hot brand, I could never risk a romantic relationship. What would a kiss do to me?

More critically, what would it do to *Linden*?

Unless . . . unless I was willing to learn to control it, like Yarrow said I should.

"Siria. Your teeth are chattering."

Linden's low voice, just a few inches behind my head, made me jump.

"It's just the wind."

His laughter was quiet and slightly muffled.

"Want to share my extra blanket?" There was nothing suggestive in his tone—nothing to imply the proposal was anything other than what a friend would offer another friend—but my heart rate leapt into a trot.

"I don't think anyone should touch me," I mumbled.

There was a pause. "You don't have to touch me, Weedy," he said quietly. "Anyway, even if you did burn me, I'd probably thank you. I'm turning into an iceberg."

Cold tremors jolted through me now. I gritted my teeth to stop them from clacking.

"Look," said Linden, "I'm just going to drape this one over both of us and lay with my back against yours. Does that sound okay? Just to keep us from freezing to death."

"Okay," I breathed. "But don't blame me if I set you on fire by accident."

There was a shifting of covers, and a moment later I felt the weight of another layer settle over my blankets. Then the solid, warm feel of Linden's back pressing up against mine.

He was shivering almost as badly as me, and for a few minutes we rattled against each other like branches in a high wind. Finally the combined body heat seeped into us both, and the trembling subsided.

"Thanks, Linden."

He laughed softly. "My motives were not entirely selfless."

I was sure he only meant warmth, but still, despite all my rationality and reservations, it was hard not to hope his words had a double meaning. I pressed myself the tiniest bit closer to him and let my eyes drift shut.

I woke confused, parts of me very warm, other parts very cold. It took a moment of blinking before I realized my head was tucked beneath Linden's chin, my nose and forehead snug against his neck. His arms were tight around me, and his breathing was deep and steady, though I could feel him trembling at the cold.

And cold was an understatement.

My back was numb from it, despite the combination of my blankets and Linden's, both our cloaks, and his body heat. It felt like tiny needles were jabbing into my feet, and though my legs were pressed against Linden's, they were icy. I was so cold I couldn't even feel stunned at the fact we were lying curled together.

I flinched at a draft of frigid air and realized the cloak covering my face had shifted slightly. I opened my eyes and sucked in a sudden breath: The crack was letting in *light*.

Sitting up, I pushed the cloak aside.

The dark forest was white with snow. It reflected the faint light seeping through the Darkness so that it seemed twice as bright, illuminating more than I had seen in weeks—perhaps more than I had *ever* seen.

I gasped, and Linden's steady breathing caught. He stirred, gave a jerky shiver, then groaned in piteous misery. "Oh Light," he slurred. "I think my ears have frozen off." He whimpered. "Everything hurts."

"It snowed, Lin," I breathed, and he gave a mirthless bark of laughter.

"Of course it did," he croaked. "Everything's been so easy so far—we obviously needed a bit of a challenge."

A giggle rose in my chest.

"And you're laughing," he said, still in that deadpan voice. "My eyes are frozen shut and Siria thinks it's funny. What a testament of friendship. See if I share my blanket with you again."

There was an almost undetectable change in his tone at this last sentence, the flippant sarcasm softer, and it brought reality speeding back to me. The snow's spell broke, my laughter trailed away, and my face flooded with heat.

Any false move, any lapse in control, and I might burn Linden to a crisp.

Quickly as I could without seeming unnatural, I drew away from him and got to my feet, shivering hard as I wrapped my cloak and blankets all the way around myself. Linden groaned again, his body giving a convulsive shudder as he pushed himself to sitting. He blinked at me, tiny white icicles clinging to his eyelashes, and one corner of his mouth twitched very slightly. His eyes held mine for a moment, and then he looked down and began breaking the ice from his lashes with careful fingers. I let out an unsteady breath.

A rush of heat blazed behind me with a sound like roaring wind, and I turned to see Yarrow pointing his Runepiece at the firepit. Flames leapt up on the new logs lying amid the snow-covered ashes of last night's fire, quickly melting away the white mounds and sending up hissing steam.

Across the circle, Merrall stepped close to the fire, hugging her bare arms. She wore no cloak, and until now it had not seemed to bother her. As I wondered whether I ought to offer her my blanket, she scowled at the fire and stepped away from it, traipsing a few steps off into the snow. I watched her thin shoes and bare legs disappear into the drifts with my mouth hanging open, but a moment later she had spread her fingers and pointed her palms toward the snow, and I remembered that snow was, after all, just a type of water.

Merrall's palms glowed blue, and the snow began to drift upward from the ground around her as though it were falling in reverse. At first the flakes were lazy and sparse, merely floating. But then they swirled faster, thickening, and after a moment the naiad had surrounded herself in a miniature blizzard, so her darker shape was no longer visible within it. Just as I was beginning to wonder whether she might try and travel that way, the snow settled and calmed again. Merrall emerged through the whirl of white wearing a new garment: a glittering, long, hooded cloak made entirely of snow.

I gawped at her, but Yarrow barely glanced up. "I told you to bring a cloak," he muttered.

"This will be much better," she said. "Warmer for me."

"Must be nice," Linden mumbled. He'd stepped into the firepit to get closer to the new flames and was now crouching over them.

"Can't you make us any warmer, Yarrow?" I said.

"My magic will only warm my own body. I can give you a hug, but I think you'd have better luck with the fire." He raised an eyebrow. "Or your own magic."

After a moment's hesitation, I stepped into the firepit too. I would try my magic, but not until I was a safe distance away from the others.

To our relief, the snow did not stay long—though its departure pitched the forest back into gray monotony. By the end of the day it had melted into the ground, remaining only on rocks and branches. Sounds of snapping wood and falling limbs increased with the weight of the snow, and we spent half the day on edge, listening for ominous cracks overhead, ready to jump out of the way.

Linden, once thawed, reached heights of cheerfulness even I had never witnessed. And despite the mix of awkwardness and longing that clawed at me whenever I thought of spending the night curled against him, I felt more normal around him than I had in months. Every time he caught my eye and smiled, the dimple dancing in his right cheek, more of my worry seemed to drop away.

That afternoon, true to his word, Yarrow began what I couldn't help thinking of as sunchild lessons. And despite my fears, I was riveted.

He taught me history—both of Luminor and the sunchild species—and I learned that the powers of a sunchild were all in some way or another connected to the sun itself. Some, he told me, had less direct correlations someone might not understand if they didn't know what the sun itself did: Healing, for one, because the sun was a powerful enemy of disease and promoted strength and health. For another, the ability to lift people's spirits and improve their moods, because of the way sunlight impacted the balance of our bodies. This was the magnetism Iyzabel's witchcraft had perverted into manipulation. Also, I could aid the growth of plants that already existed in some living form or another—different from the elf gift of manipulating them or calling them back from death.

Flight—which I had already experienced once, briefly, at the canal in Umbraz—had a slightly more obvious connection. It wasn't self-propulsion, Yarrow said, but rather an effect of being drawn to the sun. He reminded me that plants grew up toward the sun because they, too, drew their energy from it. "When sunlight hits you," he said, "it draws you upward, like a flower or a tree. Only you don't have roots, so you leave the ground." But once airborne, I could manipulate the sun's energy like a water current and turn myself in whatever direction I wanted, so long as I was not disconnected from my energy source.

Traditionally a sunchild could not fly in the shade; they needed direct sunlight to remain in the air. Yarrow looked askance at me when he said this, as though he wasn't quite sure what to make of me. As had become usual since my transformation, his gaze faltered at first. Not that I could blame him: one look in the mirror had been enough for me. At last he said, "It's possible that, kept in the dark for sixteen years when you ought to have been forming a dependence on direct sunlight, you . . . evolved."

"Evolved?"

He frowned. "I think Iyzabel hoped her Darkness would weaken you, but it appears to have done the opposite. Your body seems to have used all that time in the dark to form a connection with the sun that can penetrate even the tiniest cracks in Iyzabel's enchantment. Those little chinks in the armor of her Darkness were unavoidable; without any sun at all, this whole kingdom would have died in the first year of her reign, with or without false warmth. You're lucky your body seems to know how to reach through the cracks."

I supposed he was right, but I was terrified to feel upward through the Darkness to test his theory. Linden's neck and face—now healed to a mottled burgundy patch in the vague shape of my hand—bore witness to the horrors I could inflict, and the idea of doing worse to him or anyone else made me sick with dread. Yet I also couldn't deny the allure of Yarrow's promise that practice would make me safe. If it did, wasn't it possible to imagine Linden and I might have a future together?

When Yarrow stood and watched me, demanding I practice moving my energy from what he called the sunspot in my chest—where it always lay curled like a cloud of heat—to the edges of my skin and back again, I ever so carefully obeyed. This we did several times a day, with varied success. But though Yarrow told me to practice on my own as well, I only felt secure enough to do so in those rare moments when I was off collecting firewood or relieving myself: far enough from everyone else to guarantee their safety.

For three weeks we held this pattern, and eventually it began to feel like we had been repeating the same cycle for all of time: We woke in the cold—Linden and I slept with plenty of space between us now, since the weather had thawed somewhat—and ate a hurried breakfast before hiding the evidence of our camp. We then commenced the day's walking through the barren trees, which was no longer difficult for me, as my body had finally exchanged much of its softness for muscle. Through the day, Linden made jokes, Yarrow attempted to train me, and Merrall occasionally regaled us with strange and wondrous stories about the sea and the far South. We sometimes stopped to eat a midday meal, other times walked while we ate; and at all times, Linden's hands twitched toward his bow, ready to shoot any small animals that might keep us from starving to death. In the evenings, Merrall found water to soak in, I built a fire, Linden prepared our supper, and Yarrow consulted his compass and map to track our course.

Were it not for the gradual changes in the forest, I might have believed we had been trapped in some enchantment that would keep us locked in an unchanging pattern for the rest of time, doomed to repeat the same day over and over. But the trees soon started to look different: they were thicker than before, with more color and signs of life. There was also more variety in the kinds of trees, and after two weeks of travel, I even began to see living leaves.

"The Darkness is thinning," said Yarrow in satisfaction the first time I pointed out a leaf—a true, green leaf sprouting from a high branch. "Good. It'll be easier for you to reach the sun soon."

My stomach squirmed.

But it was hard to remain oppressed by even self-inflicted anxiety when every day the colors in the forest grew brighter, the branches and leaves thicker, and the world around us lighter. By the third week we were walking on springy moss, purple heather, and green grass, picking through underbrush and listening to small animals scurry through shrubs that looked soft instead of prickly. There were even noticeable changes in the daylight now, with the gray sky becoming almost silver at midday and only utterly black at night. I was even beginning to feel what I could only assume were traces of true warmth: dry and fresh and clean on the breeze when it blew from the north.

"Are we nearly there, Yarrow?" I asked him one day. "It's so light here. Surely we must be close."

He patted me roughly on the back in that way that seemed to say, *Buck up, you poor, naïve creature.* "Not close at all. I'm sorry, Weedy."

I slumped in bitter disappointment. "I'll never make it all the way to the mountains."

He gave me a sidelong smile. "You will. I've found you can do just about anything when you have no other choice."

23

CHAPTER

The next day the landscape became rockier and more sloped, and Yarrow said we were drawing nearer to Myrial Lake, which was surrounded by an intricate natural cave system. He explained that the area had been heavily populated by magical species in the days before the over-throw, especially dwarves and naiads, and some of the caves were famous for their beauty.

"I doubt we'll meet anyone out here now, though," he said. "Iyzabel raided these caves almost as thoroughly as she did Luminor."

Around midday, he led us all into a narrow fissure that opened up just a few paces into the rock. The cavern was enormous, with hewn stairs leading down into a cave that glittered like bronze and diamond in the lantern light, its depths disappearing into darkness. What we could see appeared to be some kind of banquet hall with a dais at one end and several carved stone chairs upon it, and a range of long tables, many upended or cracked. As I peered around, I could see that the place had been largely untouched since whichever invasion had interrupted its last feast, and though fifteen years had taken its toll, there were still many golden plates and goblets scattered about beneath the dirt and cobwebs. It was sobering to think that Iyzabel had left so few survivors to her purge that, in over a decade, no one had returned to so much as loot the place.

I felt someone brush past me and saw Merrall traipse down the stone steps, her garments fluttering in the cold subterranean air. She dropped to her knees in the dust of the banquet hall, bowed her head, and began to speak quietly in the guttural sounds of some language I didn't know. Praying, perhaps, or offering her respects to the dead.

Yarrow didn't say much, and after a few moments of peering around from the top of the steps, he turned and made his way out of the cave again, looking solemn. Merrall followed him, and I thought I saw the glimmer of tears on her cheek.

"I'll be right out, Yarrow," said Linden, raising his lantern as he picked a path down the stone steps and crossed toward the dais. I hesitated a moment before following to see what had caught his attention.

He was holding the lantern up to one of the carved chairs, which seemed to have an insignia etched into its back.

"What is it?"

He gestured at the symbol. "I saw this in Beq's house, and I wondered if it was the seal of her chief. Dwarves don't have kings, you know, but instead elect chiefs. Beq must have belonged to this clan before the overthrow."

"Do elves have kings?" I asked, glancing sidelong at him as I tried to remember what Yarrow had said about elves when I had asked as a child.

"Certainly. Why?"

"Just curious." I had a sudden vision of Linden dressed

in fine silks and sitting on a throne like this one, hair neatly combed and topped with a crown. I barely repressed a snort. "Are you related to any?"

He laughed, the sound echoing through the cavern and filling me up like sunlight. I chewed back a smile.

"No," he said, grinning and nudging me with his shoulder. "I'm just a peasant. I hope that doesn't bother you too much."

My head was starting to swim from the way his eyes poured into mine in the little halo of lantern light, holding them mercilessly.

"Why should it?"

"Oh, well, I just thought a royal personage such as yourself might not want to associate with the dregs of society like me, so I was going to offer to remove myself from your esteemed presence if you—"

The laughter burst out of me, and as his grin widened, I tried to push him away. He caught my hand and held it loosely, sending a bolt of heat up my arm. Somewhere in my brain, a distant voice was telling me to pull away from him, but I barely heard it.

Somewhat tentatively, Linden took hold of my other hand too. His fingers were gentle, and his eyes held mine, searching, uncertain. I was beginning to find breathing difficult, so I looked away. The light inside me swelled and billowed, expanding through my limbs, and the awareness cleared my head a little. Soon, I remembered, it would seep through my skin . . . and that would not be good. I tried to remember my training.

But then his thumbs skimmed over the insides of my wrists, lighter than the brush of leaves, and just as quickly my head became muddled again. I looked up. In the glow of the lantern, his green eyes roved over my face. I could see uncertainty there, but for the first time I was sure I could also see his own longing, the mirror of mine.

I wanted him to kiss me more than I had ever wanted anything in my whole life.

My hands trembled as he slipped his fingers into my palms again, interlacing them with mine. I could feel his pulse against my wrist, as strong and wild as my own. His eyes softened so much they seemed to send spidery cracks through my entire body, breaking me into fragments held together by skin.

He leaned toward me—and I jerked away just as the cavern exploded with light.

Both of us stumbled backward as I gasped and yanked the sunlight back into myself, reeling with shock and horror. For a moment the lantern light was useless as my eyes struggled to adjust, and then at last I began to see shapes again. Linden was standing against the table, looking agitated.

"Siria?" he croaked. "Are you okay?"

My eyes burned with tears of shame and self-loathing. How could I have been so stupid as to think I could ever learn control over this force, this insane power? Linden would never be safe from me. "Fine," I stammered. "Did I burn you again?"

"I'm fine," he said dismissively. "But you . . . do you . . . ?" In the shadows, his face was a mask of confusion and doubt.

"I'm sorry," I said, my voice breaking.

"Ah," he said, with rare awkwardness. "So you don't want . . . you don't . . . feel the same, then . . ."

My stomach lurched as comprehension caught up to me. He had interpreted my silence, my pulling away, my blazing light as a negative reaction. And though my immediate impulse was to assure him I *did* feel the same, I realized a second later he had given me an opportunity I could not waste.

His shoulders were slightly hunched, and in the tumble of dark hair over his forehead I saw traces of the little boy I had known as a child. My best friend. The thought of what I must do next made me feel like someone was smashing my heart with a rock. I swallowed against the lump in my throat and forced myself to look at his neck, at the mottled handprint beneath the stubble. If I told him the truth, he would say he didn't care—that a few burns didn't bother him—and how would I have the strength the resist him then?

"No," I choked, squeezing my eyes shut. "I don't."

And then, before I could take back the lie, I turned and hurried through the cavern, my footsteps echoing as I ran. I was so distracted by the roaring inside my head, by the pain tearing me apart, that I did not hear the other noise until I was a dozen paces out of the cave and into the forest. But then it reached me—a sound that made me feel as though a gust of frozen wind had blown through the trees. It was a note: a long, high, unearthly note that wavered and swelled on the air, unlike anything I had ever heard before.

I stopped and whirled just as Linden appeared through the fissure of the cave, his eyes so cold and hard I almost couldn't believe they were the same ones I had been lost in moments before. But then he heard the sound too, and his face drained of color. Chills rolled down my spine.

"What is it?" I said. "What's that sound?"

"Get to the others," he said hoarsely. "Run!"

In three strides he had caught up with me. He pushed

me ahead of him, and we began to sprint, our footfalls thundering out an accompaniment to the voice that rose as we ran.

"Together!" Yarrow bellowed from the dimness ahead. "Get together! Siria! Linden!"

He and Merrall came into view as we rounded a stand of beeches, drawing together just ahead of us. The strange music was all around.

"What is it?" I panted as we reached them, and Linden pushed me between himself and Yarrow. My shoulder jammed against Merrall's back, and Yarrow squeezed in on the other side. I realized they were trying to keep me close to the center, protected. The eerie music rose another octave and swelled to a volume that made gooseflesh erupt all over my scalp.

"It's a banshee," said Yarrow. "A herald of death."

24

CHAPTER

Most of what I knew about banshees I had learned from girls at Gildenbrook, who had, in any case, always been more interested in scaring the wits out of each another than exchanging real facts. All I could recall was that banshees wailed when someone was about to die.

I shivered again. At the moment, that seemed all the information I needed.

Prying at Linden's arm, I tried to squeeze myself free. I didn't know what I could possibly do to help without using my hideous powers, but I couldn't let them all die trying to protect me . . .

But Linden refused to budge. "They're only heralds," he hissed, shaking off my scrabbling fingers. "They don't kill people, they just announce an approaching death."

"Well, they've got it wrong!" I said, panic tightening my throat. "No one here is going to die!"

"Hush, Siria," Yarrow snapped.

The keening grew louder and closer. Wild terror swirled in my chest as I struggled against my companions—Linden and Yarrow, whom I loved so much, and Merrall, who had sacrificed years of her life to help me, despite our mutual dislike—wondering who the wailing was meant for, and how it could possibly be for any of them. Or was it for me? Were Umbraz soldiers lurking nearby? I wanted to scream for the sound to stop; it was unbearable.

Evidently Yarrow thought so too.

"Cease!" he bellowed suddenly. "Stop, banshee, and show yourself!"

To my astonishment, it did stop. The eerie wail broke off, followed by a long moment of silence in which only the breeze could be heard. Then a voice—thin and uncertain— called, "Don't any of you feel . . . a little bit, maybe . . . like you might die?"

I looked at Linden and Merrall, whose faces were uncomprehending, and then stood on tiptoe to peer in the direction of the voice. In front of me, Yarrow lowered his Runepiece.

"No," he said warily. "We'd all planned to go on living, actually."

A new sound came then: a sniffling noise, and then a sob.

Through a gap in the trees ahead, a pearly, silver light appeared. As slowly as if it were drifting on the breeze, a small, slender figure approached, bright as a will-o'-the-wisp, its head bowed. It stopped just beneath the shadow of a thick maple tree, crying softly.

"That's enough," said Yarrow. "Come out and explain this nonsense."

With a choked, gulping sound, the weeping ceased, and the figure wafted out of the trees to hover in front of Yarrow. It was a young girl, and she was not silver, as I had believed, but emitting a lustrous light from her ghostly pale skin. She was petite, even for a child, and her long, gray, wispy hair hung in curtains around her face, ending in the middle of her back. I thought her wide eyes and draping, tattered gray dress made her look a little bit like Merrall, though Merrall herself obviously thought no such thing; she was giving the newcomer the same sort of look she gave Umbraz soldiers.

Very slowly, our group broke apart and edged closer to the banshee, though Merrall kept well to the back.

"What's your name, child?" asked Yarrow.

The banshee gave a sniff and said, barely audibly, "E-e-elegy."

"Hello, Elegy," Yarrow replied, sounding torn between exasperation and curiosity. "I'm Yarrow Ash, and these are my companions. We stopped when we heard your song, as you might expect, but we remain in suspense: Might I inquire whether any of us is actually scheduled to die?"

At this, Elegy dissolved into fresh sobs. Her whole body shook with them, and she seemed to struggle to hold herself upright. Yarrow gave an impatient grunt, and on a sudden impulse I ducked around him and took hold of the banshee's hand.

Two things happened at once: The ghostly silver light around the girl vanished as instantly as if it had been blown out, and she stopped crying. She looked up at me with her bottom lip trembling, as solid as any of us, and drifted down to stand on the ground. "Y-you're not afraid of me?"

"No," I lied, hoping this was the right answer. "I just want to know why you're crying, and why none of us have died yet if you're a banshee."

Elegy stared at me, eyes very wide. Up close I could see they were a stormy shade of violet. "It's b-because . . . I'm . . . I'm a b-bad banshee." Her lip quivered dangerously again.

I crouched down to look her in the face. "Why would you say that? Did you do something terrible?"

Elegy shook her head. "No, I'm bad at *being* a banshee." She took a deep breath. "I'm twelve, and I've never predicted a death. Most of us do before we can walk, so . . . I-I've been banished."

"Your family banished you because you can't predict when people will die? And you're *twelve*?" I imagined a pale, straight-backed couple in gray clothing sneering down at this banshee child with the same impatient expression I had so often seen on Phipps's and Milla's faces. A sudden and surprising desire to shield the banshee girl from her family's disapproval rose up in me, and I bent closer to her, brushing a tear from her death-white cheek.

Elegy started at the contact but raised her eyes to mine. "It's not that unusual," she admitted. "Banishment is one of the ways we can learn to find the Sight, if we don't have it already. And if we don't succeed, we can go find another life—" She faltered. "Away from our own kind, whom we have disgraced."

"You haven't disgraced anyone," I said firmly. I didn't know what surprised me more: that I believed what I said, or that I wanted her to believe it too. "Come with us. Maybe we can help you."

"Siria." Yarrow's voice was full of warning.

I turned to him, mutely pleading.

"Excuse us a moment, Elegy," said Yarrow, giving her a little bow before towing me back toward the others. Linden looked conflicted, but Merrall was staring at me as if I had sprouted tentacles from my eyeballs. We all retreated a few steps and faced each other.

"I am sorry, sunchild," Merrall burst out at once, "but this I will not permit. We cannot take in a banshee."

"Hush!" I hissed. "She can hear you!"

"They bring death," she railed, not troubling to lower her voice. "They are bad omens, bad luck. Their power makes them filthy, an abomination."

"Bad luck?" I said, starting to feel angry now. "She's a little girl! And she's no filthier than any of us—probably a good deal cleaner than me, at a guess."

"Siria," said Yarrow wearily, "banshees are notoriously secretive about their practices. Even I know very little about them. For all we know, banishment is a very effective way to inspire the Sight in those who lack it. Be careful meddling in things you don't understand."

"You want to leave her alone in the woods?" I said incredulously. "A child, with no one to help her, who's *crying*? Anyway, since when is it 'meddling' to offer to help someone?"

He seemed to deliberate. "It may be meddling to assume that what we can offer her is help. She could very well be worse off with us than on her own."

Merrall ranted on, ". . . banshees have a terrible reputation—"

"So do I!" I interrupted, rounding on her. "Anyway, you heard her—she doesn't even have any magic yet. And she's completely alone. Maybe we should let her prove for herself whether she's worth all this judgment."

I flushed at my own words, knowing I must sound like a terrible hypocrite. All of us knew quite well how prejudiced I was against even my own power. But for the first time in my life, fear of what someone else might think of me was not uppermost among my concerns. This child—banshee or not—needed someone to help her, just as I had needed someone when I was a little girl. Yarrow and Linden had come to my aid then, and I could come to her aid now.

"I think Siria's right," said Linden quietly.

Merrall rolled her eyes and looked at Yarrow. "We have enough hungry mouths without adding another. And what if she has been planted? What if Iyzabel sent her?"

Yarrow glanced back over his shoulder. "Iyzabel has never had anything to do with banshees," he said quietly. "They have no magic apart from their Sight, so they aren't useful as a weapon. I don't think she's a plant." He sighed, then looked at me. "We can't take any added risks. If she comes with us, she can't leave. And it must be her choice. I won't have you coercing her against her will."

I nodded eagerly.

He scowled at me, and his voice became even quieter. "Hear me when I say she'll *have* to stay, Siria. If she comes, she will hear things, learn things that we could not risk anyone else discovering. If we take her in, she must stay with us faithfully until we release her."

"I'll ask her."

Elegy was still standing at the edge of the trees. Without her pearlescent glow, she looked even smaller than before. Her lip trembled as I approached, but when I smiled, she returned the gesture tentatively.

"It's your choice," I said, crouching in front of her again. "If you want to come with us, you're welcome. But you can't leave if you do, at least not for a while. And it might be dangerous, but—" I looked back over my shoulder at Yarrow, whose wiry eyebrows were raised over his spectacles; Linden, who quickly tried to hide his miserable expression; and Merrall, who looked as if she had just been force-fed entrails. I took a deep breath. "But we'll take care of you and protect you. If you don't want to be alone, you don't have to be."

She studied my face, her wide violet eyes taking in my freckles and unwashed, fire-bright hair as though they would give her clues as to my trustworthiness. I didn't know if she had ever heard of a sunchild before, or if it would matter to her if she had. It was plain she had not, at least, heard that the queen of Terra-Volat was in the process of tearing her kingdom apart in search of a girl who matched my description.

It was also clear by her expression of mingled disbelief and hope that she had not often met with a person who didn't disapprove of her.

"I'll come with you," she said in a small voice, and then flinched as if waiting for me to revoke the offer.

I stood up and offered her my hand. "Good," I said. "Come on. You can walk with me."

25

CHAPTER

At first Elegy was about as talkative as a rock, though Merrall's frequent dark and forbidding looks couldn't have been much encouragement to speak. She walked mostly beside me, either keeping her eyes downcast or sneaking furtive glances at the rest of us.

"How did she get through your defenses?" I heard Linden ask Yarrow not long after we set off again, his voice low and worried. Yarrow's reply was too quiet for me to hear, but I could tell he was disturbed. Elegy might not be a threat, but if she could penetrate Yarrow's enchantment, who else might? I saw more evidence of magic spreading out from Yarrow's Runepiece as we walked on into the night, bracken occasionally glowing white or blue beneath my boots.

After another few days, however, we relaxed again—all except Linden and me, who politely avoided each other with an effort that, on my end, felt like having a splinter perpetually embedded in my chest—and Elegy began to seem more comfortable too. I learned she had come from a large colony of banshees near Myrial Lake, and that her mother was a harsh, unfeeling matriarch who thought success was only to be found in the number of deaths one accurately predicted and the subsequent swoons caused by the heralding of those deaths. I ached as I listened; Elegy's mother sounded a lot like Milla, though perhaps more liberal in her criticism.

The fourteenth of fifteen children, Elegy had always preferred a sweeter kind of singing—less like a dirge than other banshees, she said—and from the very start had suffered her mother's disapproval.

"I'd been wondering for a while if they might banish me," she said. "So I guess it wasn't much of a surprise."

In return for her confidence, I told her that until recently I hadn't known I had any powers at all, and admitted I was still reluctant to use them. She seemed to know very little about sunchildren, but still gave me a confused look when I'd said this.

"You don't want your powers?"

"Well," I said, looking over my shoulder to judge whether Yarrow was within eavesdropping distance. "I mean, it's more complicated than that. My powers are really dangerous, you know? I've already hurt Linden, and who knows what else I might do before I figure out how to control myself. *If* I figure it out. It's not exactly that I don't *want* my powers, I guess . . . I'm just— I just . . ."

"You're afraid of them."

My shoulders slumped. I hated hearing it spoken. "I suppose."

Elegy squinted up at me, and the judgment in her face both shamed and annoyed me. I knew how it must sound to someone who wanted her own powers so badly, but she really had no idea what it was like to be a danger to the people you loved.

"I didn't think you were a coward," she said, her words soft, not meant to be cruel. They stung anyway.

I chuckled bitterly. "Well. You obviously don't know me very well. I've spent most of my life quaking in fear of things—literally quaking, half the time—and I can't remember the last time I went a whole day without being afraid of at least one thing."

"Being afraid doesn't make you a coward," said Elegy, sounding surprised. "Everyone's afraid of things. It's how you react that makes you a coward."

I snorted.

"I'm serious! You stood up for me to your friends, which was brave. But hiding from the things you're afraid of . . . that's what's cowardly."

I didn't reply, but I could feel the flush in my cheeks.

Elegy patted my arm, and I was surprised to find her smiling. "I was wrong," she murmured. "You're not a coward. You're just not being as brave as you could be."

Sometime during the afternoon, Linden shot a pheasant, which was the first game we'd had in weeks that wasn't rabbit or squirrel. The prospect of roasted pheasant that evening lifted everyone's spirits, and by the time we stopped to make camp, we were the liveliest we'd been the whole course of the journey.

Linden was warmer toward me as we built up the fire, cleaned the bird, and stewed the root vegetables Elegy had found along the trail, all of us reminiscing about our favorite foods from home and dreaming of the things we would eat when the world was right again. I wished for the thousandth time I was able to tell Linden the truth, but every time I con- sidered it, I saw the outcome as clear as reality: Linden's hurt would turn to determination, and that look would come back into his eyes—the melting, burning look that stole the bones from my legs—and before I could stop him, he would follow through with the almost-kiss from the cave.

He would kiss me, and I would kiss him back, and by the time I came to my senses there would be nothing left of his face but charred, blackened bones. It was impossible. Not for anything would I risk Linden's life.

When at last we sat down to eat, Elegy opened up a bottle she had inside her satchel and offered to share it with the rest of us. It turned out to be some kind of banshee draft that did nothing whatsoever to the tiny, fragile-looking Elegy, but made the rest of us slightly giddy. It was the first time I had ever heard Merrall laugh, and the sound was unexpectedly bright, like bells. Linden looked more relaxed than he had in days, and I found myself smiling at him from across the fire. He tentatively smiled back.

And then, while we all whooped and urged him on, Yarrow turned his Runepiece into a fiddle. With his lit pipe clamped firmly between his back teeth, he wedged the instrument between his shoulder and jaw and raised a silver-gray bow to the strings.

Anyone who had never heard Yarrow play before, I thought as my blood rose and hummed to the first barely grazed note, had never properly heard the music of the instru- ment. The bow flew over the strings like a flame dancing on the wick of a candle—leaping up and skimming across, diving down and running back and forth, so fast it was barely visible. The strings sang with a voice that seemed to come from the world beyond the worlds, for it was wild and elegant at once; sometimes keening so high it was almost a screech, but never too severe; other times dragging low and resonant and so rich the sound echoed through my bones. If I hadn't heard him play an ordinary fiddle so often before, I might have believed the Runepiece instrument was magical.

For a moment after he began, everyone went motionless, as still as the trees that surrounded us. Merrall's mouth sagged open, and Elegy looked spellbound. But then Merrall laughed and jumped to her feet, offering her hand—to my complete amazement—to the banshee, who stared at her in just as much surprise. In another moment, Merrall had pulled Elegy up and was teaching her how to dance a jig.

Linden's laugher rang out at this miraculous development, and he got up to come sit beside me. My heart started to bang off the walls of my chest—should I dance with him?—but before I could think what to do, he nudged my shoulder gently with his. I turned, wondering how I could possibly avoid touching his skin, but instead of offering me his hand, he smiled. "Sing with me?"

When we were young, and nights in front of Yarrow and Linden's fire were a regular event, Yarrow had often played while Linden and I sang. If we didn't already know the words to his songs—which was often—we made up our own. But it had been years since we'd had a night like this; the ritual had stopped when I went to Gildenbrook.

I nodded and Linden's eyes glinted, making him look like a much younger version of himself. Something so sweet it was almost painful swept through my chest. The smells of wood smoke and pipe tobacco joined with the music to press the clear image of that old cabin into my mind: I could see the carved table and the woodstove, the brick fireplace, the hanging bunches of herbs and haunches of salted meats, the mud-encrusted spades, and gunnysacks filled with seeds. I could see Linden, boyish and confident, laughter in his eyes and dirt beneath his fingernails as he sat before the crackling fire. I could hear our voices, so familiar to one another then, and Yarrow's violin weaving through them like golden thread.

And now we sang together again, breaking off periodically in fits of laughter when one or both of us got the words wrong. I was careful not to touch Linden, but my skin threw scattered light over all of us as the energy in my chest expanded, and I did not bother to pull it back in.

Yarrow twinkled down at us through the haze of pipe smoke, and began another song—sad and beautiful, but one I knew well, though I had not heard it in many years. Linden's eyes were bright when I looked at him, and for the first time since the cave, they did not drop away.

We began quietly, but our voices strengthened as they mingled with the crescendo of the violin. Linden's husky tenor rose and fell with the melody, echoing Yarrow's strings, and I sang the harmony, blending my alto with Linden's voice in each verse.

I first met Sweet Sadie in moonlight;
Though perhaps it was she that did glim.
The blue silk of her gown that flowed to the ground
With her ankles barefooted and thin.
Her green eyes alight as she moved through the night,
Oh Sweet Sadie of the Glen.

No shadow upon her could fall;
She appeared as though in matins.
Her pearly face glowed as if heaven were showed,

But dimly through the veil of her skin.
And to me I called the fairest of all:
Sweet Sadie of the Glen.

It was a folk song, old and familiar to me as Yarrow himself, but I faltered as the lyrics fell off my tongue. Well though I knew them, they suddenly blazed with new meaning. Linden caught my gaze, held it, and I saw with amazement that he had understood them all along.

Her hair was the color of fire,
And raged as a flame from within.
In her voice could be found a musical sound,
A softness that ruptures and rends.
If praise could be higher, I would not be a liar
For Sweet Sadie of the Glen.

I'll soon be with her always
As the envy of all men.
For to be close to that beautiful ghost
I've drunken a dram of black poison.
As the world turns to haze I begin my days
With Sweet Sadie of the Glen.

We sang the last note together, and I heard our voices cease at precisely the same time. As the song trailed away and came to a trembling halt with the last stroke of Yarrow's violin, I stared hard into the red embers of the fire. I didn't need to ask. I knew now that the song was about—had always been about—a sunchild.

For a moment, no one spoke. Then Merrall said, her throaty voice constrained, "That was very beautiful."

I continued to gaze into the fire, all my nerves tingling. My chest ached. Linden did not move; he remained sitting beside me, elbows on his knees while the air between us hung thick and tremulous—as real as the music had been—and my entire left side pulsed with awareness of him. The others began to get up around us, stretching and yawning and muttering about sleep, but Linden and I seemed carved out of stone.

When he touched my hand, I jumped, even though his fingertips were soft as breath. I turned to look at him, fighting to contain the rampant sun energy inside me, which had swelled as we sang. The expression in his eyes was inscrutable, a wild mix of hope and doubt and confusion and longing, and I knew I was doing a bad job of upholding what I had claimed in the cave. The mere fact I was glowing had to be a clue to my real feelings, even if by some chance he couldn't see them written in my face. I ducked my head, trying to fight off the haze of banshee wine and music long enough to think what to do . . .

What would happen if I told him the truth? Was it possible there was some way to truly control this power, to keep myself from being a danger to him?

I drew a breath, opened my mouth, lifted my eyes to his—

And he dropped his gaze and turned away. Doubt seized me, but before I could react, he cleared his throat and stood up. "We need sleep," he said gruffly, and walked off toward the others.

I felt as though I had been emptied of all but my bones, which now seemed to be made of some cold, clanging metal. Were it not for my conscious control of it, my light would have blinked out all at once; but I dimmed it slowly, drawing it in by degrees so I would not make Linden suspicious.

This was for the best, I told myself as I followed him toward the aqua orb and bundled shapes on the ground that were Merrall, Yarrow, and Elegy. Let Linden stay angry; it was far better than being maimed or dead.

The campfire had burned almost out, and the early spring night chill had its grip on the forest. As the emptiness inside me expanded, I was relieved to lie down beside Elegy and wrap myself in my blankets, squeezing my eyes shut against tears.

My dreams were unsettling. Elegy pinned me with an accusing violet eye and said, "Coward. You are a coward, sunchild."

She turned into Linden, who leaned in to kiss me, but then drew back at the last second. He became a beautiful woman with silky black hair and green-painted lips, who smiled darkly before pressing her mouth to my cheek.

"Not a coward at all," she said in a low, purring voice. "It takes courage to resist using your powers. No one understands that, do they?"

The spot she had kissed burned cold.

26

CHAPTER

The next day was foggy and slate-colored, like my mood, and no one spoke much until we stopped for the midday meal. I sat down beside Merrall, as far away from Linden as I could get. The naiad had been silent all day, and she, too, was staring absently into space. But as I watched her in a vague, detached way, I realized her chin had begun, very slightly, to tremble.

"Merrall—are you all right?"

She actually jumped, as if she had completely forgotten I was there. I watched her warily and was alarmed to see tears glittering in her huge aqua eyes.

"Fine," said Merrall in almost a bark. "I am fine. I was just going to go look for a stream. I can hear one . . . down the ridge."

I hesitated, then said, "Do you mind if I come along?"

Merrall looked startled. "I—I suppose not. If you want to."

We picked our way down a rocky slope toward the trickling sounds of a stream, and I wondered if the naiad's health and mood were tied to the water in the same way mine seemed to be tied to the sun. Perhaps going so long without her usual amount of time underwater was taking a toll.

"Is it hard for you?" I asked as we neared the stream. The trees here seemed healthier than the ones farther up the incline, and large patches of soft green moss grew along the banks. "Traveling over land for so long?"

Merrall shrugged. "It is not terrible. There have been enough brooks and streams along the way. Do you want to swim, sunchild?"

"I—n-no thanks," I stammered. The memory of our icy excursion through the Umbraz canals still haunted me. "You go ahead, though."

Merrall gave a smile that did not reach her eyes and walked straight into the water.

The change was immediate. Where they touched the water, Merrall's feet turned deep fuchsia, widening and flattening into a pair of fins even before the rest of her legs were submerged. Glittering scales sprang up on her ankles below the fluttering seaweed garments, spreading as her legs fused into one appendage and flicked with tremendous power, propelling her into the greenish water. As Merrall plunged beneath the surface, the reedy-brown strands of her hair turned brightest violet, shimmering in the gray air as her head reemerged. Every part of her had intensified, had become a more radiant version of itself, and her skin flushed dazzling blue.

"Merrall," I said, stepping carefully to the bank's edge and sitting on an outcropping of rock. I left my rucksack on my back, fearful of getting it wet. "Is everything all right? You seem a bit . . . sad."

Merrall's eyes flashed toward me, but her defensiveness faltered when she saw I was sincere. She looked away.

"I understand if you don't want to talk about it," I said, already half hoping she didn't. My relationship with Merrall had improved over the last month, but we were still a long way from friends.

Merrall swam closer to my rock and rested her elbows on a mossy boulder. "Sometimes," she said, without looking at me, "life can be overwhelming, and sometimes it catches up to you. Do you know what I mean?"

I gave a humorless laugh. "Yes."

Merrall lifted her face to regard me. Her eyes narrowed, and she seemed to deliberate something. Finally, she let out a long breath. "When I was young," she said, "I lived with my mother on the western coast of the Elder Bay. We had a small cottage in a cove and spent every day in the sea. Life is endless and deep and dazzling in the open water . . . Not like rivers.

"One day I ventured farther than I ever had before and came upon a fishing boat that had caught a seal in its nets. I watched from behind a driftwood log as the fishermen debated what to do with the creature. Most of them wanted to sell its skin, but one young man said they should release it. He fought with his companions, and the argument grew loud and violent. The young man—Brinn, I learned his name was—drew out a knife and cut the seal loose. The creature went free, but one of the fishermen lashed out, slashing Brinn's face, and hit him hard across the head. Brinn toppled out of the boat, and his companions sailed away, leaving him to die.

"I caught him before he sank too deep and towed him to the surface, then swam him back to the cottage. My mother was still out, but I nursed him back to consciousness and dressed his wounds. By the time Mother returned, he was sitting up and talking again.

"He stayed with us a month. By the time he left, we

were in love, but he had no money for marriage, and said he would be back for me after he returned home to claim his inheritance. Three days later, Luminor fell."

I did not need Merrall to explain further. As a naiad, she would have been in immediate peril.

"My mother and I fled north through the canals and rivers to the resistance camp we heard had formed in the Northern Wilds. But Mother became sick on the journey . . . She only lived for a week after we reached the rebels."

"I—I'm so sorry, Merrall. What did you do? Once . . . once she was gone?"

"Without Mother, I wanted work—I wanted to be busy. I was assigned to be a spy in Umbraz, and I left with half a hope that Brinn would find me, that his love would drive him to search every corner of the kingdom. But the years passed . . ." She swallowed. "I still have not seen him again."

At a complete loss for what to say, and feeling words were probably inadequate anyway, I gazed at Merrall for a long moment, then reached for her wet hand. She flinched slightly but did not pull away.

"Sometimes," she continued in a very tight voice, "certain things make me more aware of the loss of him than I usually am. It has been fifteen years, after all. But that song . . . the song you and the elf sang last night . . ."

My stomach clenched.

"It cut into the old wound, and . . . and it made me remember."

All I could think to do was to squeeze Merrall's cold fingers. My mind strayed back up the bank to Linden, and it suddenly seemed stupid to keep my feelings from him when life was so short and full of uncertainty. There was no guarantee any of us would survive the next week—let alone the rest of our lives—and what did it matter if my power kept me from kissing him? He should at least know the truth.

Merrall and I did not speak again, but after another few moments, the naiad hefted herself onto the bank and transformed back into an ordinary-looking—albeit dripping wet—woman. Side by side, we made our way back up the slope.

My head was so full of her story and my own new resolve that it wasn't until Merrall lurched to seize my arm that I heard the screams.

27

CHAPTER

We exchanged one horrified look, then started to run, stumbling over loose stones and tree roots and pulling each other up by turns as the cries grew louder, then mixed with the clanging of steel and the twang of bowstrings. My chest felt like it was shrinking, too small to contain my knocking, throbbing heart. I was almost dragging Merrall.

We came over the rise and ran straight into an Umbraz soldier. He bellowed and charged, but Merrall acted quickly. With a flick of her hand, she pulled a sphere of glittering blue water out of thin air and flung it at him. It did not break; instead, it settled on his head like a bizarre water helmet, distorting his features and his voice, even as he opened his mouth to shout again. He clawed at the bubble, his fingernails slipping off its surface as if it were glass, and as he choked and his eyes began to bulge, I realized what would happen next. A bolt of horror shot through me.

"Come on," said Merrall grimly, pulling me away as she drew her aquamarine stiletto.

Through the trees I could see Yarrow, the Runepiece in his palm glowing white as he fell soldiers like toy dolls.

Linden's dagger was out, and he commanded the legion of crawling vines that swarmed over the ground toward the soldiers' feet, entangling them and dragging them down. His skin, like Merrall's, blazed with evidence of his magic. Elegy crouched near him at the base of a tree, as if she was trying to make herself as small as possible.

Iyzabel's soldiers were everywhere. They outnumbered us twenty to one at least, and I felt dizzy as I tried to comprehend their presence. How had they found us? Had it been our singing the night before? Had Yarrow's enchantments failed?

It was a moment before I realized the ground beneath me was shuddering.

I turned, and as I saw what was causing the ground to shake, my body seemed to disconnect from my mind. I had expected pursuit, and I knew Iyzabel had many dark creatures at her service, but I had never thought to expect this one. He wasn't hard to identify; he figured prominently in many children's tales, and his hundred claw-footed legs were as infamous as the twenty-foot-long, muscular pale body that wound through the tree trunks, as well as his spiky, horned head. According to the stories, he had wings too, and if you were a bad child, he might arrive, flapping and twisting at your window, ready to break the panes with the flat armor on his head and force his snakelike neck inside—at which point he would either devour you or fill your room with cold black flames from his maw.

A Night Wyrm.

I stood with my arms hanging at my sides. How had the soldiers managed to bring him all the way here?

"Kill them all—except the girl! Leave the sunchild!" one of the soldiers bellowed, some distance to my left.

I suddenly realized Merrall was no longer beside me. As I looked wildly around, terror and adrenaline churning in me like boiling water, a roaring sound came from the Night Wyrm's direction, and then I heard absolutely nothing at all. Some instinct made me throw myself behind a tree trunk, and then the world was black and silver and a brilliant, shocking blue, and I smelled sulfur and charred flesh. My limbs became immobile as a roiling cloud of chill white fog swallowed up the forest, denser than smoke, with billows that burned so cold they were almost hot.

"*Linden!*" I screamed, choking on the dry, frozen fog.

The white smoke ebbed slightly away, and I flung myself out from behind the tree, sprinting over crunching, icy bracken in the direction I had last seen Linden. Through the thinning fog I could see that every tree within sight was now thick with ice on the side facing the Night Wyrm, and I knew that anyone who had been directly exposed to the beast's frozen fire died instantly. My heart felt like it might break out of my rib cage, and I screamed a curse at the whirling white smoke that was still too thick to see through. What had happened to my friends? Had they taken shelter before the black fire—

Something collided with my right shoulder, sending me to my knees so quickly I didn't immediately realize I had fallen. And then heat and pain blazed through my entire arm, and for a moment I was oblivious to everything but the sudden swell of nausea that made both ground and sky seem unfixed. I threw out my left arm to catch myself as I fell forward, and lights popped before my eyes. Every nerve in my right side was agonizingly ablaze.

I heard men shouting somewhere nearby. The Night Wyrm gave a chilling, guttural screech as I lurched to my feet again, trying to ignore my arm, and I managed several more steps before I staggered once more. Another wave of dizzying pain shot through my limb. I forced myself to look down at it.

My stomach heaved.

A thick, black arrow was speared through my upper arm, protruding straight out on each side as if the flesh and muscle were no more substantial than upholstery. Dark, glutinous blood covered the shaft beyond the exit wound, rapidly soaking into my clothes.

My mouth opened—a shudder ran the length of my body—I was going to be sick—

Something red and brighter than flames exploded through the trees just ahead of me, and I looked up. Yarrow was there. He had turned his Runepiece into a long, pale knife—the source of the red light—and he glowed like wrath incarnate as he drew it in a wide, arcing ring around himself, sending a wave of crackling crimson speeding out over the whole forest.

It caught me in the chest. The world trembled, shimmered.

And disappeared.

PART THREE

"The light shines in the darkness, and the darkness has not overcome it."

JOHN 1:5

28

CHAPTER

I gasped and blinked furiously. I was lying on the ground. The red imprint still glowing on my eyeballs told me no time had passed since I had been in the midst of the frozen trees, but my surroundings had changed entirely. There was no ice, no shouting, no red light. I remained in the forest, but the trees around me were thinner, younger. The air was fresh, and I smelled dirt rather than cold smoke. Birdsong began tenuously somewhere above me, and I saw a field stretching just beyond the trees in the foggy gray light of the afternoon.

As I tried to push myself upright, pain tore through the fibers of my right arm, churning my gut and obscuring my vision again. I had just enough presence of mind to drop back onto my side so I wouldn't choke on my own vomit when my vision flickered out and my hearing faded.

I was lying on a scratchy surface that smelled of sheep. The right side of my dress clung wet to my skin, and I was shivering. Beneath the numbness spreading like frost through my body, I could feel a dull, pulsing pain in my right arm.

"Light above," breathed a man's voice, very near at hand. "There's no good way to get at it. Bronya, hold her still, won't you? I'm going to have to break it in half."

I opened my eyes. Leaping, dim firelight flickered all around, giving the impression I was lying inside a giant lantern. A ceiling of wooden beams gleamed far above me, and blurry faces swam in and out of my sight. I raised my left arm to rub my eyes, but found my fingers gritty with blood and dirt.

"Lie still if you can, sweetheart," said a woman's soothing voice. "Roark, can you snap it cleanly without doing more damage?"

"I . . . think so."

I could feel hands slipping beneath my head, lifting it gently and propping me against something. Fingers found my left hand and closed around it.

"It's okay, darling," said the woman's voice. "It'll be over in just a minute, and then you'll be fine. Hold my hand."

Someone lifted my right arm and the pain redoubled, shooting up and down the limb as if a thousand hot needles swarmed inside it. And then the needles became swords as something thick and inflexible moved inside my arm, between the muscle and the bone. I screamed.

"Shhhh," breathed the woman, holding me as I tried to jerk away. "Hush, love. You must be brave . . ."

Brave? I was not brave. I tried to tell her, but my tongue felt thick and uncooperative.

The man's voice was swearing fluently. "Damn it to the bloody Chasm, what's this thing made of? It won't break!"

"Could you cut it with something?"

"I'd have even less control . . . probably tear something in her arm."

"Try one more time."

The foreign thing inside my arm moved again, and I thought I would die from the pain. I screamed again, but the sound got tangled up in a sob. A loud *crack* echoed around the room, someone gripped my right arm firmly, and the thing inside it began to slide . . .

"Roark, the blood," said the woman sharply.

Darkness washed over me, and I plunged into blessed oblivion.

I roused after what seemed several long years. I was dry now, and wrapped in warm, clean blankets, lying on the same slightly lumpy surface as before—which I now recognized as hay. I was inside a barn.

I reached to scratch my cheek and discovered my hands and face were clean. All of me seemed to be clean, in fact. The nightgown I was wearing was not mine. My right arm still throbbed, and when I peeled away the cocoon of blankets, I saw that it was bandaged in strips of cloth. Dried blood bloomed over the wrapping like spilled ink.

My stomach growled. How long had I been here?

I sat up so abruptly my head whirled. How long *had* I been here? And where was *here*? Some dim gray daylight faintly lit the barn, but now there were short wooden walls on all four sides of my hay-bed—a stall. The scent of farm animals was pungent, and I could hear something grunting and shuffling nearby.

I strained to remember what had happened, but all I could recall was the Night Wyrm and the cold and the arrow in my arm. I tried to push myself up, but I crumpled again almost at once, shaky and panting.

What had happened to Linden and the others? I squeezed my eyes shut, desperate to remember, and came up with a bright red light. I had found myself in a different patch of woods, away from the ice and fog and soldiers, hadn't I? Yarrow's work, surely. Had he scattered everyone, or just sent me away to save me?

A horrible, twisting pain bloomed in my chest. I would never forgive Yarrow if he had sacrificed himself and the others just for me. *Never.*

Trying to steady myself, I put my head in my hands and realized I was burning with fever. The arrow wound must have become infected. But I didn't have time to be sick. If I didn't go find my friends now, it might be too late.

Then, I thought, it might be too late anyway.

Tears scalded my cheeks. I tried again to stand, my legs trembling as I scrabbled to pull myself up by the stall wall, but I fell again at once. The sunspot in my chest was empty and darker than the skies of Umbraz.

If the others were dead, I was alone. If they were dead, I had lost all the people I loved.

I wept where I fell, clutching straw in my fists until the dry stems snapped and poked into the skin of my palms. I drifted back into a stupor of sleep, thinking vaguely of my supposed ability to heal myself with sun energy, and wondering why, with so much emotion, I hadn't already summoned enough sunlight to heal—or burn—the whole world.

29

CHAPTER

I didn't realize I had fallen back asleep until I woke again. People were talking nearby, their voices tense. It was the man and the woman—the ones who had removed the arrow from my arm, presumably the ones who owned the barn, the nightgown, and the blankets.

"I'd find it very hard to believe, even if she admitted it," the woman was saying. "It's been fourteen years, Roark. It's just a coincidence."

"I don't believe in coincidences," grunted the man, Roark. "But even if I did, I'd have a hard time thinking this was one."

The woman was quiet for a moment. "I don't actually think it's a coincidence, either," she said at last. "I'm going to talk to her."

I suddenly realized that the "her" in question was me.

"Wait. It's dangerous, Bronya. I—" His voice faltered. "I don't want to lose you too."

Bronya's voice was gentle when she replied. "I know, my love. But talking to her can't hurt anything."

A door creaked on its hinges, and a glow of light spilled into the dark barn. In another moment, my stall door opened and the gold light resolved itself into a lantern held aloft by a short, curvy woman. At first all but her outline was obscured by shadow, but as she stepped into my stall, I could see she was middle-aged and pretty, with a heart-shaped face, smooth umber skin, and thick black hair pinned into a bun at the nape of her neck. She smiled.

"I didn't know you were awake."

"I heard you talking," I said, too weary to pretend otherwise. "And I know your husband thinks I'm dangerous. He's right."

I wondered if Iyzabel had been spreading propaganda about me in the month I had been tramping through the woods, and it suddenly occurred to me that this Bronya could, in all likelihood, turn me in for a substantial reward.

"Not you, my dear," said Bronya. "He doesn't think *you're* dangerous. That is, he knows what you are, of course."

She looked almost excited—unless it was a trick of the lamplight. I tried to think how I might escape if I learned they were planning to turn me over to Iyzabel, but even the idea of trying to run right now was exhausting.

"Oh, my dear," Bronya said in a suddenly constricted voice. "Oh, sweet child. Your mother would be so proud of you."

I stared at her. "Milla?"

"Milla?" Bronya repeated, looking blank. "Oh! No, no, not Milla. Oh dear, I thought you'd know by now—"

A funny tingling swept through my chest. "Wait," I interrupted. "Wait, you knew my *mother*? My *actual* mother?"

The barn spun around me. It was one thing to imagine my long-dead queen of a mother as a character from a story, or to weave fantasies about what she might have been like, or how my childhood would have been different had she lived . . . But to think that someone still living might have *known* her? Forgetting my weariness, I sat up, breath short and fearing that Bronya might turn out to be a dream.

Her eyes filled with tears. "Oh, sweetheart, you look so much like her. I thought at once it must be you—the kingdom's been crawling with soldiers searching for you this last month, and anyone can see what you are—but goodness! You even *look* like Elysia—apart from the hair and the freckles. That'll be the sun, of course." She laughed, but there was a barely controlled sob in the sound. "I can still picture her face on the day you were born. Never in all her life did she imagine she'd bear a nymph child. You'd think she'd just given birth to the sun itself, the way she looked at you."

My thoughts were thick and ponderous, and I put a hand to my head to stop the spinning. I didn't understand who this Bronya was, or how she knew these things, but I couldn't mistake her sincerity. As her words sank into me, warm and rich as steamed milk, everything else faded to insignificance.

My mother had loved me from the first moment she saw me.

Not tolerated me. Not hoped I might advance her standing at court. Not set impossible standards by which I might hope to earn her approval.

Loved me.

My mother.

Before I could stop them, tears were sliding hot and fast down my cheeks, and I bent forward to put my head into my lap. Bronya gave a choked "Oh!" and I felt her arms around my shoulders. She drew me against her as she plopped down on the hay and cried too, her sobs soft and gentle.

"I'm sorry," she sniffed after a few moments, releasing

me so I could sit up again. "You must think I'm mad. Here I was going to be proper and controlled, and what do I do? Come in and start blubbering without so much as a how do you do!"

I dragged a sleeve across my face, hiccupping slightly, and looked at her. Her eyes were a deep, soft brown, and there were laughter lines at the corners. Though I could still see unshed tears glinting above the lower lids, she had regained her smile.

"I'm sorry," she said again, her voice choked. "I don't know what's happened to you, but I can see you've been through a lot. Let me start over." She took several deep breaths and sat back cross-legged, her plain muslin skirt spread neatly around her. "My name is Bronya Dell, and my husband Roark and I live and work on this farm. We found you badly injured at the edge of our land, and we've done our best to fix you up. So long as you don't leave the barn, you'll be safe until you recover. No one knows you're here."

I nodded, repressing a smile at her sudden formality. There were a hundred questions I needed to ask—how long I'd been here, where we were, what the queen had been doing to find me—but the words that spilled out of me had nothing to do with any of that.

"How did you know my mother?"

Her posture melted slightly, and her hands twitched as if she wanted to pull me into another hug. Instead she clasped them in her aproned lap. "We were childhood friends," she said, decorum gone in another rush of emotion. "Elysia was a commoner, you know. Daughter of a cobbler. And your father—oh, your father was so good to her. Theirs was a fairy tale sort of love story. The prince courted the cobbler's daughter as if she were a duchess, and she may as well have been, as kind and good as she was. She was my dearest friend. I held you the day you were born, you know, Princess."

I was back to feeling lightheaded. "Siria," I mumbled.

"Siria," she repeated, as though trying out the name. "Yes, that's what the broadsheets call you, isn't it?"

"Shouldn't they?" I said, trying not to look stunned at the idea of broadsheets with my name on them.

She looked surprised. "Well, it's not your real name, of course."

I blinked at her in shock. It made perfect sense that Phipps and Milla had been the ones to call me Siria, but somehow it had never occurred to me that my original mother and father might have given me a different name. Had Yarrow known? Bronya seemed to guess at some of my thoughts, because she gave a kind smile and put her palm against my cheek.

"Helena. You are Princess Helena of Luminor."

For a few moments I sat with my eyes closed, pretending the hand against my cheek belonged to Elysia of Luminor, my mother, who had loved me from the first moment she saw me. Who had named me Helena. Who had been the daughter of a cobbler, and who my father, a prince, had treated like a duchess.

I opened my eyes again, taking several shaky breaths. "How long have I been here?"

"Four days," Bronya said, folding her hands in her lap again. "You've been very ill."

"*Four days?* Has—has anyone come looking for me?"

"No more than usual," she said, sounding surprised. "Just the average patrol of soldiers. Princess, what are you doing?"

I had clambered to my knees and was trying to disentangle myself from the blankets. "Call me Siria," I said, pulling frantically at a quilt. "And I'm sorry, really I am, but I need to leave right away. My friends—I don't know what happened to them. Yarrow cast some enchantment, and I ended up at the edge of your field, I guess . . . And if something's happened to them . . ." I broke off, struggling to get a grip on myself. Tears were rising behind my eyes again, both at my sickening worry and at the idea of leaving this woman who had known my mother.

"Yarrow?" she said, eyes widening. "Yarrow Ash?"

I froze and stared at her. She looked odd—startled and sad and hopeful all at once.

"You know Yarrow?"

She nodded slowly. "I did . . . once. He didn't approve of Roark and me leaving the resistance, and I haven't seen him since. But at one time we were . . . good friends."

"The resistance?" I gasped, forgetting my haste in a new wave of shock. "You and Roark were part of the resistance group in the north?"

"A long time ago. But . . . things happened, and we left, and . . . Well. Never mind that. How do you know Yarrow?"

"He as good as raised me," I said, my chest aching. I wanted to stay here with Bronya and hear about why she and Roark had left the rebels, how she knew Yarrow, what my mother had been like . . . but I knew I would never forgive myself if Yarrow and Linden died because I had not come to find them. I resumed my weak attempts to stand.

Bronya looked amazed. "So they went through with the plan, then? They sent out guardians to watch over all the girls? I'm very glad Yarrow is the one who came to you. Your parents would have been pleased."

I stopped again. Had *Yarrow* known my parents too and never said so?

"Siria, please," said Bronya, startling me out of my thoughts. "You really can't leave yet. You're not well enough. The fever may be gone, but you haven't eaten anything in days. Stay a little longer—please. Get your strength up again before you set out. What if Yarrow sent you here on purpose?"

I gave up and sat back down, impressed by this argument. It *would* be like Yarrow to do something like that. And I had to concede she was right: no matter how desperate I was to find my friends, it was obvious I was too weak to travel. The simple struggle against my blankets had defeated me.

I nodded. "Thank you . . . for taking care of me. I think I would have died otherwise."

Bronya reached for my hand and squeezed it. Hers was small and soft but callused like Linden's hands—evidence of hard work. I squeezed back.

"I'll bring you some soup," she said. "But stay in the barn. There's a royal warrant for your arrest, you know. Anyone catches sight of your skin or hair, you'll be on your way to Umbraz before you can say 'sunchild.'"

CHAPTER

The people who farmed Terra-Volat did not have much to live on, but Bronya was an excellent cook. It amazed me she could turn a few pale vegetables and a pot of water into a savory soup, or a handful of grain into a loaf of soft, sweet bread.

"We're better off than some," she admitted when I marveled over the quality of her cooking. "Most people outside of Umbraz barely have enough to keep them from starving. But some farmers, like us, produce more than the standard, and we're rewarded with a little extra food."

"Why do you produce more?"

"Roark and I farmed long before the overthrow, and we know how to get the best results, even in poor conditions. Most who labor for Iyzabel worked in other trades before she took control, and they don't really know what they're doing. Fifteen years is long enough to learn to get by, but nowhere near long enough to master a trade without tutelage."

Yet Bronya did not seem to be doing much farming during my stay. For two days she spent nearly all her time sitting with me in the barn, telling me stories about her childhood with my mother. I learned that, like me, Elysia had spent many of her formative years running wild out of doors, playful and curious. When she turned eleven, my grandfather had insisted she start learning his trade, but she had resisted because she didn't like wearing shoes, and his craft was making and repairing them.

Unlike me, however, my mother had been bold and fearless. That was why she caught Prince Auben's heart a few years later. He was an insecure and fretful teenager, and when the king and queen hosted Luminor's annual Festival of the Sun, he had disguised himself as a tanner to escape public notice. At the first night's outdoor revelries, he'd been asked to dance by the dark-haired cobbler's daughter, who thought he was handsome, and though he was too bad a liar to keep the truth from her, it didn't seem to make any difference in how she treated him.

He fell in love very quickly.

Bronya also told me all she could remember about my brother Eamon, and though I knew he would be different now that he was a grown man, I drank in every word. Her stories made me feel a new kind of longing to reach the Northern Wilds. Suddenly it was more than just the promise of safety and sunlight and meeting some abstract person who was my brother; it was getting to know the dark-haired boy who had learned to swordfight almost before he knew how to walk, who had hated carrots so much he snuck them from the table into his pocket and threw them from the highest tower window, and who had solemnly promised our mother at my birth that he would protect his baby sister even if he had to fight a sea serpent to do it.

On the morning of my seventh day in Bronya and Roark's barn, I told her, with a regret so strong it surprised me, that I felt well enough to leave. Her face fell, but she hid her disappointment behind an understanding smile. I had only seen her husband once since I'd been awake, and I suspected he feared what I might ask when it came time for me to go.

I asked anyway.

"Come with me? You and Roark, I mean. Help me find Yarrow, and then come with us to the Northern Wilds."

Bronya squeezed her brown eyes shut. Then she sat down beside me on the rickety bench beside the dairy cow's stall.

"Siria, I want you to know that meeting you and talking with you these last few days has been one of the greatest joys of my life. When I learned, all those years ago, that you had survived . . . I used to pray I might see you again one day." She paused and drew a deep breath, as though preparing to dive underwater. "But I made a promise to Roark, and I won't break it. Nor will I leave without my husband."

"Why doesn't he like me?"

She smiled again. "Oh, my dear, it's nothing like that. He—we lost a great deal in service to the rebels. Roark decided then that no cause was worth the loss of loved ones. We left the north and began farming for Iyzabel, because that was the only way he felt he could keep me from harm." She sighed. "He's afraid you'll pull me away from safety again."

"Oh." I swallowed. "Who . . . who did you lose?"

Bronya looked down at her hands, twisted in her lap. "Iyzabel has many eyes and ears, and in those days we were working to infiltrate her spy network. Roark feigned interest in her service . . . but she found out that we were loyal to Luminor. We had . . . children . . . in those days. Two little girls, and—" Bronya's voice cracked, and she broke off.

I could only stare at her, horrified, as she cleared her throat and continued.

"Roark blamed the rebels, even though he knew it wasn't their fault. It was easier for him, I think, to imagine that leaving them would in some way bring justice for his daughters. He thinks the resistance is doomed. I don't agree entirely, but I do think it will take miraculous power to overthrow Iyzabel. Our people are too weak to fight, and so many have been seduced by the Darkness. Its power strengthens year by year."

Bronya's expression was dark, and I dropped my gaze to stare into my own lap. It was sickening to think about. I had felt Iyzabel's seductive power myself, and it had taken both transformation and loss to shake me out of the longing to serve her. A sudden and unexpected stab of sympathy for Phipps and Milla pierced my thoughts: their behavior may not have been right, but perhaps it was at least understandable in light of Iyzabel's influence. If she could spread that kind of power through her Darkness, I doubted whether we could ever overturn her rule. Surely the people would revolt if we tried.

And yet, Yarrow believed . . .

But Yarrow had been disappointed in Bronya and Roark for leaving the rebels, even after their children had been murdered. I felt a squirm of disquiet at the thought. Did that make Yarrow deluded, or callused . . . or cruel? Was he ignoring the odds and leading me to my death?

"Bronya," I said after a long time. "I'm sorry about your daughters."

She looked at me with wet eyes, and started to speak, but couldn't. This time I wrapped my arms around her shoulders and held her as she cried.

That evening, both Bronya and Roark came to the barn, each with an armful of supplies. Between them they carried a full waterskin, several days' worth of dry food, a small pouch of gold coins, and the clothes I'd had in my rucksack when I arrived—freshly laundered, mended, and smelling of sweet woodruff. And several things more.

"Something to cover your face," said Bronya, handing me a thick, knitted scarf. "It's cold enough, you shouldn't look out of place. If you wear your cloak and hood, and dress like a boy, I think you'll go pretty well unnoticed."

"And this," said Roark, his deep voice kind, though his wind-weathered, pale face looked concerned behind his black beard, "is for you to protect yourself. If you can, try and wield it with your left hand until that right arm is fully healed."

He was holding out a dagger in a copper sheath, completely engraved with intricate, swirling patterns. Set in the hilt was a yellow stone, gleaming dully in the lamplight.

I stared at it.

"This is already yours, actually," said Bronya with a smile. "Your mother had it made after you were born. It's the traditional weapon of a sunchild. The citrine in the hilt provides some kind of link to you, and you can use it in ways ordinary humans can't."

I stared at her. "Yarrow told me about this . . . But how—?"

"Elysia gave it to me a week before the overthrow, though she wouldn't say why. All she said was that I was to keep it safe for the future, just in case. I thought she was being paranoid. Now, of course, I know she had learned of Iyzabel's desire to kill you and intended to do what she could to protect you, at any cost." Bronya looked wistfully at the dagger, still extended toward me in her husband's hands. "I almost forgot I had it. Perhaps you were meant to come here."

I took the weapon, turning it over reverently while I examined the scrollwork. My mother had once held this dagger in her own hands.

"Thank you. Thank you both." I hugged Bronya, breathing in the clean, herby scent of her as she held me tightly, stroking my back. If only she could have adopted me instead of Milla. I wished I could give her something in return for the care and generosity she and Roark had shown.

At last I pulled back and smiled at her. Her eyes were wet.

"I hope I see you both again someday," I said, offering Roark a hand to shake.

But he smiled through his beard and pulled me into a hug as well, his arms and chest broad enough to swallow me up. "Take care, lass."

"Be safe," whispered Bronya, reaching up to kiss my cheek.

At the door of the barn, she and Roark both stopped. As solemn and formal as courtiers, both swept me a low bow.

I stood still, facing the inside of the door long after it had closed, the citrine dagger hanging loose in my hand as I struggled to master my emotions. After a few moments I realized the barn was lit with bright, golden light.

31

CHAPTER

I crept out of the Dells' barn as soon as I could sense the sun rising beyond the Darkness the next morning, wearing my cloak, deerskin jacket, and Linden's old leather trousers. Bronya's scarf was wrapped several times around the lower half of my face and my neck, and I had rubbed dirt into the visible skin around my eyes so my freckles wouldn't draw attention. I pulled my hood low, hair wrapped in a linen scarf beneath it, hiked the rucksack higher on my back, and set off.

Despite the danger, I had decided to take the Queen's Road north, continuing toward the rebel camp, rather than search the forest for my friends. If they were dead, their bodies would have been taken to the queen as proof; and if alive, Yarrow's magic would most likely keep them hidden. But they would be looking for me. I resolved to leave them clues and hope for the best.

The first afternoon, as I was walking between two fields of scrawny-looking cornstalks in the hazy half-light of the day, I felt and then heard the shudder of hoof-beats approaching behind me. I looked wildly around for someplace—anyplace—to hide, spotted a stile in the weathered stone wall of one cornfield, and sprinted off the road.

Vaulting over the stile, I stumbled upon landing and threw my momentum toward the scrubby weeds beside the wall. I fell with a crunch and pressed myself as close to the cold stone as I could. Golden light seeped from my skin, and I heaved it back inside with a monumental effort.

In moments the cacophony of hooves was level with my hiding spot—twenty or thirty horses at least, by the sound—and my heartbeat matched their pace. But they did not so much as pause, and after another few moments lying trembling with my face in the weeds, they had gone. I lay in the silence a long time, then finally, still shaking, pushed myself up. Sitting with my back to the wall, I breathed in and out as steadily as I could.

Coward, I thought, shame trickling in as my fear ebbed away. I knew it was not foolish to hide, since even disguised as a boy I might be stopped and questioned, but none of those rational thoughts had driven me to fling myself over a wall and lie quivering in the dirt. That had been pure, raw fear, controlling me like a puppet. The light was proof of that.

I thought of what Elegy had said that day in the forest: *Being afraid doesn't make you a coward. It's how you react that makes you a coward.*

I could not—*would* not—be ruled by my fear. I could use it, I could heed its advice, I could even let it fuel me . . . but I could not allow it to control me.

I would be brave, like my mother.

I sucked in several more deep breaths, and then swallowed hard.

After triple-checking to make sure no one was in sight

on the road or in the fields, I sat down again, closed my eyes, and allowed my thoughts to drift upward through the gray fog, to the ever-present force that hung like a shroud between me and the sun. Anxiety bloomed in my chest, making my hands shake, but I reminded myself there was no one around I could hurt. This was safe.

As Yarrow had told me, and as I had sensed, the Darkness was not a solid wall; rather, it was like layers of netting, shifting and sliding over each other to let in hints of sunlight that kept the world from dying. I probed the weak points with my mind, surprised to find how natural the impulse felt, and as the Darkness shifted I sought my way through the gaps. After a few moments' focus, I felt my consciousness unfurl on the other side.

Though I could not see it, I felt the sunlight with the tendril of my thought that had wriggled through the Darkness, and as I let myself rest there, a glorious image of light and endless, golden sky bloomed in my imagination. It was unlike anything I had ever seen with my physical eyes, brighter than any light I knew of. Far from overwhelming me, though, it filled me with a powerful, startling joy. I wanted to stay sitting against this stone wall, pouring my mind into the sun for the rest of my life.

I opened my eyes and gasped. My skin was blazing once more, illuminating half the cornfield in front of me. Panic exploded—the heat in my palms flared—and I gave a cry, jerking them up, but too late. The weeds beneath them were smoking, burned to cinders. Trembling, I severed my connection to the sun and jerked all the light back into my body.

Dismay battered me, but I took long, deep breaths until I felt steady again. Then I looked down at the charred weeds.

I *had* to learn to control this. Yarrow had said I could help existing plants grow—perhaps I could repair the damage myself. Lack of practical experience notwithstanding, I knew *a lot* of theory. The basic idea, I recalled, was to use my emotions instead of letting them use me.

I gave a hollow laugh. *That* was difficult even in theory.

A quick check to make sure the road was still empty, and I placed my palms back over the spots they had burned. I loosened my careful grip on my fear and horror and felt the rush of sun energy swirl and bubble inside me like water coming quickly back to the boil. Instead of letting it run wild, I tried to focus that whirl of power and draw it under my control.

My first attempt failed miserably. So did my second. But on the third try, I finally got the knack of catching hold of the energy with my thoughts, and I gathered it carefully to the center of me, making sure I did not glow. Then I imagined the little blackened, prickly stalks becoming green again, growing taller, sprouting seed heads, then sent the energy slowly, carefully, down my arms to my hands.

Something tickled my left palm, and I lifted it to find three little stalks of grass wavering up out of the charred ground. Unexpected tears pricked my eyes. It was a long way from perfect, and my right hand still lay upon ruined earth, but even so, I had done it.

I had made something good.

An idea sprang up in me as suddenly as the weeds had grown in the earth.

I knew how to leave clues for Yarrow and Linden.

32

CHAPTER

At six years old, I had decided it was not fair for Linden and Yarrow to be named after plants when I was saddled with a name that had once belonged to a cantankerous great aunt.

"Give me a plant name," I demanded of the pair of them, who were busy tilling the barren earth in Phipps and Milla's garden. "I want to be named after this one."

And I yanked up the only thing that would easily grow in what little light the shadowy moor offered: a thick, spiny stalk with papery leaves and a prickly white blossom on top I thought rather pretty.

"That's starthistle, Siria," said Yarrow, glancing back with a hint of a smile. "It's a weed."

"So? Name me after it."

"You want to be a weed, Weedy?" giggled Linden.

"No. Starthistle. I'll be Starthistle."

"Certainly, Weedy," Yarrow chuckled.

Much as I protested, the name had stuck—especially when my height surpassed Linden's for a few months during my early adolescence.

And though I had not been called Starthistle once, I

knew Yarrow and Linden would spot the significance—
though I doubted anyone else would. I therefore set to work
as I walked, using my newfound skill to draw up starthistle
blossoms every twenty paces or so. Their stalks were abun-
dant along the road, and although it was too early for them
to bloom, it was not difficult for me to encourage premature
flowering. I knew Linden at least paid enough attention to
local plant life to notice if something new appeared.

If he's still alive to notice anything, a small voice whispered in the back of my mind.

While I drew up starthistle blooms, I tried my hand
at another unobtrusive skill Yarrow claimed I possessed:
healing. The wound in my upper right arm was still sensi-
tive enough that it hurt to even clench my fist, so I began
sending sun energy to that spot and imagining it knitting
the tissues back together, healing. This was more complex
work than growing weeds, however, and required more concentration. By the end of my third day on the Queen's Road,
I could not feel much difference—and for all I knew, the
progress I'd made was my body's natural healing.

At night I snuck into sheds or livestock pens to sleep,
and during the day I spoke to no one—though most of the
people I saw were also dreary, downtrodden foot travelers.
When I had to pass through towns or villages, I always
waited to go through with a crowd, trying to look incon-
spicuous as I walked past Iyzabel's soldiers. So far, I had
not encountered any guards from Umbraz; these men were
all rural patrol soldiers, stationed in the outlying towns to
oversee production and shipment of the kingdom's food. I
wondered if our being discovered in the forest had drawn
most of the Royal Guard to search there.

But on the fifth day since I'd left Bronya and Roark, I

came around a bend and spotted the silver-and-black livery I had come to fear almost as much as the queen herself. Stifling a gasp, I ducked beneath the shadow of a stand of hemlock trees, relieved to see that the four soldiers—all standing on the road beside gleaming black mounts—had not noticed me. Their attention was fixed on a lumpy pile of something at their feet, just off the dirt track. As I watched, the pile stirred feebly, and I heard a voice that was too high and thin to possibly belong to any of the soldiers.

It was not a pile of anything. It was a person.

My impulse was to run farther into the trees and hide until the soldiers had gone, but I balled my fists and crept closer to the soldiers while remaining in the trees' shade. I could at least get near enough to hear what they said.

"You saw someone," barked one of the soldiers. "On the road—*this* road—you said you saw someone yesterday." He kicked the heap, and I heard a yelp of pain.

It seemed to be an old man, I thought while squinting at the colorless tunic, knobby legs, and wispy white hair. Even from this distance, I could see that he was emaciated— either ill or starving. Or both.

"Oh yes!" said the wavering, weak voice. It was not the frightened sound I expected to hear, but eager and desperate. "Oh yes, I did! But please . . . I don't know where she went. I would have followed her if I'd known it would help. Please, I want to help! My queen . . . I want to help my—"

But he broke off on another cry as the first soldier kicked him again, this time landing his boot squarely in the man's face.

I turned away, but not fast enough to avoid the sight or sound of the impact: blood sprayed from his lips, and there was a horrible crunch. I felt sick, and realized my hands were shaking. I directed some of my attention to controlling the light within me.

"Oh please," said the old man, his words now slurred and muffled by whatever damage had been done to his mouth. I looked back to see him raise a trembling arm, as if he wanted to be helped up. "Oh please, take me to her! I love my benevolent queen . . . I wish to gaze upon her! You've seen her . . . haven't you? What is she like? Tell her—when you see her, tell her that I love—"

This sentence, too, was cut off abruptly as another soldier kicked him in the stomach. Furious tears burned in my eyes, and I took an unconscious step forward.

"Useless," said the soldier, sounding exasperated. "Shall we kill him?"

"Why bother?" said the first man in disgust. "He'll be dead soon anyway. Look at him."

The four soldiers swung into their saddles and cantered off up the road heading north, eventually disappearing around another bend. I ducked out of the trees and hurried across the road to the old man.

Tears were spilling down my cheeks before I was halfway to him. As I knelt, I saw that his breath came in labored wheezes, and he seemed to be weeping silently. His jaw looked wrong; there was blood pooling around his head, staining his thin white hair and making mud of the dirt. I choked on a sob as I laid a hand on his bony shoulder, afraid to turn his head. His eyes rolled, struggling to find who was touching him, and at last swiveled up to look at me.

"They wouldn't . . ." he slurred, voice weak. "They wouldn't take . . . me to her . . ."

I shook my head, appalled to find that his adoration for

Queen Iyzabel was genuine. It was just as Bronya had said: many of the people toiling under her dominion were still overcome by the power of the Darkness. This man had been so swayed that he longed for the favor of the very woman responsible for his starvation and pain. Was the delusion more powerful because he was physically weak?

"It's okay," I heard myself saying in a cracking voice as I stroked his skin-and-bone shoulder. "It's going to be okay. I'm going to help."

"My queen?" he said, eyes widening.

"No," I said. "A friend."

His eyelids fluttered and he began to choke. I was crying so hard I could barely see him now, and by the time I had blinked the tears away, his coughing had stopped. He had gone still, his eyes glassy and wide, staring up toward the cold gray sky and the Darkness above.

I shook as I rose to my feet, hearing my own promise echoing in my ears. *It's going to be okay. I'm going to help.*

I never could have done anything for him, of course. I had known it was an empty promise. But the words burned in my mind.

I'm going to help.

I *could* help. Not him, but others like him. Others who could not resist the lure of the Darkness in their hearts, others who labored and starved for a queen who thought they were disposable, who only cared about their ability to produce her food and resources.

Yarrow said I had the power to stop this tyranny. This Darkness.

I looked upward, hating the curse that hung over this kingdom—*my* kingdom—and felt resolve harden like steel inside me. For the first time, and with an equally new sense of responsibility for the country I lived in, I was glad to have a power that was strong and dangerous.

Because the Darkness was strong and dangerous too, and I needed to be a match for it.

CHAPTER

The old man's death fused something inside me, uniting at last the conflicting parts of myself that had kept me from accepting my gift. Everything was now in accord, focused by a growing obsession with reaching the Northern Wilds, meeting my brother, and seeing the sun with my own eyes. There was a new ache inside me too; it had been there since the day I sat at the edge of the cornfield and reached through the Darkness for the sunlight. I ached, in a way that surpassed even my childhood infatuation with Yarrow's stories, for the presence of the sun in my world. I practiced using my gift constantly, in every way I could think of that didn't involve actually showing my light. And though I paid for it in increased exhaustion, I also saw small improvements day by day. When I was sure I was alone, I even tried to let the sun draw me up off the ground, like it had done in Umbraz. It never worked, but I still tried.

On my ninth day of travel since leaving the Dells' farm, I came upon a garish, bright purple caravan trundling along the road ahead of me, pulled by an ancient-looking cart-horse whose pace was slower than mine by at least half.

I soon caught up to them, and a window in the side of

the caravan swung open. A black-haired boy about my own age leaned out of it, grinning.

"Hallo, traveler," he said cheerily. "Need a lift?"

I glanced at the plodding carthorse. "That's all right," I said, pitching my voice lower to match my now filthy boy disguise.

"Where you headed?" asked the boy, leaning on his forearms as if he frequently conducted conversations through the window of his moving caravan.

I gestured vaguely ahead.

"Polter?" he said in surprise. "Don't take kindly to common folk there, they don't."

"Even less kindly to actors," muttered the stout woman on the driver's bench, flicking her whip in a routine sort of way.

"Aye. We avoid the place. Too many soldiers, and soldiers never pay nothing. Plus," the boy added, raising his eyebrows meaningfully, "dangerous times, if you know what I mean, what with everyone looking for that escaped sunchild girl. Dangerous. Not that I'd mind meeting her, o' course. They're meant to be a sight to see." A dreamy look came over his face.

My cheeks were hot beneath the scarf.

"Hear about them other travelers they tried to get in Slaye, though?" put in the woman driving. "Escaped, but it was a near thing. Strange times."

I stumbled. Other travelers?

"Where was this?" I asked, trying to sound casual rather than desperate. "Who were these people?"

The woman glanced back at me. "Slaye, like I said. Last town back from Polter. Only last night too."

"I heard it was nymphs," said the black-haired boy in an

impressive tone. "Wild nymphs. Two men and two women. They'll be setting up checkpoints next, you mark my words."

I could barely breathe, but I forced my voice to sound indifferent. "Right," I said, with a shrug. "Well, you can't always trust gossip. Best of luck to you."

I strode on, outpacing them easily, and hurried toward Polter while hope unfurled, wild and giddy, in my chest.

As I entered the village, I was alarmed to see a few of the broadsheets Bronya had mentioned nailed to the gates: Two of me—reasonably accurate, but much fiercer-looking than I was—and one that claimed to be Yarrow, though the illustration showed a man at least twenty years younger than the mage I knew. Both read, "Wanted by the Queen: Dead or Alive." I pulled my hood low and adjusted my scarf more securely.

The streets were crowded and loud, full of traders, travelers, and soldiers, though I didn't see any workers—or indeed, anyone who looked like they had missed a meal in the last year. Feeling uncomfortable, and thinking of the actors' warning about Polter, I hugged the side of the road and tried to affect a careless, boyish shuffle, letting my eyes dart around for familiar faces.

I saw none.

For the rest of the afternoon, I wandered the streets, giving soldiers a wide berth, but otherwise letting the crowd sweep me along in its current. Once I felt someone trying to pickpocket me, and when I jerked around to confront the thief, I found it was a young man about my own age. His eyes met mine with a malicious expression that first widened and then narrowed in suspicion before he disappeared into the crowd. I felt jumpy after that and pulled my scarf up all the way to my eyes.

Evening fell, and the vendors began to pack up their wares. I passed a bread merchant, and the sweet smell of yeast made my stomach ache with hunger. But Polter—and the traveling players' warning about it—was making me edgy, and I was afraid to stop and talk to anyone, even if only to buy bread. I supposed I would just have to leave and hope I met Yarrow and the others in the next town.

But how?

I veered down an alley, hoping to cut through to the far gates, but found a dead end. I turned back, ducked down another street, and hurried past merchants who were beginning to look curiously after me. Panic rose in my chest. What would I do if I couldn't find my way out?

Three more streets, and the dim buildings were all starting to look the same. I couldn't even find the gate I had come through that morning. I turned abruptly to retrace my steps, hurried around a corner—and ran hard into someone on the other side.

Panic mushroomed in my veins, and I gasped an apology as I looked up into the face of the lean man I had plowed into, now grasping at my shoulders to steady himself.

His familiar green eyes widened in shock.

34

CHAPTER

Light, Siria!" Linden gasped, and crushed me against him, long arms wrapping me up like a cocoon. "I was afraid—I thought you were . . ."

"I thought *you* were dead," I said, pushing back and pounding my fists against his chest. "Almost two weeks I've had to wonder whether you were captured or tortured or even alive . . ." Tears blurred my vision.

"You think I've had it any better?" His voice edged toward hysterical, and he hugged me so tight against him I thought he might crack my ribs. For a moment or two we stood there, locked together with twin pounding hearts and trembling limbs while the twilight deepened around us. Then Linden muttered, "Let's get out of here." But he seemed reluctant to let go of me and took my hand as soon as we pulled apart. "There's an inn at the edge of town that's safe. We can talk there."

It was indeed at the very edge of town, though it looked more like an abandoned townhouse than an inn, with a crumbling brick façade and dimly lit windows three rickety stories high. Linden dropped my hand before we entered, and I checked my scarf and followed him into the shabby, fire-lit common room. There were only three people inside, each of them hooded and sitting on various pieces of broken or sagging furniture, and they all looked up nervously when we came in. At least we were among kindred souls, I thought, pulling my own hood lower.

"My brother and I'd like a room, please," Linden told the innkeeper, plunking a few coins on the bar while I stared at the threadbare rug. "And if you could send up whatever supper you've got, we'd be grateful."

"'Course," said the man, inclining his head. "Just this way, please, lads."

Our room was a small dormer on the top floor, with one sagging bed, a low table, a wooden chair with mismatched legs, and a cold fireplace. Though I had no idea where Yarrow and the others were, this room and its one bed seemed to indicate they would not be joining us tonight.

One bed.

I swallowed, faintly lightheaded at the thought of an entire night alone with Linden. I was better now than I had been at controlling my power, but I'd also had precious little practice under emotional duress. Could I tell him the truth of how I felt? I bit my lip and moved to look out the window. Behind me I could hear him lighting the lamps.

"Siria," he said after a moment.

I turned around slowly, hood and scarf still up. My heart had become erratic, like a spooked rabbit in a cage.

But before Linden could speak, a knock sounded at the door. A serving boy came in with a tray of hot food and a basket of firewood and made quick work of reviving the hearth. When he had finished, Linden slid all three bolts into place behind him and turned again to face me.

Now that the intensity of finding each other had cooled,

he seemed uncertain how to proceed. I shifted, wanting to take off my hood, but feeling like it would be suggestive if I started pulling off articles of clothing while he watched.

"I'm sorry for hitting you," I said. "I've just been worried about you. And Yarrow, I mean," I added, a little wildly. "And the others, obviously—"

I felt stifled by my hood as my face flamed. Jerking the scarf away, I flung it onto the chair and threw back my hood, shaking the hair off my sweaty neck. "Sorry," I said. "I was boiling."

To my surprise, Linden laughed. "I was wondering how long you were going to leave that thing on."

In the clearer light of the room, I could see that there were deep purple shadows under his eyes, like bruises on his slightly darkened gray-brown skin, and at least two weeks' worth of stubble covering his jaw. Had he slept at all since we'd been separated? His nut-brown hair was wilder than ever, and despite the obvious fact it hadn't been washed in many days, I couldn't quite repress the desire to touch it. I balled my fists, watching him watch me, and wondered if my thoughts were written all over my face.

"The others are fine," he said, still standing by the door. We were like pieces on the board of some invisible game, immobile, each waiting for the other to move. "They didn't think you'd stop in Polter, so they went on to the next town. Yarrow and I argued, but in the end, he let me do what I wanted."

"You know me well," I said, trying to sound lighthearted. His eyes caught mine again and held them a moment longer before I ripped my gaze away, feeling like I was drowning.

He shrugged. "I ought to, after ten years." Though there was a practiced carelessness to his tone, I heard tension beneath the words, like he meant them slightly differently than they sounded.

I ought to, but I'm not sure I do.

I chewed the inside of my cheek.

"You should eat," he said, an edge of irritation in his voice now, though I wasn't sure if it was for me or himself. "You look like you haven't had a decent meal since you left us." He gestured toward the table and the food tray.

"Half of that's for you." My stomach was a tangled knot, but hunger had nothing to do with it.

Tell him, I thought. *Be brave. Be brave like your mother, like Queen Elysia.* I sought his eyes, but he was avoiding my gaze.

"I'll eat when you've had your fill," he muttered, and moved to the bed, where he began to unpack and repack his rucksack, getting out a pair of buckskin trousers and a woven shirt that looked only slightly cleaner than the mud-stained ones he was wearing. Facing away from me, he set to unclasping buckles and loosening laces until he had shrugged out of his bracers, lined leather jacket, greaves, boots, and various belts, sheaths, and quivers, all of which he folded or stacked neatly and replaced in his pack.

I watched, mesmerized. In the gear he'd been wearing since we left Umbraz, Linden looked like a mountain ranger or a seasoned huntsman: strong, tough, and capable. But stripped down to his thin shirt, half untucked and open to the collarbone, his filthy trousers and his bare feet, he was just an eighteen-year-old boy again, flesh and bone. Not invincible, not all-knowing. Just my friend Linden. Familiar, beautiful . . . and confused.

It was not his job to understand me without my help.

I waited as he checked over his bow and quiver,

unstringing the former and propping it against the wall, but he still did not turn around. Before I could stop him, he mumbled something about a washroom and left, leaving me to pick at the food on the tray in increasing agony.

A quarter of an hour later, he returned with wet hair and several dripping pieces of clothing he seemed to have washed. He draped these over the screen in front of the fire, making rather a business of arranging them.

His damp, tousled hair seemed to mock me. But even as my fingers twitched to touch it, I wondered how long it had been since *I'd* had anything like a bath.

"Um," I said, "where was that washroom?"

Linden didn't turn around. "Down the hall to the left. But lock the door, and be careful in the corridor. The last thing we need is someone spotting you."

"Right." I swallowed. "I'm finished eating. You should have the rest."

He glanced back briefly. "Be careful in the hallway."

"You said that."

"Sorry." His voice was terse.

I stood up to leave, but hesitated. "Linden?"

He turned, jaw clenched as if steeling himself for something.

"It's really good to see you."

The hard expression loosened like dry earth beneath a sudden rain, but without it, I saw profound sadness in his eyes. He gave me a weary smile. "You too, Weedy."

He turned away from me again.

I stared at his back for a long moment, and then left.

35

CHAPTER

I spent the entirety of my cold and rustic bathing experience obsessing over what I should say to Linden when I returned. My hands trembled and my heart thrummed as I left the grimy washroom and retraced my steps to our room.

Be brave, I thought as I bolted the door and draped my own semi-clean, wet clothes over the fireplace screen.

Linden was sitting on the bed mending a sock, and he looked up warily when I came in. His hair was nearly dry now, but standing up in all directions, as if he had been raking his fingers through it the entire time I'd been gone. I smoothed the front of my wool dress—still clean, as I had only worn trousers since leaving Bronya and Roark—and went to sit beside him.

He stood up and moved to the hard, wooden chair across from me. I dug my fingernails into my palms. *Be brave.*

"Wine?" I said, indicating the untouched flagon the kitchen had sent up.

Linden ignored this. "Tell me about the last two weeks."

"I think you could do with some wine, frankly."

"Tell me about the last two weeks," he repeated, "before I go insane wondering what happened to you."

I frowned but didn't argue. And Linden listened to my story with a solemnity I had rarely seen in him, his jaw set and green eyes fixed on my face as I spoke. He flinched when I told him about the arrow, briefly shutting his eyes and bowing his head, but he did not interrupt. When I was finished, he leaned forward onto his knees and put his forehead in his hands, fingers curling into his hair.

"Linden?"

"We should have done more," he groaned. "We should have split up sooner, tried harder to find you. What if you'd been recognized or questioned on the road?"

"But I wasn't."

"And what if that couple hadn't helped you?" He looked up through his fingers. "You could have died from that infection."

"But I didn't." I stood up and stepped toward him, taking his hands from his face. Heart banging, I held on to them. "You did all you could, and I was fine. Better than fine. Think about it, Linden. I'd never have worked so hard at my powers—never stopped being so afraid of them—if all that hadn't happened."

He looked for a moment at our hands, interlocked, before he squeezed my freckled fingers and brought them to his lips. Heat jolted through my body, equal parts terror and desire, and I suddenly understood in a new way what Elegy had meant when she said bravery was acting in spite of fear. As Linden lifted his eyes to mine again and made to release me, I screwed up my courage and gripped his hands tight.

His eyes grew round. A flock of birds seemed to flap

inside my stomach as I met his gaze and did not look away. His brows contracted. Then, slowly, deliberately, never once taking my eyes from his, I lifted his long, callused hands to my own mouth and pressed my lips against his knuckles.

Linden was on his feet in one fluid movement, hands slipping through mine, cradling my face as if it were made of glass.

"Wait," I gasped as the light flared within me, and he stopped, eyes scorching mine. "I don't want to hurt you."

His expression froze, then closed, and his fingers went rigid against my skin.

A beat of confusion—then, "No!" I cried, clasping his wrists. "No, no, Linden, not like that—I mean *literally!*"

He blinked, still immobile. "Hurt me?"

For answer I released him and traced the handprint, just visible as a darker smudge beneath the rough stubble on the left side of his jaw and neck. Comprehension kindled in his face, and then a rainfall of unreadable emotions seemed to wash across it.

"You're afraid you'll burn me again." He sounded stunned, disbelieving. "You told me in Beq's house that I shouldn't touch you, but I never thought . . ." His mouth fell open. "But Siria, what you said to me in that cave . . ."

I ducked my head, but he leaned toward me, searching out my eyes. "You didn't mean it?" His expression was half desperate, half jubilant.

"I was trying to protect you," I whispered.

He stared at me for a long moment, eyes darting back and forth between mine as an incredulous smile spread over his face. Then he threw his head back and laughed, an exultant sound. "Weedy, you know I'm not fussy about a burn or two. There are far worse ways to get injured."

"But *I* care," I insisted. My whole body was weak with relief, and I was fighting hard to keep the sunlight contained. "How do you think I'd feel if I did worse than that to you? This power can kill people, you know. Even now, I barely have it under control."

"Now?" He sounded fascinated. "You mean it's almost coming through right now?"

"Yes!"

"Really? Because of *me*? In a good way?"

"Linden, you're a clot-head."

He laughed again, as if turning me into a lethal, blazing torch was the greatest triumph of his life. Holding me slightly away from him, he looked down into my face, and for a moment he seemed unable to keep his eyes away from my mouth. I took a shaky breath, knowing I would not have the willpower to resist him if he kissed me. But then half a smile quirked his lips, he swept his eyes up to mine, and his expression became very earnest.

"I understand," he said. "And I know you're still figuring it out. But I also think it won't be like this forever. Yarrow and I will keep helping you, and you'll get the hang of it." The grin was back, and he released me to put his right hand over his chest, as though making a vow. "I therefore promise not to kiss you until you're ready. Until you think it's safe. Unless, of course, we're going to die anyway. Then I want a mercy death by burning."

I laughed, both relieved and the tiniest bit disappointed he had surrendered the point without a fight.

"But can I ask you a question?"

I raised an eyebrow at the familiar thread of mischief in his voice. "Maybe."

"All those times you've lit up like a candle . . . Weedy,

were those all because of me?" His grin was fiendish now, and it broadened as I flushed and glared at him. "They were, weren't they!"

"*No*, you arrogant toad!" I tried to fend him off as he reached for me.

"That's as good as a confession!"

"Linden Hatch, I do hate you."

"I know." He smirked, slipping his hands around my waist and pulling me close. "You hate me so much it makes you glow."

It was going to be hard for either of us to uphold our agreement at this rate, so I made him pull the wooden chair several paces back from the bed while he told me what had happened to him and the others after we were separated in the forest.

I'd been right: Yarrow had indeed scattered us all with an enchantment, to get us away from the Night Wyrm and the soldiers. But it had been an insane thing to try by the laws of his magic and should have failed. As it was, the spell had sapped Yarrow's powers and energy for almost a week, and when Linden, Merrall, and Elegy had found him at the bottom of a ravine, they'd feared he was dead. Of our company, Yarrow and I had been scattered farthest, and though they found Yarrow within two days, they could discover no trace of me.

They agreed to canvass the forest in that area as well as they could while avoiding the increasing numbers of soldiers, and when they still didn't find me, decided I must have landed outside the woods. They began to worry I had been captured.

"Yarrow didn't speak for days after that," said Linden, tracing patterns on my palm with his finger. He had pulled the chair close to the bed and was holding my hand on his knee. "I don't think he'd have forgiven himself if you'd been taken. But we decided to try the road, just in case you'd gone that way, and eventually we noticed starthistle growing where there'd been none before. Yarrow almost cried."

They had followed the starthistle trail, he said, searching towns along the way, and sleeping as little as possible in order to catch up.

"Tonight, of course, Yarrow felt we'd better move on, since Polter was so swamped with soldiers. We also had some trouble last night in Slaye when someone recognized Yarrow."

"I heard about that! How'd you get away?"

"Magic." Linden grimaced. "So I think they'll tighten everything up along the Queen's Road soon. We'll have to be even more careful tomorrow."

When holding Linden's hand no longer felt too risky, I made room for him on the narrow, lumpy bed and we sat curled together atop the thin blankets, propped against the headboard. We sat for a while in drowsy silence, then I asked, "Was it lonely, growing up with just me and Yarrow?"

He paused in the act of brushing a curl back from my forehead, and I felt a pinch of painful realization. "You gave up a lot to come south, didn't you?" I said. "No one could ever find out what you were. That's why you didn't go into the village, didn't have other friends . . . Linden, I'm sorry. I never realized. You must have been so lonely."

His fingers resumed their lazy twirling of my hair. "I had some friends," he said, "but no, never for long, and never very close. Naturally I had friends before I left the north too, but I barely remember them." For a long time, he was silent, and I wondered what the last four years had been like for him while I was at Gildenbrook learning to be a snob. Eventually he squeezed my shoulder. "I was never lonely when I was with you."

I twisted around and put my arms about his neck, pulling him closer. Then, making sure my sun energy was well contained, I tilted my chin up and pressed a kiss against his temple.

I felt his breath catch, and then his chest rumbled with laughter. "Testing my promise already, are you? Trying to make me trip up? Well, you won't find *me* so easily swayed, Siria Nightingale. Do your worst, sunchild. I'll resist your wiles."

I laughed too, and had to give a sudden internal snatch at the light that tried to spill off my skin. It was not, I realized, from being curled into Linden's arms, or feeling his hands against my back, or his chin against my hair. It was not even from the release of letting him know how I felt about him.

It was from the joy of being with my best friend.

The firelight was glowing soft gold against my closed eyelids when I slipped into dreams beside Linden, his fingers still woven into my hair.

36

CHAPTER

L inden woke me when it was still dark.

"We need to leave with the laborers," he said in a croaky voice. "Even Polter has some of those, and they'll all leave town before dawn to get a full day's work in."

So before even the landlord was awake, we slipped out of the inn and into the streets to join the small, shambling parade of sleepy-looking men and women filing out of town toward their various labors. No one so much as glanced at us.

"Linden, we need a plan," I murmured as the ever-thinning crowd of workers dispersed into the fields and farms surrounding the village. "You said it'd be more dangerous today."

He nodded. "Yarrow and I agreed to meet at an inn just below the northern pass, but it's two days from here. I think we'll be stopped before then."

"How far if we cut through farms or the forest?"

"At least an additional two days. But I'd be surprised if they didn't have patrols out there too." He looked furtively around. "If we managed to commandeer a supply cart, we might go unquestioned . . ."

I glanced around as well and saw something large and trundling take shape on the road ahead, its hideous purple paint visible even through the gloom of early morning.

"Linden!"

He jumped and looked both relieved and irritated to find me smiling. "What?"

"I have an idea."

The players' carthorse was walking so slowly that Linden and I caught up to the domed wagon within a few minutes. We slowed to a jog behind it, and I grimaced at Linden before rapping sharply on the back door. After a moment, the upper half of the door swung open, and the same black-haired boy I had spoken to before looked out, rubbing sleep from his eyes.

His mouth fell open at the sight of us, and even though I had intentionally pulled my hood and scarf down, remembering what he'd said about sunchildren, my stomach plunged as he gaped at me.

"We met before!" I said quickly, lengthening my stride to keep up. "On the road! I was dressed as a boy, and you told me not to go into Polter, but I had to find my friend"—I gestured at Linden—"and now we need help. Can you help us?"

The boy seemed torn between terror and awe. "You—you're that sunchild, ain't you?"

"Yes. Please, can you help me?"

"Gareth, what is it?" called a woman's voice from within the wagon.

"Some . . . people . . ."

"You don't have to harbor us or anything," I said, looking back over my shoulder so often I was getting dizzy. "It'll be quick. Just—please let us in, and I'll explain."

He opened the lower door and stepped back, looking

like he didn't know what else to do. Three other actors were crammed inside the wagon—stuffed floor to ceiling with fold-down beds and tables, miscellaneous set pieces, and drawers bursting with bright fabrics—and they all stood in alarm at the sight of us.

"What's going on, Gareth?" demanded an old man with fluffy white hair. He was staring at me with eyes as round as wagon wheels.

"They need our help," said Gareth, sounding slightly more confident. He turned back to me, the eagerness I had counted on bright in his eyes. "What can we do?"

I forced myself not to look at Linden as I gave Gareth a warm, lingering smile. "We need to be disguised," I said, feeling both relieved and guilty to see Gareth's answering interest as he stared at me. "Completely, and very quickly. Can you do that? We can pay you."

Gareth smirked at his companions. "Can we do that?" he repeated with a cocky wink. "Oh, I think we're probably up to the job. Just you sit down, beautiful, and we'll fix you right up."

A quarter of an hour later Linden and I jumped out of the wagon as entirely different people, waving our thanks to the actors, and the rest of our money, as they trundled away—Linden tight-lipped and irritated after the kiss I had given Gareth in thanks, which had prompted the actor to vow undying silence and secrecy on our behalf. Neither Linden nor I recognized each other when the players had finished with us, so I felt optimistic that Iyzabel's soldiers wouldn't either.

Linden was sporting a false beard and black, bushy eyebrows, as well as a stringy wig, a straw hat, and a reeking pair of overalls the actors claimed they had found in an abandoned farmhouse. He had swapped his rucksack for an old grain bag, and his handmade shirt for a nastier one with some questionable stains. With his usual swagger replaced by the shuffling slouch that betrayed his bad mood, he looked every inch the downtrodden Volatian farmer.

I had undergone a more difficult transformation. Since being hooded and veiled would likely raise suspicion, I had allowed the players to dye my hair jet black with an indigo paste that had left it greasy and gritty, as well as cover my skin in a face cream they sometimes used for their productions. It would eventually wash off, but for now I was as sallow as Linden again, every last one of my freckles hidden beneath a layer of makeup that itched as it dried. I wore a pair of thick, foggy spectacles to obscure my vivid eyes, and a rather stained farm dress that had been stuffed with my own clothes in the hips and bosom to disguise my telltale boyish figure. It was a little awkward to walk in, but I decided an ungraceful gait would add authenticity to my new persona.

Linden was sour for the first part of the morning, but for me the effect was somewhat lessened by the absurdity of his false beard and scraggly wig. After a while his scowls started to make me giggle, and Linden's frown gave way to a smirk.

"You look ridiculous," I informed him.

"Well," he said, rolling his eyes, "it's too bad they only made *one* of us look silly. What were they thinking, making you so stunning after they'd turned me into this travesty of facial hair and grease?" His eyes fell on my hair, and he grimaced. "I still can't believe they did that to you."

"It'll grow back the usual color," I said, mostly to keep myself from regretting what I had done. Survival was far more important.

Now that we were alone again, I was increasingly distracted by thoughts of last night in the inn. I was almost as self-conscious as I had been at Gildenbrook, and Linden kept taking his hands out of his pockets and putting them back in again, as if he didn't know what to do with them. I wondered with a rush of paranoia if he was having second thoughts about me. Our conversation had opened a door onto a new landscape of warmth and intimacy, but the night's sleep seemed to have shut it, and I wasn't sure how to nudge it open again.

We kept to the road, and our fears were confirmed as the day passed: dozens of horsemen thundered past us in one direction or the other throughout the day, sometimes in small groups, other times alone. They all wore some variety of Umbraz attire, though only a few bore the polished silver-and-black armor of the city. Several times, these soldiers stopped at the sight of us and jumped down to look for signs we were the people they sought. But our disguises worked like a miracle—especially after we found a pile of horse manure to rub on our clothes.

About midday, the sky lightened to a pearly, dark silver color that illuminated something I had been longing to see since we left Umbraz: the mountains. They were all the more overwhelming for the way they seemed to suddenly appear, massive and hulking on the horizon, the light having been too weak to bring them into view slowly over time. I stared at them over the rims of my thick spectacles almost constantly for the rest of the day, straining to pick out the peaks through the clouds. I couldn't believe they would get even larger as we drew nearer, as they were so impossibly big already. My fascination seemed to amuse Linden; he kept chuckling to himself as I gaped.

"Why does no one know how beautiful the north is?" I said at some point, marveling at the combined effect the view, the fresh scents, and the bright air were having on my mood. "All I ever heard was that it was a dangerous wasteland beyond the Battlements, full of sickly, weak folk. If they're sickly and weak, it's only because Iyzabel's starving them, not because of the weather."

Linden grunted. "She keeps a tight lid on it. Has to, doesn't she? The only people who travel so far out are her guards, and they're paid well to keep their mouths shut. Otherwise she'd have all her most loyal subjects running off to build country estates in areas where her Darkness has less control, and before long she'd lose her grip on them. They'd see that her nonsense about light and dark was just that: nonsense."

When the sun began to set behind the Darkness and the mountains were lost again in shadow, Linden pointed out a cluster of buildings rising dimly ahead of us on the road. Outside the wall surrounding the town, a crowd swarmed before the gates.

"They've set up a checkpoint," Linden said, squinting.

I groaned. "Should we take the long way around?"

"If they're checking everyone entering the village, I'm sure they have soldiers surrounding it as well. Getting caught trying *not* to get caught would go much worse for us."

He was right, but I still felt cold at the thought of submitting to an inspection that had been set up for the express purpose of finding me. "All right, then. Slouch," I told Linden, doing the same myself. "Try to look more defeated. You're far too confident for a poor farmer."

"Yeah, well, that's because I have this irresistible beard. All the lady farmers love a putrid, lice-infested beard."

"And your bow, Linden . . . what if they find your bow?"

"What if they find your dagger?"

Another spasm of panic. Bows and arrows were common enough for travelers, but the citrine dagger would never pass an inspection. Linden's agate-hilted knife was concealed in the bottom of his boot, making him limp, and I suddenly wished I'd opted for the same discomfort.

"Put it in your ample bosom," he suggested. "If they do too much exploring, the game's up anyway, Madame Falsehood."

In the end I decided my padded hips were more suited to the task of hiding the dagger, and I secured it to my real hip as well as I could while Linden rubbed dirt into his bow to disguise its intricate carvings. When we joined the clump of people waiting to enter the village, Linden was slumping with convincing hopelessness, and I was chewing a fingernail with as bored and vacant an expression as I could muster behind my foggy spectacles.

The guards seemed to become more alert when it was our turn, presumably because I was a young woman, and they grabbed hold of me at once, looking me over like a horse at auction. I didn't have to feign terror.

"Hey," said Linden with an impressive blend of timidity and indignation, "that's my wife you're handling, sir."

The soldier who had me by the arms gagged at the reek of horse manure and released me, but then seized a handful of my hair and peered down at it. Beneath another guard's raised lantern, he rubbed the strands between his thumbs, and I bit my lip so hard I tasted blood, praying the dye had worked. Finally, with a repulsed look at the grease coming off on his fingers, the guard shooed Linden and me away. Linden immediately pulled me under his arm and led me through the gate, shooting looks over his shoulder that seemed to shame the guards for intimidating his poor, young wife. But I could feel his arm shaking.

"You could join the acting troupe," I muttered, my legs like pudding.

"Nah," he said, his voice a little weak. "They didn't take a shine to me like they did to you. Of course, *I* didn't kiss any of them . . ."

I wanted to laugh, but couldn't quite manage it.

Our disguises were efficient, but it was the horse manure that saved us in the end. We passed three more checkpoints before we reached the road that split off up the mountain, walking through the night and the whole of the next day, and not one of the checkpoints detained us for longer than it took to rub a lock of my hair or swish it around in a bucket of water. Each time they seemed impatient to get rid of us, faces contorted in disgust, and I began to feel a perverse kind of fondness for the pungent odor.

By the time we had climbed the main road of a remote hilltop village and stopped in front of the pub Linden said was our destination, I was so tired my eyes would barely focus, even without my false glasses. But he squeezed my arm and gestured at the sign creaking on rusty hinges above the door, and my head seemed to clear a bit.

Chipped and weathered, it bore a sphere of yellow on a red field, with a number of thin yellow brush strokes stretching out from the sphere to the edges of the sign.

The same design Yarrow had taught me to draw when I was eight.

A sun.

"Welcome to the Rising Sun Tavern," said Linden.

37

CHAPTER

When we walked into the common room, painted boldly in the banned colors of red, yellow, and gold and well-lit by many lamps, I saw that only a few of the circular tables were occupied. A toothless, wispy woman holding a cat sat at one, a pair of cloaked, whispering men at another . . . And three people I had feared I might never see again were hunched over tankards on the other side of the room.

I practically ran toward them, my throat tight. But they looked up at me with alarm—not the relief and joy I had expected—bristling and reaching for weapons, and I wanted to smack myself for forgetting my disguise. But Yarrow had frozen, eyes focusing on my face instead of the hair, the glasses, and the filthy clothes. I whipped the glasses off. Tears were already spilling down my cheeks.

Elegy was quickest out of her chair, and she hurtled into me so hard it punched the air from my lungs. I hugged her gray head to my chest, but my eyes were on Yarrow. His mouth worked furiously, and his eyebrows drew so tightly together that his whole forehead seemed to be wrinkling over them, like an old tortoise. His eyes had turned to liquid silver behind their round spectacles.

Finally, he pushed himself out of his chair and stumped toward me. Elegy stepped back and I felt like a fragile stem swaying alone in a strong wind. But then Yarrow pulled me against his chest, and I couldn't tell whether it was him or me shaking with sobs, because we were both crying even though Yarrow never ever cried. And I realized that Phipps Nightingale's indifference was no longer an open wound in my heart, because he was not my father.

Yarrow Ash was my father. He had been since I was six years old, when he appeared at Nightingale Manor and took it upon himself to love me as no one else ever had.

After a long moment, Yarrow released me with one arm and pulled Linden in as well. "That's a fine beard you've grown, my boy."

Linden laughed, and I heard Elegy say to Merrall, "They smell *terrible.*"

When we broke apart, I found Merrall standing beside the banshee. "It is good to see you," she said, smiling. "But you will surely clear the whole tavern if you do not change out of those clothes soon."

"She's right," said Yarrow. "Elegy, why don't you take them upstairs and show them where to wash? I'll bring some food up."

Sitting in a blissfully hot bath fifteen minutes later, I scrubbed hard at the paint still coating my arms and face. Close as we were to the Northern Wilds, my thoughts now settled on my brother with the same looping repetition as a child learning to play a few chords on an instrument. Soon I would meet him; soon I would know what he looked like, how his voice sounded, whether he was funny or serious or brave or dull.

I fidgeted with nervous energy. Soon I would know

whether he approved of me as his sister. Yarrow and Linden had become my family, but Eamon, I couldn't help thinking, truly was. We had been born in the same palace, kissed by the same lips, sung to sleep by the same voices.

Once upon a time, we had both belonged to a family. And now we might belong to each other.

Between the heat of the bath and my restless thoughts, I was a little dizzy when I stepped out of the tub, rubbing a towel over skin that had returned to its normal, freckly state. My hair was still resolutely black, but the dye had been worth its weight in gold for the protection it gave us at the checkpoints. I stepped in front of the mirror as I toweled the wet curls—and went very still at what I saw.

There had been no mirror inside the Polter inn. I had not seen my reflection since the carriage ride out of Umbraz, and that had been a short glance in a dim coach. And though I expected the unfamiliarity of black hair, I could not stop staring at the total stranger now looking back at me out of the cracked, wood-framed mirror.

My face was thinner, and the cheekbones starker than before. My collarbones and the tendons in my neck were more pronounced, the soft, pampered contours replaced by sharp angles and lean muscles. I was fitter than I had ever been, but I couldn't help noticing I also looked a bit too thin. Away from Gildenbrook, I was growing malnourished, just like the rest of the kingdom.

And though I was now used to the freckles on my arms and hands, seeing them on my face, neck, and shoulders— covering every inch of my skin—made me reel. My eyes, too, had dimmed to normalcy in my memory, but I saw afresh that they were like lit gemstones, twin whirlpools of glowing peridot and sapphire, struck through with veins of amber. And black though my hair was, the damp waves and spirals falling over my shoulders were distinctly firelike, flames made still.

I was beautiful, I thought in surprise. There was no vanity in the notion, because I felt no sense of ownership over the person in the mirror; I had almost never seen her before. But my reflection was so striking, so peculiar—even without the gold-and-copper hair—that it was stunning to behold. Not like the perfect specimens in Iyzabel's court, or the girls I had envied at Gildenbrook. I was still as far from them as it was possible to be, and a long way indeed from perfection.

But—I felt a rush of exhilaration as I realized it— something had changed in me, and I no longer wanted to be perfect. I was glad to be what I was. Because *I* liked me.

A small victory, perhaps, but I was in a mood to take any victories I could get.

I gave the sunchild in the mirror a small, bracing smile and left to get some sleep.

38

CHAPTER

When we filed out the inn's front door the next morning, a bright silver sky was already shedding misty light over the path up the mountain. I stopped at the sight. It was the lightest morning I had ever seen, and the range of color on the mountain—the hues of deep purple, rich charcoal and slate grays, shadowy greens and dark blues that comprised such towering heights—was a visual symphony. And the temperature . . . I was sure that this, at last, was what Linden had meant when he described true warmth: free and open, soft against the skin, and tantalizing as ribbons of gold borne on a lazy breeze. I wished I could stand in this spot all day.

Apparently immune to the scene ahead, Yarrow faced us all, looking stern. "This path is the most treacherous in all of Terra-Volat. It saves us a week's journey over the mountains, and will put us right in the middle of the Northern Wilds, but it's largely disused because it's so dangerous. My magic will help, but I want all of you alert and careful."

He waited for a nod from each of us before turning back to lead us up the path. "Weedy," he said over his shoulder. "Come walk with me."

The winding path was flanked by evergreens—full, strong, *healthy* evergreens—and I took so many deep breaths of the sharp, fresh-smelling air that I soon became woozy. As we rose higher, the occasional gaps in the trees revealed sweeping mountain-laced landscapes, spread out on either side of us like works of art, snow-capped or clothed in green. I was giddy from looking around so much—from *seeing* so much. It was difficult to keep from spilling sun energy over everyone.

Not unexpectedly, Yarrow asked almost at once for my account of the last two weeks. He was very quiet at first, and I tried to soften some of the harsher details to make him feel less responsible. When I reached the part about Bronya and Roark, however, he missed a step on the rising path and nearly fell headlong into the gorse.

"They said they knew you," I offered as I helped him up, hoping for his side of the story.

He was very pale. "Yes," he said. "Yes, they did know me once. Though I'm not sure I knew them."

I frowned. "Bronya wondered if you'd sent me to them on purpose."

"I didn't have . . . much control over what I did that day," he said, looking agitated. "I wasn't even sure it would work. But as you know, magic is often controlled by thought and emotion. In the chaos, perhaps I remembered that they farmed near the forest."

"I tried to get them to come with me, but Roark thinks our cause is doomed."

Yarrow grunted. I could see an angry flush creeping up his face beneath the scraggly white beard.

"Iyzabel killed their children, Yarrow. Don't you think that gives them some excuse?"

But this only seemed to make him angrier. He glowered in silence until my story left Bronya and Roark well behind, though he was shocked to hear of the citrine dagger, and at the end of my account he asked to see it as well as my arrow wound. He frowned at the latter, and promised to teach me more about healing next.

Midmorning, I finally saw what he had meant when he said our path was the most treacherous one in the kingdom. So far, we had merely been climbing over rocks and shale, occasionally passing drop-offs we could easily avoid. Now, however, the path left the forest behind, and continued for an appallingly long stretch on a two-foot-wide strip of ledge that was carved into the side of the mountain like a thin belt, hugging the sheer face of the peak.

To the left of this path was a vertical wall of rock, climbing ever upward into clouds toward the pinnacle. To the right, a drop-off whose depths disappeared in shadowy fog.

It was wide enough to cross, but only if you walked carefully, as one would walk along a roof's peak.

Yarrow tapped his Runepiece—a walking stick for the moment—on the rim of the ledge, and I saw a vivid teal light expand from the point it touched and shoot along the ledge. "That should keep anyone from missteps, at least, but I don't know how much more it will do," he said. "Be careful, all of you. Take your time."

I edged out onto the lip of rock after Yarrow and reached behind me for Linden's hand. Glancing back, I was grateful to see that he had offered his cloak for Elegy to hold. Merrall was grim-faced and lockjawed behind the banshee, both hands searching for nooks in the side of the mountain as we inched along.

When Merrall had progressed several paces over the

open void, and the rest of us were far enough along that Yarrow was approaching the very middle of the ledge, I heard a sound that made me feel like my stomach was falling all the way down into the chasm of fog below us.

It was the unmistakable creak of a bowstring, though none of us was holding a bow.

My head snapped back toward the trees, and I saw something shift in the shadows. A man appeared through the branches, the iron tip of his arrow glinting as it caught the filtered light from the clouds. Behind him came a second man with a sword, and with a nauseating swoop of recognition I saw a third, this one holding a loaded crossbow. They were the men from the tavern last night, who had been whispering at a table together when Linden and I arrived.

I turned away to hide my face, cold terror rushing through me.

"Where's the sunchild?" said one of the men, his voice deep and aggressive. "We know you're her companions. Tell us where she is and we'll spare your lives."

It was small consolation he had not spotted me, and my mind began to fumble for ways I might use this to our advantage. Our advantages, however, stuck as we were like training yard dummies on the side of the mountain, seemed limited.

"She is dead," said Merrall evenly. "Your people shot her."

"Liar," breathed the man. I heard the crunch of rocks and guessed he was stepping forward. My hands started to shake.

"She *is*—" began Elegy.

"*Liars!*" bellowed the man. "She was seen in the village of Polter, heading north not three days ago!"

The pickpocket.

There was a twang and a thunk from the crossbow, and I ducked reflexively, turning in spite of myself to see what had happened. Merrall had flung up a whirl of water to catch the arrow, but she staggered back, off balance, and bumped into Elegy.

I watched in frozen horror as the banshee teetered uncontrollably, still clinging to Linden's cloak. The second soldier lunged forward and swung his sword at Merrall, who twisted her airborne water into a rippling aqua blade and parried the blow. But the wave of movement was too much for Elegy, who flailed her arms for balance even as Linden wildly grasped to catch one of them. They knocked into each other, Elegy gave a terrified scream, and a piece of the ledge crumbled away beneath her foot.

In a flash of silvery-gray hair, she fell backward, over the edge into the abyss, and her shriek tore through my bones.

I was more afraid than I had ever been in my life. Still, I hesitated only long enough to glance at Linden, who was staring in whey-faced shock at the place Elegy had fallen.

Then I threw myself off the side of the mountain, into the fog after her.

PART FOUR

"*For a while they stood there, like men on the edge of a sleep where nightmare lurks, holding it off, though they know that they can only come to morning through the shadows.*"

J.R.R. TOLKIEN,
THE TWO TOWERS

39

CHAPTER

I plummeted like a boulder, but Elegy had fallen first. There was no time to be afraid, no time to do anything but what I *must* do if we were to survive.

I had flown once since my transformation, and then only by accident. Now, somehow, I had to do it on purpose.

Turning my mind to the clouds, reaching through the thin Darkness, I yanked sunlight into my body until it burned in my limbs. Terror made it easy. Then, like a falcon diving for prey, I pressed my arms to my sides and propelled myself faster, ever downward, into the terrible, thickening fog that masked the bottom from view.

"*Elegy!*" I screamed, and heard her shriek back, a little to my right, slightly above me.

I had gone too far.

Focusing hard on the sun energy coursing through me, I remembered what Yarrow had said about flight: I could manipulate it like a water current as long as I was connected to my source. Thinking of swimming, I swerved right through the mist, grateful for the blazing light of my skin, and saw the blur of gray that was Elegy just in time to throw out my arms and catch her against my chest.

I felt my sternum crack as she hit. I tried to gasp, but could not draw breath, and the pain was sucking my sun energy away, making it impossible to focus on summoning more. And then Elegy and I were plunging together, and there was nothing I could do to save us.

"*Siria!*" Elegy screeched.

And then air filled my lungs again—blessed, wonderful air—and I sucked life back into my chest. Pain tore through my sternum, but if I could breathe, I could cope with pain. I seized the sunlight again and pulled it through my body in a rage of determination—and it coursed from my hair to my feet. With the last vestiges of my control, I held it back from the edge of my skin, protecting Elegy from burning.

How to stop us?

Fear was all I could feel, blinding and clawing as we shot downward.

We were going to die.

I gritted my teeth and seized the terror I felt. I imagined Elegy and I stopping—heaved us upward—with every ounce of energy I had. The air began to slow around us, and as if we were grinding to a halt on some unseen surface, we finally, *finally* stopped falling altogether. My limbs felt like water, but the task was only half finished. Thankful someone bigger had not fallen, I adjusted my grip on the banshee and turned all my energy toward raising us upward again. At first nothing happened, though I could feel the fire burning in my veins. Then we began, very gradually, to climb again. Elegy's dead weight dragged at us, and I shook with exertion as we drifted higher with agonizing slowness.

But we were rising.

I was flying.

When at last we broke through the fog, Elegy gave a

shriek, and I looked up just in time to veer out of the way of another falling body.

My stomach flipped over, but it was only the soldier with the sword—and he was already dead. *Up*, I commanded myself, jaw clenched, and we continued to rise. A second body toppled over the ledge just as we reached it, and this time it was the crossbow-wielding man who screamed, quite alive, as he fell.

Yarrow nearly collapsed against the cliff face as Elegy and I drifted into view, and Linden put his head in his hands, looking as if he might throw up. Then they were reaching to pull us up as Merrall followed the last man—the first soldier, with the longbow—flinging shards of ice at him as he ran back through the trees in the direction of the tavern.

When at last Elegy and I stood on the ledge, both of us trembling so badly we had to be supported, there was a long moment of stunned silence. Elegy, who still seemed too shocked for tears or speech, clung to me like a child to its mother, and Yarrow seemed capable only of staring at me with his chest heaving. Linden was grayer than a corpse, and still looked in danger of vomiting, but he stepped close enough to take hold of my hand and squeezed it with shaking fingers. Then, when everyone seemed in better command of themselves, Yarrow led us on as quickly as we could safely go. Solid ground, when we finally reached it, had never been so welcome.

We stopped in the shelter of the trees to wait for Merrall, and Yarrow turned to me at once, his face twisted with emotion. "What were you *thinking*, Siria?" he demanded, and though his voice was weak, he looked furious. "You told me yourself you hadn't figured out how to fly. You could both have been killed!"

"If I hadn't . . . Elegy definitely . . . would have," I wheezed, sinking down to sit on the ground while I covered my sternum with my hands. "And speaking . . . of powers . . . now might be a good time . . . to teach me . . . healing."

Yarrow's anger melted immediately—either at the truth of what I said, or at my obvious pain—and crouched beside me to talk through the process of mending my bones with sun energy: a continual and focused effort to pull sunlight down and imagine it knitting the injuries together. It could take weeks, he said, but if I was determined enough, I might manage it more quickly. And though I grimaced and gasped, exhausted by so much effort to use my power, a few broken or aching bones seemed light compared to the price Elegy and I had nearly paid.

It wasn't until Linden sat down beside me and gathered me gently into his arms, tripping my calming heartbeat into a stutter again, that I realized what else had happened. "It's good to have you back to normal again, Weedy," he said, pulling a lock of hair over my shoulder. I stared at it in amazement. The burst of sun energy I'd summoned had burned away the black dye completely, returning my hair to its usual vivid spectrum of coppers that flickered and glowed like living flames with the power still running through me.

"Also," he muttered, putting his forehead against my temple and closing his eyes as if he, too, were recovering from an internal injury, "please never do that to me again."

I could only manage a nod, but I took hold of his hand and held it tight.

Merrall soon joined us with the unwelcome news she had lost the third scout in the woods. Though she was willing to return and search further, Yarrow shook his head.

"He'll be back to the tavern before you can catch up, and then heading south on horseback. We'd better go on. Linden, I need your best work covering our tracks. When he returns with more men, we can't give them so much as a bent twig to follow."

To my surprise, Merrall came to help me up, looking down at me with unmistakable approval. "Most people would have let the banshee die," she said baldly, offering me her hand. "But you did not. You are a worthy leader, sunchild."

Finally, Elegy burst into tears.

We pursued a downward slope for several hours—slowly, for my benefit—and then veered directly west into the trees. They were even fuller here, and the myriad green hues within their needles and new spring leaves were varied and deep. I thought that if I had been magically transported from Gildenbrook to this forest without having watched the slow progression through the Forest of Eli, I might not believe that these belonged to the same family as the skeletal, withering trees on the moor.

"Is this the Northern Wilds?" I asked.

"Officially everything beyond the pass is the Northern Wilds," said Yarrow, just ahead of me. "But we're still several hours from the resistance camp."

I thought of my brother—a mere *several hours* away—and had to reach out for a passing branch to steady myself.

Before long the underbrush grew denser, and we fought our way through brambles and tangled vines. My ribs and chest smarted with every step, though I worked constantly to heal them. I could feel the sunlight inside me like a billowing cloud, but either I was doing it wrong, or it would take even longer than Yarrow guessed.

Linden worked too, always half a dozen steps behind the rest of us, his eyes glowing green and his skin swirling with lines and whorls as he meticulously regrew every leaf and stalk we flattened along the way. It was difficult to keep from watching him. He was beautiful even at his most bedraggled, but clean and rested as he was now, with the uncanny changes his magic made to his appearance, he was hard to ignore. I found myself wanting time alone with him more than I even wanted to heal my chest.

As the day wore on, I could tell we were drawing near to that final tapering away of the Darkness. The enchantment above the trees felt more like a screen than a barrier, and I could sense something farther north that was like a cliff, only it dropped upward instead of down. It pulled at me, as if a tapestry hook had caught the center of my being and drew me inexorably on, toward that bright gulf.

Near evening, Yarrow held up a hand to indicate that we should stop. I stretched my arms cautiously—skin warm from using so much internal sunlight on my cracked bones—and gazed around. Yarrow looked as if he was expecting something, but the forest appeared no different here than it had all day; we were not even in a clearing.

But then—out of thin air, it seemed—two men appeared, hooded and clad in earthy greens and browns. Before any of us could speak, they raised loaded crossbows, and pointed them straight into Yarrow's face.

And he smiled, as if this were exactly what he had been hoping for.

40

CHAPTER

Name your business, strangers," one of the men said.

"We are not strangers," Yarrow said. "I am Yarrow Ash, Mage of Caritas, and these are my companions. We are your allies."

The men considered him doubtfully for a moment before they noticed me. They exchanged looks. Then one of them nodded curtly to the other, who said, "Follow me," before turning to walk in the opposite direction.

Unlike us, the rebel men passed over the leaves and bracken in complete silence, leading us farther into the thick trees like soft-footed foxes. We came to a clearing, and I could just make out the violet-tinged clouds above the tree-tops, growing darker as the sun set, unseen, behind them. Even hidden, the sun was so close now I could genuinely smell it; a fragrance on the rich air that was new, and yet more familiar than any scent I knew.

My heart beat hard against my temples. Soon I would see it.

And soon I would meet my brother.

I was utterly terrified.

One of the rebel men gave a sharp, birdlike whistle that

echoed around the clearing, and three more men appeared between gaps in the trees, raising their own crossbows.

"Allies," said the man who had whistled. "Look, Sedge."

The man he addressed was short and middle-aged, with sandy-brown hair and a tan face disfigured by scars. He frowned skeptically, but when his eyes fell on me, his mouth sagged open. "Incredible," he breathed. "The whole forsaken country out looking for you, and somehow you outwit them all. How did you find us?" He looked at Yarrow. "Who are you?"

"Yarrow Ash," he said. "I was trained and apprenticed in the city once known as Caritas. This is Merrall of the Elder Bay, who has spent the last fourteen years as a spy in Umbraz for our cause, and Elegy, a banshee from Myrial Lake who was banished from her clan."

The rebel men cast Elegy looks of alarm, and several stumbled in their haste to retreat.

"Linden Hatch is an elf from the northeast," Yarrow went on, frowning at them, "whose family was murdered in the overthrow. He left this camp with me ten years ago for the purpose of traveling south to watch over one of the girls the resistance thought to be the missing sunchild."

All the men were gawking now, looking from Yarrow to me, and back again.

"And in case you haven't already guessed," he said, gesturing at me, "*this* is that girl: Siria Nightingale, princess of Luminor, the last sunchild in Terra-Volat."

I blushed as the rebels stared at me, and in their silence the chorus of insects and birdsong around us grew much louder. One of the men turned and disappeared into the trees. The scarred, sandy-haired rebel cleared his throat and strode forward to lift a lock of my hair, which he examined.

He then took hold of my wrist—Linden started, but Yarrow held up a hand—and raised it to eye level while he peered at the freckles. Then he spat on his thumb and rubbed it hard over my skin, as if trying to scrub away paint.

It was much like the treatment I had received from Iyzabel's soldiers, though in reverse.

"Satisfied?" I said, tugging my arm away.

He didn't seem remotely abashed. "Yes," he said, bowing deeply. "Thank you, my lady, for permitting the impertinence. I had to be sure." He turned to Yarrow. "We sent scouts below the mountains near two months ago now, hoping to aid the princess when she came. No one scented a hair of you, though."

Yarrow frowned again, but before he could reply, sounds of snapping branches came from the brush behind him. A moment later, three more people crashed into the clearing, with two fumbling to restrain the third: a tall young man with black hair.

"Get *off*, Reef," he was saying, trying to shrug out of their grip.

But the man called Reef had caught sight of me and relaxed his hold. The black-haired man pulled free and looked up.

I stared. There was something eerily familiar about him . . . about his long nose, the shade and shape of his hazel eyes, his mouth . . .

He stared back at me and took a slow step forward, gazing intently, as if he was afraid I might disappear if he blinked.

I took a guess. "Eamon?"

And then the mouth that was so similar to mine broke into a wide smile, and he charged forward with a roar of delight.

41

CHAPTER

Is it really you?" he cried, seizing my hands in his broad ones. "My sister? Helena!"

My hands stiffened in his, and I felt suddenly very foolish. In my weary, dull-witted state, I didn't know what to do with the name that was both mine and not mine. Though I had imagined this moment many times, I had never thought of the inevitable confusion over what I should be called. As I tried to assemble a response, confusion crept into his face, followed by a look of comprehension. He squeezed my fingers.

"Oh Light, I'm sorry," said Eamon, eyebrows bunching. "I should've realized you wouldn't stay Helena. Never even occurred to me." He gave an apologetic smile. "Tell me, then: What's my little sister called now?"

The tension wound tight throughout my muscles eased. His little sister. I had an older brother. Amazing how you could know a thing in your mind, but not understand it until it was standing before you. I smiled back, lips trembling.

"Siria," I said. "Until a few weeks ago, the only name I'd ever known was Siria Nightingale."

And then something crumbled inside me, and I fought to hold it up, acutely aware of all the people watching us. I did not want to cry in front of them. But I had a newfound name, and a newfound brother, and once we had been part of a family together. I'd had a mother and a father who loved me, who wanted to spend time with me, who had named me Helena. And a sister. I'd had a sister too, I remembered with a sudden, piercing sorrow.

I blinked rapidly, trying to bring Eamon back into focus. He was still smiling, but his eyes—exactly the same shade of hazel mine had been before I transformed—had grown very bright.

"Siria?" he said, and I nodded through half a laugh, half a sob. He laughed as well. "It's so wonderful to finally meet you. I'm Eamon."

"I know," I said, and my tears came at the same moment his did.

I forgot everyone else as my brother pulled me against his chest, and I clung to him as I wept, as if he might keep me from drowning in the joy and grief now thundering through me like the currents of competing rivers. There was something so familiar about him, even about the sound of his voice, that made me feel calm; that, even as sobs shook my body, seemed to encase me in warmth, like someone singing a lullaby. I wondered if his voice was anything like our mother's, and if it was her I recognized in him: the voice that had woven through my growing bones and knitting fibers in the womb and sang to me in the first unremembered months of my life.

When at last he released me, I turned to my friends, uncertain how to proceed. But Eamon took the lead.

"My sister's companions?" he said with another warm

smile, stepping toward them and shaking hands with Merrall and Elegy as I introduced them.

"And this is Yarrow Ash," I said. "He's—" I broke off, another wave of tears blurring my eyes as I caught Yarrow's familiar gray ones behind the old spectacles.

"Siria's become like a daughter to me over the years," he finished for me, his voice gruff as he shook Eamon's hand. "It's a pleasure to meet you at last, Crown Prince." I expected Eamon to wave down this formal address, but he seemed not to notice it.

He turned to Linden, and I felt heat rush into my face. How in dark night to introduce him? "Surrogate brother" seemed wrong, and "best friend" wasn't quite enough. Yet I could hardly call him "the boy I had fallen wildly in love with a few years ago, and who probably, maybe, hopefully, loved me back."

"Linden Hatch," said Linden, sticking out his hand with a grin before I could attempt to sum him up. He and Eamon were precisely the same height, though my brother's build was thicker than Linden's wiry frame. "Your sister's my favorite person in the world."

I blushed, my stomach swooping at his words. His grin widened as he caught my eye, the dimple pressed hard into his cheek, and Eamon threw his head back and laughed.

"I like an honest man," he said, clapping Linden on the shoulder. "Or elf. Best of luck to you, friend."

I felt dazed, but there was no time to gather my wits, because Eamon was naming the rebels around us, and there was more handshaking to be done. Every time I caught Linden's eye, a wicked smile flashed across his face.

Once everyone in the clearing had been formally introduced—including Sedge, the man with the scarred face, who seemed to be a leader of sorts—the resistance party led the way west, toward their camp. The sun had long since taken any trace of light with it beyond the horizon, and the forest was dark but for the glow of lanterns as our procession wound between trees, around thickets, and over chattering streams.

When we came to the edge of the resistance village, I did not recognize it as a living space. The people had disguised their homes so well that when Eamon gestured to an enormously thick maple tree and said, "That's one of the watch houses," I thought he was making a joke, and laughed.

"She doesn't see very well in the dark," said Linden, obviously trying not to laugh himself. "Sunchild, you know . . ."

"I can see perfectly w—" I began, but Linden pulled me a few feet closer to the maple until I could see that the trunk had a large gap at its base, where a moss-covered structure had been built to look like an extension of the bulbous roots. I stopped in surprise.

"And look up," said Linden, brushing my arm with his forefinger and making my skin tingle.

High in the branches, I could pick out a second structure, which had been built around the growth of the tree, ingeniously settled in the natural nooks of the branches that appeared sturdiest.

"Oh," I said.

Eamon chuckled from behind us. "Farther in, they're less heavily disguised, but all our buildings try to work around the trees that already exist. Wood nymphs helped a good deal with construction in the beginning."

We jogged to catch up to the others. The path seemed to follow a broad sort of lane that wound along the forest floor like a village main street. More houses were discernible now, and as Eamon had said, every structure I saw was built either around a trunk or in the branches of the trees.

"This is the East Lane, since it feeds from the eastern pass," Eamon was saying. "But there are a lot of us—near a thousand now—so people live all over the forest. The village goes on for miles."

Lanterns bobbed on hooks outside most doors near the heart of the camp, and smoke issued in curls from chimneys, making me think of comfortable evenings in Yarrow and Linden's cabin. I gazed around as we walked, and had just turned to ask Eamon where we were heading when I caught sight of a face in an upper window—a little girl—who shouted at the sight of us and disappeared again.

A moment later she and her family spilled out onto a high porch, the father still clutching a leg of some roasted meat, and I heard the girl say, "There! That one!"

Face hot, I looked straight ahead. As we passed other houses, more people came out, their whispering like a strong breeze through tall grass. I had the uncomfortable idea that many were not retreating back into their houses but trailing after us instead.

"Eamon," I whispered. "Are they following us?"

"Yes." He sounded solemn. "You can see why, I'm sure. We rarely have visitors, and your appearance . . . well, it's bound to cause a stir. The sunchild story is a bit of a legend here."

By the time Sedge led our group into a wide clearing, the crowd behind us had swelled to the size of a small army. Another man had joined our party as we walked, but he stood beside Yarrow with his head bent, speaking with him in low tones.

Thick clover blanketed the ground here, and a great,

wooden pavilion loomed to the right, encircled by glittering lanterns on poles and lit by a roaring fire in a pit. The pavilion was as big as the dining hall at Gildenbrook, and I could see one long table inside it, dark and glossy in the firelight, surrounded by wooden benches and chairs.

"Gather up, please!" said Sedge, motioning for us to cluster around him. "You too, nosy busybodies!" he shouted to the crowd. "Can everyone hear me?"

There was a chorus of assent. I craned around to see the people behind us, surprised to find they encompassed all ages, from infants to the nearly infirm. Most wore rough, homemade garments like Yarrow's, but some of their clothes appeared to have been crafted by a more graceful hand—like Linden's—and these, I could tell, were nymphs. Quite apart from their clothes, these folk flashed periodically with evidence of their power—shades of blue glowing in the cheeks of the naiads, tree-bark lines racing over the skin of the elves, and sourceless breezes fluttering the hair and clothes of the winged pixies—magic apparently more frequently accessed here than anyone would dare below the pass. But all the people here were markedly different from those below the mountains, and not just because of their clothes. Their faces were fuller, alive with color you never saw below the mountains, even in the far north. In Umbraz every face looked as if it had been dusted with ashes, no matter what skin tone a person had. Here, the faces radiated depth and life, boasting a clear spectrum from flushed peach to burnished copper to deep, glowing sable, and they seemed healthier, stronger . . . happier. By comparison, everyone else I had ever met looked like a ghost.

"Our guests have traveled a great distance to get here," Sedge was saying. "And while I feel certain they will want to join us in celebrating their arrival, I suspect they might prefer to rest first."

A smattering of chuckles came from the crowd.

Sedge threw a glance at the older man talking to Yarrow. He was tall and very lean, a bit like an aged scarecrow, with skin like cracked leather and hair sticking out in silver tufts beneath a buckskin hat. "Tomorrow night . . ." said Sedge, and the scarecrow man gave a barely perceptible nod. "We will meet here." He raised his arms. "To feast, dance, and celebrate our guests. Please bring food to share and spread the word. We will begin at sundown. Good night!"

I felt a tingle of unreality at his use of the word *sundown*. Like the sun was not a fable here, but a presence. Like they had access to it; real, direct access to an unveiled sun.

A shiver ran the full length of my spine.

Soon, so would I.

42

CHAPTER

The crowd scattered back into the trees, and Sedge gave our group a rueful smile. "I hope you don't mind a bit of a party on your behalf."

Linden laughed. "I think you just used the word *feast*. You couldn't keep us away with a pack of dragons."

"Speaking of food," said the scarecrow man, turning away from Yarrow and addressing the rest of us. His voice was raspy, but slow and calculating, as if he weighed every word. "I imagine you are hungry now. If you don't mind waiting in the pavilion, I will see to your supper and lodging for tonight."

"Thank you, Briar," said Yarrow, and though his tone was light, the crease between his wiry brows did not disappear. "We would be grateful."

We wandered into the pavilion and took seats near the far end of the table, closest to the fireplace. Sedge went to build up the fire, and Yarrow watched him work with a distant, abstract expression.

"There's so much I want to know," said Eamon with a small laugh. "I can't believe you're here."

I smiled. "Neither can I, frankly."

Yarrow turned to look thoughtfully at my brother. "It's been a long wait for you, I suppose. And with less and less news as the years have gone on?"

It was an odd question, I thought, but Eamon nodded. "When I was young, people were constantly going and coming, planning and scouting and bringing news, but there's been less of that most recently. I used to wonder why, but Briar explained we had to wait for my sister to turn sixteen before we could help her." He smiled at me, affection warm in his hazel eyes. "I've never been good at waiting. I used to try to sneak out at night, to run away and find you. But I always got caught, and eventually they posted guards around my rooms and barred my doors and windows." He laughed ruefully. "I guess they didn't want to have to rescue *two* Luminorian royals from the Witch Queen."

Careful to control the light swirling beneath my skin, I reached for Eamon's hand and squeezed it. He clasped my hand in both of his and held it tight.

Briar returned in three quarters of an hour, during which time Linden and I summarized our two-month journey for Eamon, who proved a rapt and invested audience. Three other people came with Briar when he arrived: a tall, white-haired elf woman and two men bearing smoked ham, cheese, crusty bread, and apples.

"This is Freda," Briar said in his raspy, measured voice while we helped ourselves to the food. The wood nymph smiled at us, eyes kind in a wrinkled mahogany face. "She has volunteered her house for you to sleep in. It's just off the East Lane, and near the river, for the naiad's use."

"What added protection have we given our borders for the night?" said Eamon.

Briar frowned. "Do you think our border guard insufficient?"

I was surprised to hear scorn in Briar's voice, but Eamon either didn't notice or didn't care. "My sister just told me they've been pursued by Iyzabel's forces nearly their entire journey—even as far as the mountain pass. Siria is the most wanted person in Terra-Volat, and if any of the queen's men find this place, they'll raze us before we have time to dust off our swords."

Briar scowled, and I wondered suddenly if he, at least, was not pleased the Crown Prince had grown up to be a man to whom leadership was a natural quality as much as it was a birthright.

"I told you to send out scouts, Briar," said Yarrow, almost indifferently. "That soldier who got away at the pass will have gone back for more of his men. They'll be at your borders within a month, and they'll tear apart the forest to find you. This safety you think you have is an illusion."

"Paranoid nonsense," scoffed Briar. "In fourteen years, we've never been discovered. Why should they find us now?"

But Sedge was looking at my brother. "We'll reinforce the guard tonight," he said, and Eamon nodded his approval.

Briar flushed, looking irritated.

We left the pavilion in the dying light of the fire and traipsed back down the path that led to the village lanes. My brother fell into step beside me, but I strained my ears to hear what Yarrow was saying to Linden just ahead of us.

". . . too comfortable," I heard him mutter. "Pigheaded. It'll be their doom."

I glanced at Eamon, but again, he didn't appear to be listening.

"What was it like, growing up here?" I said.

He smiled at me and puckered his dark brows in thought. "Lonely at first. Scary. And I missed everyone terribly." He shrugged. "But I got used to it, and eventually I heard about how things were below the mountains, what sort of life you were probably living. So I stopped feeling so sorry for myself." He winked, but there was something sad and slightly bitter in his expression. "Still. You're here now, and that's what matters, eh?"

I nodded, though I wasn't exactly sure whether I agreed.

Freda's house turned out to be a one-level cottage built into the low branches of two thick trees, about six feet above the ground. A winding staircase twisted up from a covered garden into the house itself, which was entirely wooden with a thatched roof and open, curtained windows. Everything inside was ingeniously constructed out of natural material, from the grass-woven mats to the woolen blankets and tree stump tables.

"I'm afraid I don't have much room," said Freda, after we bade Eamon goodnight and piled through the front door. "But I do have one bed, a cot in the bedroom, and the settee out here." She smiled kindly. "There's food in the cupboards, and more blankets in the hall. Please make yourselves at home."

"Thank you, Freda," said Yarrow. "We truly appreciate your hospitality."

She nodded and strode toward the door but stopped with her hand on the knob. "I know I'm only one person," she said, looking back over her shoulder at me, "but I want you to know that I'm with you—all of you—in what you've come to do."

I blinked at her, but before anyone could reply, Freda was gone.

I slept fitfully beside Elegy in the house's only bed. My chest and ribs ached, and my dreams were strange, full of Eamon, the rebels, and the men from the mountain pass. I woke while it was still dark but found I could sense the sun as a distant presence in the east, below the horizon. Its proximity was calming, and I lay in bed for a solid half hour, letting it seep into me while Elegy breathed, deep and rhythmic, beside me. Gradually, I fell back asleep.

After breakfast, I went to find Eamon, and we spent the afternoon on a grassy bank of the river, dangling our feet into the water and comparing childhoods. I told him about Phipps and Milla, and then how Yarrow and Linden's arrival at Nightingale Manor had upended my dull, lonely life. He told me about growing up with nymphs and rebels and people who had known our parents; how it had been both balm and sting to be constantly surrounded by people who had loved them.

After a while, a companionable silence fell between us, and I dug my index finger into the dirt, idly drawing a star-thistle blossom from a barren stalk. My control was getting better and better. I barely noticed myself holding the energy back from my skin anymore.

"Kysia," I said eventually. Her name was like a lyric to a long-forgotten song. "Tell me about our sister Kysia."

Eamon beamed. His memories of our dead family were clearly not a torment to him anymore, but rather a source of joy. It was true he'd had fourteen years to grieve, but I could tell my brother was not the sort of person to let his pain rule him.

"Kysia," he said, settling back on his elbows in the grass. "Well, Kysia would've run the kingdom if she'd had the chance. She was two years younger than me, but by the time she could talk she was already bossing me around, telling me what to do and where to go. She looked more like Father, but had all of Mother's personality.

"Father was quiet and kind, but often unsure of himself. But Mother"—he chuckled—"Mother was decisive and frank and bold. When you were born, Kysia already had half the palace bending to her funny little toddler whims."

"I'm more like Father," I said, feeling oddly disappointed by the conviction. *Quiet* and *kind* were very admirable qualities, of course, and I was glad to know I had inherited things from both parents. But *bold* and *decisive* and *brave* . . .

"You're like both of them, I think," said Eamon, and I looked up to find him studying me. "I know I haven't had much time to observe, but you seem to have the best blend of them. Father's kindness with Mother's conviction. Mother's bravery with Father's introspection."

"You think I'm brave?" I said, astonished.

"You think you're not?"

"I think . . . I think I *want* to be brave, but I'm always afraid."

"Well, that just means you're wise," said Eamon. "I don't think someone who wasn't brave could have come all this way and through as much danger as you did."

I mulled this over, feeling a quiet happiness settle into me. For a moment I wished I didn't have to go back down into Terra-Volat. That I could just stay here in peace, with my brother, with Linden, with Yarrow and Merrall and Elegy, in an elf-made tree house, with the sun. The idea was enough to make me hurt. It was almost everything I had wanted since I was a child.

But staying would neither make nor keep me brave.

43

CHAPTER

Midway through the afternoon, Linden brought us a picnic lunch and news. The feast Sedge had announced the evening before, he told us, was to be postponed.

"Why?" asked Eamon.

Linden shrugged, but I could see he was uneasy. "Something about preparations, and there being business to settle between Yarrow and Briar."

"Nothing to worry about, I'm sure," Eamon said, clapping him on the shoulder.

Linden smiled a little abstractedly, then turned to me. "Yarrow wants to use the next couple of days to teach you some practical skills. He asked me to tell you not to run off in the morning."

I nodded. "Where is he now?"

"Went to meet Briar. Said he wouldn't be back before supper."

We invited Linden to sit with us the rest of the afternoon, but his distracted mood persisted, even after we collected Merrall and Elegy and went with Eamon to eat supper with some of his friends in the lavish tree house mansion he called home.

"What's wrong?" I asked Linden quietly while Eamon and his friends roared with laughter together over some memory.

He shook his head. "I don't know. Something just feels wrong about all this. When I was here before, it was different. I know I was young then, but—the people seemed . . . less comfortable."

I could see what he meant. Eamon's house was not a palace compared to the Black Castle, but it was nothing to sneeze at either. It made Yarrow and Linden's cozy cabin at Nightingale Manor look like a hovel.

Linden trailed a finger lightly across the back of my hand, and sunlight leapt in my veins. "No point worrying yet, though," he said with an unconvincing attempt at levity. "Worry ruins good ale."

He raised his mug to me, and Eamon's spirited friends followed suit.

"To the sunchild!" one cried.

"To ale!" said another.

"To more nights like this one!" proclaimed a third.

Yarrow was tired and cranky the next morning, so I followed him outside to a clearing with some reluctance. But I was surprised to find his manner much gentler than usual, and I wondered if whatever had made him grumpy had also increased his sympathy for me and my ignorance.

He didn't waste time repeating the things he had told me during our journey. Instead he faced me across a distance of several yards, drew his Runepiece, and told me to do whatever occurred to me. Then he sent a ball of green fire speeding through the air toward my face.

What occurred to me was to yelp and duck.

"Weedy!" he said in exasperation as I picked myself up off the grass.

"I'm sorry! It was so sudden!"

He rolled his eyes. "Do you think Iyzabel's going to warn you before she attacks?"

"No, of course not." I sighed. "Try again."

I dodged the second fireball before I could even think to stop myself, but whirled to fire a blast of sunlight after it as it fizzled out among the trees. It missed. Grimacing, I turned back to Yarrow—but he had already hurled a third green fireball at me.

This time I reacted out of sheer terror. I threw my hands up, feeling heat rush out of my core, down my arms, and into my palms. The next second there was a sound like damp cloth on glass, and a shimmering, faintly golden, concave barrier—thin and glossy as a mirror—materialized in front of me and absorbed the fireball like a pool catching a droplet of water. I stood still, chest heaving.

"That's more like it," Yarrow grunted. "That's a sunshield, Weedy. You see how it acted as a defense rather than a weapon? You need to master that one."

And so we practiced it, over and over, until I could produce the sunshield without difficulty. By noon I was positively dropping from exhaustion, having achieved a rudimentary adeptness at producing a sunburst—which was essentially just a fiery missile—a flaming lasso, and a sun-energy sword, as well as the sunshield. Yarrow promised we would begin working with the citrine dagger after lunch.

"If I can *move* after lunch," I groaned from where I lay in the grass, feeling as if my limbs were made of wet dough.

"It'll wear you out less after you've seen the sun," said Yarrow, digging into our cold chicken and cheese. "Remember, your transformation is still incomplete, and magic will always take an extra toll on you when you don't have direct access to your source."

"Then why don't we go find it today?"

"Because I still think waiting to expose you during the equinox is the best hope we have for breaking the Darkness. That should maximize your power."

"And when is the equinox?"

"Eight days from now."

"How much time before Iyzabel's forces are here, do you think?"

There was something strained in his gaze when he looked at me. "Two weeks," he said. "Three, if we're lucky. They won't want those reprobate Upland soldiers fighting for them, so I imagine our little scout will run a few horses into the ground to get back to Umbraz for the queen's best men."

"But surely he couldn't get all the way south and back again in two weeks?" I said, incredulous. "It took us almost two months to do half as much!"

"On foot, hugging the long arc of the Forest of Eli, Weedy. They'll have horses, and the use of the road the whole way."

I nodded dismally, trying not to think about how much time we could have had to rest in the resistance village if we'd been able to ride horses along the Queen's Road. "Briar's still determined not to reinforce their borders here, I suppose?"

Yarrow's eyes were hard. "He's just determined not to take my advice, I think. Arrogant fool."

"Well," I said, "the equinox is a little over a week away. I'll have had a crack at the Darkness long before they arrive, won't I?" I shivered as I spoke, the idea almost too surreal to believe.

He nodded. "Let's hope so."

Yarrow went easier on me during the afternoon, mostly helping me master the use of my dagger, and the next day was much the same, albeit with a longer lunch break including both Eamon and Linden. When I could feel the sun beginning to sink toward the west behind the thin layer of Darkness, Yarrow stretched and groaned. "Nearly suppertime," he said. "We'd best get dressed."

The banquet was to take place that night, and we had all been given new clothes to wear, which everyone seemed to have different opinions about. Merrall grumbled as she pulled on the aquamarine silk dress she had been given, apparently annoyed to have her wardrobe dictated, but Elegy swirled around our bedroom in her new violet frock in wild delight, squealing over the detailed embroidery. I wondered whether she had ever had anything new in her life.

Mine was a sweeping white dress with beautiful gold detailing, which felt as if it had been tailored to fit me— though I couldn't imagine how anyone could have done the work in the mere two days since we'd arrived. I plaited my hair into a thick rope around the crown of my head, and Elegy, seeing it, gasped that it was the most beautiful thing she'd ever seen. With a smile, Merrall offered to do Elegy's hair the same, though I noticed she left her own untouched.

Linden looked uncomfortable in the garments he had been given, though they were finer than anything he owned and made him look absurdly handsome. Yarrow, however, had flatly refused to wear any clothes but his own, and as we all walked toward the pavilion, I thought his rough leather tunic and wool trousers made him look stubbornly shabby.

I stole glances at Linden as we went, admiring the way the new clothes set off the broad sweep of his shoulders and the lean taper of his waist. His hair had grown past his ears, and he had washed it so that the dark waves shone glossy as they brushed his collar and curled against his stubbly jaw.

He caught me looking and a slow grin spread over his face. "See something you like?"

"Just marveling at the radical change," I said archly. "Looks like you've finally found something worth washing your hair for."

He laughed, his step springy. "Ah, well, why not make a bit of effort when you're offered a banquet? Maybe there'll be pretty girls there."

He laughed louder at my outraged expression, and I strode ahead, determined to give him nothing more to smile about the rest of the night.

It was a merry feast. The long table had been removed from the pavilion, and all the chairs and benches were set in a ring around the edge. On the far end, a little knot of musicians was reeling out jaunty tunes, and there was food and wine in abundance.

"Having fun?" I asked Elegy about halfway through the evening as she collapsed into a chair beside me at the edge of the pavilion, eyes bright and smile wide.

"It's *wonderful!*" she gushed, and then jumped right back up again, apparently too excited to bother resting. I was grateful that most of the village had welcomed a banshee into their midst without complaint, and though there were still a few who avoided her, she seemed not to notice.

Linden had just been dragged away by yet another girl determined to have him for a dance partner, and I watched askance as she preened and laughed at his every word. It had always been this way at Gildenbrook. Even when we hosted mixed balls with schools of eligible young men, and Linden served punch in ill-fitting servant's livery, my class-mates hovered around him like flies at a picnic, hoping to catch his eye.

I shook my head and laughed at myself. After everything that had happened, it seemed pretty, confident girls still had the power to make me jealous.

From across the pavilion, Linden's eyes flickered onto me, and I realized he had heard my laughter even from so far away, amid all the noise. Or perhaps he had merely seen it, eyes trained to my slightest movement. My jealousy evap-orated, and I thought for the thousandth time of our night at the Polter inn, of his attempt to kiss me in that dwarf cave, of his declaration to Eamon . . .

I had been holding myself back out of fear of hurting him, but now, if I was being honest, I was holding back out of plain old fear.

"May I have this dance, Your Highness?"

A brawny young man stood over me, half-bowing with his hand outstretched. He gave me a cheeky wink, and I noticed a few other boys seated nearby, watching us with wide grins. His friends, I guessed. Maybe they had placed wagers on whether I would accept.

"Thank you," I said, smiling back, "but no."

Linden had just disentangled himself from the girl and was looking with narrowed eyes toward my suitor. *Enough of fear*, I thought, and left the young man where he stood, weaving through the crowd toward Linden. The petite brunette at his shoulder was still gripping his arm as she effused her thanks.

I swept him a clumsy curtsy. "Will you dance, sir?"

He bowed solemnly, but the side of his mouth twitched. "I will. But you're a terrible dancer, my lady." He took my hand, and the brunette stalked away, looking sour.

"That's true," I said. "But I try to help friends in need, when I can."

The dimple winked in his cheek as he led me onto the floor. Though the dance was a jig, we wove a slow waltz through the other pairs, drawing irritated glances as they swerved to avoid us.

"I hate to inconvenience you, Miss Nightingale," Linden said after a moment, his earnest voice betrayed by the glint in his eyes, "but would it be too much trouble for you to perform the correct steps to this dance? We're dancing a waltz, not stomping grapes in a winepress. It's a delicate balance, I know . . ."

I made sure to stomp his toes. "Perhaps you'd prefer one of your other partners," I said, sucking in my cheeks to control my smile. "I imagine they're better dancers than this wine-stomper."

"No, no, certainly not," he said gravely. "I'm only offering a suggestion, after all. You're a fine dancer, really . . . except for the way you move your feet."

My bursts of laughter were starting to draw attention.

"Hush, now, hush!" said Linden in mock embarrassment. Then he pulled me closer and said, still in that falsely earnest voice, "There is something else I wished to ask you." He gestured over his right shoulder to a clump of young women standing off to the side, several of them his former dance partners. They were all watching us, presumably waiting for the dance to end.

He cleared his throat. "I hate to—"

"Inconvenience me?"

"Yes, quite. But if it—"

"Isn't too much trouble?"

"You're so intuitive, Miss Nightingale. Yes, if it isn't too much trouble, I wonder . . ." He paused to give me a significant look. "I wonder if you might pretend to be *in love* with me. Then perhaps I might receive fewer invitations to dance with complete strangers."

My nerves tingled and sang. "It strikes me, Mr. Hatch, that all the other young women have acted in that precise way, and yet you've had no lapse in invitations."

"Ahhh," he said, choking on a laugh. "I see. So you think it should go the other way around?"

"Only if you wish to break a great many hopeful female hearts."

He bowed his head. "A necessary evil, I think."

And with a dramatic flourish, he dipped me and pressed his lips against my cheek. But when his mouth touched my skin, something changed.

The comfortable flirtation, the easy joking, the ambiguity—all of it—vanished like an icicle plunged in boiling water. I felt a tremor run the length of our two bodies where they touched, and all pretense of dancing was abandoned and forgotten. For a moment it was as if the pavilion and its whirling throng of people had ceased to be; we were back in the dusty dwarf cave in the lantern light, back at the inn, curled together on the shabby bed. I clung to his neck, scarcely breathing, as our faces hovered a hair's breadth apart.

But then someone knocked Linden's elbow, jarring us back into the present, and we straightened and stepped apart. As we fumbled to resume the dance, I became aware of both the number people around us and the cold, yawning distance that now separated my body from Linden's. My hands trembled as he guided me through the steps, and I could not look anywhere but at his face, and the bright, burning green of his eyes.

The dance ended, and I thought of my mother, asking the prince of Luminor for a dance.

Be brave.

I took Linden by the hand and led him, wordlessly, out of the pavilion.

44

CHAPTER

We walked in silence into the darkening trees, which were a blur of purple shadows that grew cooler as the night deepened. Insects hummed and chattered all around us, their strange cacophony a music I would never tire of hearing.

Linden squeezed my hand. "Let's go this way. I want to show you something."

If I had thought my heart could not beat any harder, I was mistaken. By the time we stopped in a small glade, equipped with an unlit lantern on an iron hook, a firepit, and two fallen logs as seating, it felt as though a battalion of military horses were stampeding inside my chest.

"I found this place yesterday," said Linden, stepping away from me to light the lamp. "Sat a while . . ."

He swallowed visibly and raked a hand through his hair as he turned back to face me—and something inside me loosened from its tight coil. Linden, with his unfailing confidence and good humor, was nervous too.

Letting out a long breath, I moved to sit on one of the fallen logs. I felt like I was on the brink of the mountain precipice again, preparing to jump. Even with near certainty of

Linden's feelings, and the long ache of my own, I was terrified to speak. And yet somehow I also *longed* to speak, so badly the words were practically clawing their way up my throat.

I smiled up at him, and his face relaxed.

"Hello, Weedy," he said softly. He pronounced the old nickname as though it were the most precious word he knew.

"Hello, Linden."

He gave a quick, lopsided grin and sat beside me, folding his hands in his lap. His knee touched mine very lightly, but he came no closer. I resisted the urge to crawl into his lap.

"Tell me what you meant the other day," I said. "When you said what you did to my brother."

The look on his face made my breath quick and uneven. I glanced away to steady myself.

"Do you remember the day Yarrow and I came to Nightingale Manor?" he said.

I looked back at him in surprise and nodded. It was one of my clearest early memories.

"You were our assignment, Yarrow and me. I'd sworn to the rebels I would protect you, and I thought meeting you would be like . . . well, like meeting a princess. I thought you'd be some delicate thing I'd be able to guard valiantly and stoically, like a knight guarding a tower."

A sound somewhere between a cackle and a hoot burst out of me.

"I've never been more wrong about anything," he said, grinning. "I remember that day perfectly. It was freezing cold . . . Yarrow and I were exhausted. We'd been traveling in almost complete darkness for days, and we came through the trees onto the moor and saw the manor house with its glowing windows and smoking chimneys . . . I don't know

why, but it made me angry to see it. I resented you for growing up there, for living in ignorance of the horrible things
that had happened to us both. But Yarrow knocked on the
door and we went into the warm parlor, and just as I was
wondering where your lavish tower bedroom was—there
you were."

His eyes glowed at the memory. "You came charging
out of the hall like a whirlwind, with all your fine skirts
askew, and said, 'Hello! I'm Siria,' while the butler kept trying to introduce you as *the young Miss Nightingale.* You
came right up to me, even though I must have looked like
a gargoyle, and you seized my filthy hands and said—"

"'We're going to be best friends,'" I finished.

Linden laughed. "I had no chance after that. You'd have
been crushed if your new best friend was mean to you, even
if he secretly thought you were turning out to be much
more than he'd bargained for."

His laughter faded, but I heard the soft echo of it in
my ears as he turned toward me and took both of my
hands in his. My heart was surely bruising itself against my
injured ribs.

"You've been my favorite person in the world since that
day," he said. "That's what I meant."

Every particle of my body yearned toward him, but
I held myself back. "Linden," I said, my voice quavering
slightly, "I'm sorry I kept away from you those last years at
school . . . I don't know why I was such an idiot."

"You thought you needed to live up to different expectations," he said gently. "I can't fault you for wanting your
parents' love."

"I wanted yours too. I just didn't think I *should.*"

His eyes held mine. "Either way, you always had it."

An acute, aching joy spread through me. I pulled one hand free from his and lifted it to his face, placing it precisely over the handprint I had burned into his skin, barely visible beneath his stubble in the lantern light.

"Siria," he whispered, flecks of gold dancing in the green of his eyes. His free hand came up to my face, the mirror image of my hand. "I really don't care if you burn me."

A laugh bubbled up in my throat as I slid forward and put my arms around his neck, bringing my lips to his. And then he was pulling me tight against him, one hand at my waist, the other tangling into the braided hair at the nape of my neck as he kissed me, gently at first, and then with the heat and intensity of ten years' buried longing. My pulse raged, and I could feel his thudding erratically in his neck as I slipped my hands into his hair.

It was overwhelming, I thought, to have felt so much for a person for so long, to have kept it hidden—and then suddenly to let it stretch inside your heart like a freed captive. I had never known anything more terrifying, or more wonderful. Sunlight thundered through my body, and I channeled it into things that could have no chance of burning him: healing energy, plant growth, flight.

I was floating several inches above the fallen log, but Linden pulled me back down. By the time we broke apart again, he was laughing, and a veritable thicket of trailing vines—both his work and mine—had grown up over the log and engulfed our legs.

"Well," he said, gesturing to the place our ankles had disappeared, "I hope you didn't want to go anywhere before the next frost."

"Not really," I said, and though I laughed too, I almost meant it.

Linden kissed my forehead, my nose, my lips again, and then folded his arms around me, tucking me against his chest. As I held on to him, feeling his heartbeat begin to slow, I could sense his thoughts returning to the shadow that had loomed over us from the very beginning.

"The equinox," he began, but I shook my head against his neck.

"Not now. Let's just pretend that the Darkness and Iyzabel and every other foul thing we've been worrying about the last two months have gone away. Just tonight, Linden . . . let's pretend we're normal people."

He started to brush a lock of hair away from my forehead, and then stopped. "What about *almost* normal people?"

"What do you mean?"

"Let me show you."

Something moved against my ankles, soft and ticklish. I pulled back and saw vines snaking up over my skirt, gently, but with determination. "Linden—"

"Just wait." His eyes burned brightest green, and deep brown patterns swirled over his skin.

The vines, which I recognized from years of gardening experiments as climbing jasmine and honeysuckle, had reached my arms. They made their way up over my shoulders and crept into the now disheveled braided crown of my hair. Linden's blazing eyes were open, but unfocused. After another few moments the funny crawling sensation retreated, slinking back down my neck, over my shoulder, and down my skirt once more. But a slight, new weight remained on my head, and I could still smell the mingling fragrances of the two flowers. Linden's eyes and skin faded to normal, and his grin widened.

I raised a hand to the top of my head.

"A circlet," he said, cocking his head to peer down into my face, "for the princess of Luminor. I'm not sure if you noticed, but these flowers are in the colors of the old kingdom."

White and gold: the colors of the Luminor standard.

"It won't last forever, but I've made it self-sufficient for a while." He surveyed his work, looking smug. "It makes you look utterly wild."

I raised an eyebrow.

"That's a compliment."

"Only from you."

We sat another moment, gazing at each other, both of us grinning like fools.

"Linden," I said. "I don't think we're very good at being normal."

"No," he agreed. "But abnormal is much more interesting."

And as the sunlight swelled once more within me, Linden pulled me to him and kissed me again.

45

CHAPTER

An hour later, we made our slow, meandering way back to the pavilion, sure the celebrations would be nearly finished. Linden held my hand, fingers interlaced, and swung it gently as we walked, glancing over at me from time to time with a lopsided grin that made the sunlight grow bright in me all over again.

We had almost come into the lantern-lit glade where the pavilion stood when he suddenly stopped, his fingers tensing. Before I could ask what was wrong, I heard it too: shouts from up ahead. Was it a drunken argument? But then I recognized one of the voices, and Linden and I dropped hands and broke into a run.

". . . overwhelming difficulties over the years—not to mention the last two months! We endured for the sake of this cause, despite terrible opposition, because we believed when this day came you would stand beside us without hesitation!"

We skidded to a halt just outside the pavilion. Yarrow was in the middle of the now empty dance floor, red in the face and shouting down an equally furious-looking Briar.

"We have learned not to be rash—" the old rebel began, but Yarrow cut across him.

"*Rash?*" He sounded incredulous. "This plan has been underway for *fourteen years*, Briar!"

The pavilion had emptied significantly, but there were still a number of villagers sitting on benches or tidying up leftover food, and judging by their shocked expressions, the argument had only just erupted. I located Merrall and Elegy sitting a little distance away from the two old men, and while the banshee looked drowsy and a bit frightened, Merrall's expression was hard and alert.

"Wait a moment," my brother called, voice ringing with authority as he stepped forward. "What did Yarrow mean, they believed we would stand beside them when the time came?"

Briar looked like he was fighting both fury and impatience. He chewed his lip, silently calculating, but it was Sedge who answered.

"Your Highness, Yarrow refers to a plan that was formed in the early years of the rebellion, when he and others left us to find and protect the princess. We thought then that we could reclaim Luminor, that with the power of the sunchild girl at the equinox, we could destroy the Witch Queen's Darkness."

My mind reeled. *We thought then*, he'd said. *A plan that was formed in the early years* . . . And my brother didn't know this plan. Which had to mean—

"We abandoned the idea as ludicrous and fantastical many years ago," Briar said scornfully. "This girl could no more destroy the Darkness than build us a bridge across the oceans to Soleador."

I suddenly felt faint. Was it possible we had come

all this way, endured so much, only to be denied help from the very people who had sent Yarrow and Linden to find me?

"Why did you want me to come here, then?" I asked, stepping forward. Briar and Yarrow both jerked around, looking startled. "You said you sent scouts—said you wanted to find me . . ."

But then I knew the answer. *Of course.* They had their own ideas of how I could be useful. Because that was what I was: A tool for other people's ends.

"You could make our safety here absolute!" one of the rebels called from the benches. He sounded excited, hopeful. "You could bring the sun back, and we could reinstate the rule of Luminor here in the Wilds!"

"Why risk more death in a war we cannot win?" said a blonde woman two seats away from the other man. "If the queen tries to invade, we could offer her a truce, promise the sunchild won't touch the Darkness below the mountains if she leaves us in peace. We could have normal lives again, and no one would have to die for it!"

Many of the rebels were now bobbing their heads in agreement or excitedly whispering to one another. I felt a rush of dizzying disbelief.

"No one wants another war," said one man loudly, to murmurs of assent. "Why should more of us die?"

"The queen doesn't know we're here, and even if she discovers us, we have the power of a sunchild on our side!"

Sedge was one of the only rebels who had not spoken or nodded in agreement; behind him, Merrall's expression was like carved ice, and Elegy had covered her face with her hands so that only her large violet eyes were visible. Beside me, Linden seemed to have grown roots. Yarrow, by contrast, looked as if he was about to erupt: His nostrils flared, and his face had gone crimson.

"Am I to understand, then," he growled, "that this community no longer claims the ideals it held fourteen years ago, when it decided saving the lost sunchild was the most important task it could undertake? That you've abandoned the passion that drove so many good people into the darkest places of Terra-Volat to try and clear the way for the future, when the restoration of the Light would once more be possible in our kingdom?"

Though several people on the benches shifted and looked away, two or three appeared ready to argue.

"I do not think that is our position, Yarrow," said Briar in his calculating tone. "We esteem the princess most highly here, and wish her to use her powers for good."

"For *your* good!" I shouted, blood rushing in my ears. And then I was striding toward him, fury swirling in me like a rising storm. "You just want to use me! And you're willing to abandon an entire suffering kingdom in order to save your own skins."

I poked Briar hard in the shoulder, and he jumped away from me with a cry. There was a ringing silence in the pavilion as we all saw the smoke curling up from the hole I had accidentally singed in his tunic.

I felt no remorse.

Briar's face lost its shrewd calm. "This will be for your benefit more than anyone else's, in case you haven't realized," he snapped, weathered skin flushing dull maroon in the firelight. "Who could prosper from the sun more than a sunchild?"

"And besides," said the woman with blonde hair, "marshaling an attack on Umbraz will likely end in death for most of us, including you. Why should we die for people we don't even know—people who are too lazy to stand up for themselves?"

I felt sick. These people had no idea what life was like in the grip of Iyzabel's manipulation, but they were willing to judge the countless souls trapped there? I suddenly realized why they had given me a dress in the colors of Luminor: they wanted me to feel I had come home, that I was their proud standard, the defender of their peace. I wanted to tear it off.

"So," I said through tight lips, "you would leave the rest of the kingdom helpless against the Darkness? You would condemn generations to die without ever having seen the sun?"

Briar bowed his head. "It is . . . regrettable, to be sure. Do not mistake me. If it were possible to save them . . ."

"It *is* possible, Briar," said Yarrow, who had beckoned to Merrall and Elegy, and turned to walk toward Linden and me. I was surprised to hear his voice was quiescent now, almost defeated. "It is. You knew it once."

I was hardly aware of the walk back to Freda's house, and barely registered climbing into bed beside Elegy. I tried to distract myself with thoughts of the sun, but that hope seemed empty now. Even if I did succeed in using the vernal equinox to crack the Darkness, I could never overthrow Iyzabel's government without the support of the resistance.

If they could even be called that anymore.

Anguish and fury boiled in me as I tossed and twisted in bed, but the warmth I felt did not diminish, even when I fell gradually into a restless sleep that should have calmed the burning. An intensifying heat followed me into my dreams, like a stifling woolen blanket I could not throw off. I tossed fitfully and smelled smoke. I was hot—so very hot.

Somewhere close, a voice cried out.

I threw myself upright, dragging my eyes open just in time to see a large section of Freda's thatched roof shrivel beneath licking, red tongues of flame. As Elegy screamed, a chunk of burning thatch separated from the ceiling and fell onto the foot of the bed, spitting embers and sending flames shooting across the floor into the rest of the house.

We were on fire.

46

CHAPTER

I scrambled out of bed, dragging Elegy after me, and scooped my rucksack off the floor as I charged toward Merrall's cot. The naiad was propped on an elbow beneath the open window, frozen halfway to sitting, her enormous eyes so wide they reflected the flames like small mirrors.

"Get up!" I cried, seizing Merrall by the arm. "Out the window, both of you!"

I grabbed Merrall's rucksack and flung it with my own out into the night, then pushed Elegy toward the window. "Climb down on the limbs," I yelled over the roar of the fire. "I'll meet you outside!"

"What about you?" said Elegy.

"I'll be fine," I shouted, spotting Linden's flower tiara on the bedside table and lunging back for it. "I'm going to make sure the others get out. Hurry!"

"No—" began Merrall.

"I'm a *fire* nymph!" I bellowed, terror for Linden clawing at my chest. His magic was useless against flame. "I'll be fine! Now move!"

For a brief moment when I had woken up, I'd wondered whether I had started the fire with my own excess energy.

But the flames had come from the roof, not from my bed, and I now feared something much worse.

Hiking up my shift, I hurdled the crackling ruin of ceiling blocking the doorway and landed, choking, in the hall. The main room seethed with black smoke and churning flames. I fumbled forward and ran straight into someone who grasped my arm and then crushed me to his heaving chest.

"I've got her, Yarrow!" roared Linden. "Get out!" To me he added, "Merrall and Elegy—?"

"Climbed . . . out the window . . ." I choked.

"Out!" Linden gasped, hustling me forward.

I inhaled a lungful of smoke as we passed through the door, but Linden held me fast, both of us choking as we hurried down the steps of Freda's house. It wasn't until we reached the ground that I fully realized what was happening.

It wasn't just Freda's house that was on fire; it was the whole forest.

Everywhere, people were running pell-mell, screams puncturing the smoky air, and in the distance I thought I heard the clash of steel and the thunder of hooves. Linden and I sprinted toward the trees.

And then, out of nowhere, three men in black-and-silver livery appeared between the tree trunks, and I felt like I had been pitched backward in time, into the Forest of Eli. The men stopped at the sight of us, staring at me as if they couldn't believe their luck. One of them took a wary step back, but the other two exchanged a look of triumph.

"Get her!" the largest of them cried, lunging forward with his sword raised.

I reacted instinctively, shoving Linden behind me and flinging up a sunshield. The sword connected with the barrier and slipped to one side. The soldier stumbled right into the golden, shimmering wall with a crackle, and his clothing ignited. He screamed and stumbled back, flailing against the flames.

As the burning soldier's comrades fumbled to help him, I withdrew the sunshield and hurled a burst of sun energy from each hand, catching both men across their steel breast-plates. They too screamed at the heat, clawing at their chests, and Linden and I bolted past them, farther into the trees.

I was shaking, trying and failing to take deep breaths. Something blurred my vision, and I blinked against it. Where were the others? And why—*why*—had Briar refused to listen to Yarrow's warnings? I clung to Linden's hand, still coughing, and then—

We burst into a clearing as three more people charged through the trees opposite us: Yarrow, Merrall, and Elegy. My legs went weak with relief. I dropped Linden's hand and started toward Yarrow just as he raised his Runepiece with a look of determination.

There was a flash of silver light, a feeling like cotton filling my head.

The world around me disappeared.

I woke with an incredible pounding in my head and a layer like parchment over my eyes. Breathing in earth and smoke, I shifted my sore limbs and blinked. The parchment obscured my vision with an odd, greenish-yellow light. Raising an arm that felt heavier than stone, I shifted the obscuring layer aside and found cool air above.

It wasn't parchment at all; I was covered head to foot in leaves.

I started and pushed myself to sitting. Leaves fell away like feathers from a molting bird. I had been lying in the narrow hollow between two thick tree roots, too tight a fit to be an accident. My skull was throbbing, and my sense of up and down felt nebulous.

I struggled to my knees and squinted through the trees, many of which were charred and blackened. Smoke drifted like fog through the branches above me, and the stench of burned wood and what smelled like meat was powerful enough to make me gag. I was still in the resistance village—I could see a burned-out elf house some distance to my right. The silver light filtering through the Darkness was fading, which meant it was late afternoon. There was no sound apart from the wind in the leaves. How long had I been unconscious? An entire day?

I swayed as I tried to stand, and put a hand to my head. Linden's flower tiara was somehow still there, though slightly crooked. I straightened it.

"You're awake!"

I wheeled to find Elegy charging toward me, her long gray hair dirty and plastered in strands to her ghostly face, which was even paler than usual and streaked with mud. Her old tattered dress was filthy—completely smeared with dirt, soot, and dried blood—but I felt faint with relief at the sight of her.

"Elegy!" My voice came out in a croak. "What happened? Why was I—?" I gestured around my feet at the leaves.

"To keep you safe," she said, reaching for my hands. Hers were cold and trembling, and her voice was shrill. "Y-Yarrow didn't want the soldiers to find you. He thought they might not kill the others if they couldn't catch you. They would want them for bait."

"Bait?" I blinked at her, waiting for her words to make some kind of sense. "What do you mean, Elegy? Might not kill what others?"

"The soldiers tracked us," she said wildly, her luminous eyes darting around the clearing. They were red and swollen,

I realized with a stab of fear, and new tears were gathering in them. "They wanted you, and Yarrow knew you'd never agree to hide, so he enchanted you and hid you—" Her fingers were trembling in mine, and I hugged her mechanically, rubbing her back with numb hands.

"It's okay, Elegy," I said, barely controlling my panic. "Just tell me what happened."

She took a few deep breaths. "The soldiers—Iyzabel's men—b-burned everything. They kidnapped a few and k-killed as many others . . . as they could. Yarrow told me . . ." She swallowed and squeezed her eyes shut. A stream of tears issued from beneath each eyelid. "He told me to hide and watch your spot . . . to m-make sure no one found you."

"You said the soldiers might spare the others? Who—" I faltered. "Who did they take?"

She shuddered. "They took c-captives . . . to draw you. Merrall, L-Linden . . . and Prince Eamon."

A funny lightness swept through my head, and the next moment I found myself on the ground again, trying not to vomit.

"And Yarrow?" I made myself look up at her. Her face was scrunched in a silent sob.

"I-I'm s-sorry, Siria," she gasped. "I'm really, r-really sorry. There was n-nothing I could do—there were so many, even too many for his magic—"

"It's not your fault," I heard myself say, my voice muffled and far away. I felt that I ought to stand up and hug her again, but I could not.

Instead I simply watched her, a pale little wisp of a girl who was far too young to bear such weight, as she pressed dirty knuckles into her eyes and wept for the best father I had ever known.

47

CHAPTER

T"ake me to him," I said eventually. Standing up felt like the hardest thing I had ever done.

Her swollen, violet eyes widened.

"It's all right, Elegy. Just take me to Yarrow, please."

Still shaking with tears, she started back through the trees. I followed, feeling like I was made of wood. My emotions were strangely inactive, as though someone had trapped them deep inside me.

We arrived on the south side of a lane of tree houses, where only the backs of a few smoldering, ruined homes were visible. Bodies lay everywhere on the churned, trampled earth, some marred by a single fatal wound, others rendered unrecognizable by fire or sword. My stomach heaved as I looked at them—people I'd eaten with and danced among only yesterday—and I immediately understood why I had smelled burned meat. My trapped emotions quavered, and my legs stopped moving. I did not want to see what damage had been done to Yarrow. But I also knew I wouldn't believe he was dead until I had seen his body.

Elegy picked her way through the corpses and stopped beside a bloody shape half-covered in a thick traveling cloak. I felt numb all over. Elegy slipped her small hand inside mine and squeezed it.

I forced my neck to bend, forced my eyes to remain open.

Yarrow's body was riddled with minor cuts and gashes, but the fatal blow had clearly been the stab wound in his abdomen, which, in spite of being covered by his cloak, had bled so heavily through the wool that the stain looked almost black. He blurred out of focus as I looked down at him—at his skin, turned yellowish-gray, his familiar mouth gaping slightly open—but I was relieved to find his eyes were closed. I did not think I could bear to see them blank and lifeless.

The anguish I had not yet felt reared its head then, but I didn't glow—didn't burn—and the pain that should have blazed like molten fire spread like ice through my veins and made me so cold and weak I could not hold myself up. My teeth clanged together until the chattering was all I could hear.

I crumbled toward Yarrow, one knee banging the ground and the other jutting alongside me like a broken wing. I felt furious he was gone, furious enough to rip my own hair from my head, yet the yawning gulf opening inside me stole my strength and kept me from even pounding my fist against the muddy ground, as I longed to do. A broken sound came from my throat, somewhere between a groan and a sob, punctured by gasps as I tried to draw in air. I did not want to be here—didn't want to be *anywhere*—without Yarrow alive. With this hole widening inside me like an abyss. My head felt like it would split from the pressure behind my eyes. It was too much to find release in mere tears.

I took his arm—the closest part of him I could reach—and pulled it out from beneath the cloak, wanting to hold his hand. His hand . . . I could feel no curiosity about it, but as I lifted it, I saw that there was something in Yarrow's hand.

Clutched in his stiff fingers, muddy and slightly crumpled, was an envelope made of black parchment.

Without really caring what it was, I tugged it from his grip. The seal was broken, but I could see what it had been: a raven set behind the letter *U*, in green wax. The envelope was addressed to The Lady of Light, Miss Siria Nightingale.

I removed the green parchment inside with cold fingers and pried it open. It was covered in swirly black script:

Your attendance is requested at the Black Palace of Umbraz
To honor the queen of Terra-Volat with a masquerade ball
To take place at midday on the date of the vernal equinox.
Celebrations to include feasting, dancing,
and a royal blood sacrifice.
SHADOW IS MIGHTY AND WILL PREVAIL

For a full minute, I stared at it. I barely noticed when Elegy pulled the parchment out of my hand to read it herself. Then my brain, like a rusty and unwilling machine, creaked into motion. What had Elegy said? That the soldiers had taken Linden and Merrall and Eamon to use as bait?

I took the parchment back from Elegy.

Celebrations to include feasting, dancing, and a royal blood sacrifice.

Iyzabel's men had come for me, but they had not succeeded in capturing me. Iyzabel had probably guessed that, failing my capture, I would want to rescue my friends and my brother, so the soldiers had kidnapped them and left Yarrow, the greatest threat to Iyzabel's plan, dead with an invitation they must have known I would find.

On the afternoon of the vernal equinox.

This meant Iyzabel knew our plan. On another day, it would have twisted my mind to think how she had learned it—Had she guessed? Were we betrayed?—but now the mystery was almost uninteresting. The queen presumably believed like Yarrow that the magic of the equinox would work in my favor if I were in direct sunlight at midday, so she had devised a plan to make certain I would come south at the equinox if her men could not capture me.

Eamon.

Iyzabel was going to kill him. The skin crawled up my arms as I remembered the queen had eaten at least one person's heart in her lifetime. What would she do to him? Did she have some sinister purpose for him, or was the threat on his life simply motivation to send me into her clutches?

Without really noticing how I had gotten there, I found myself bent forward over my knees with my face to the ground, tears making mud beneath my cheek while I clutched the invitation on one side and Yarrow's arm on the other. Rage and loss swelled, and I screamed into the sodden ground until my throat felt like it was tearing.

I did not know what to do. Despair crashed through me in waves, again and again, mercilessly. Yarrow was dead, Linden was gone. Iyzabel was going to kill my brother on the only day I had any chance of becoming strong enough to stand against her, and even if I went to Umbraz now, weak and helpless, to try and save him, I would have no defense. I was only one person—two, if I was heartless enough to drag along a twelve-year-old, powerless banshee as well—and I was empty of sun energy and crippled by grief. And the Darkness of Umbraz, I remembered only too vividly, could suck my power dry even when I was strong.

I clutched Yarrow's hand harder, because there was nothing else to hold on to, and at first I was shaking too badly to realize what was hidden inside his wrist like a miracle. But as I quieted, pressing my thumb against his veins, I began to feel it.

Faint, fading, like a guttering candle at the end of its wick, but still, somehow, there.

A pulse.

48

CHAPTER

I flung myself up, spluttering through mud and grit. "Elegy!" I gasped. "He's not dead!"

"W-what?"

I pulled her down by the hand and pressed her fingers against his wrist. Her eyes widened, but quickly clouded over again.

"Siria," she said quietly, "his pulse is almost gone. I don't need the Sight to know what comes next."

"No, no—you don't understand!" I cried, swiping furiously at the hair and dirt clinging to my cheeks. "I can heal him! Yarrow said it himself—I can heal people!"

I knew I sounded feverish, even hysterical, and judging by the look on Elegy's face, she thought I was grasping at irrational hope. I ignored her, though, and lifted the cloak from the stab wound in Yarrow's stomach. It was ghastlier than I had feared, but I gritted my teeth and covered it with my shaking hands, drawing my focus inward to my sunspot.

I had realized the energy was all but depleted, but I still swore aloud when I found it empty. I flung my mind toward the hazy clouds, even as a tense voice chanted in the back of my mind, *Hurry, hurry, hurry! He is dying, he is dying.*

I dragged sunlight into myself as quickly as I could,

feeling it burn inside my chest. With more concentrated focus than I had ever put toward any task, I closed my eyes and sent the energy into my hands, imagining it as a thin, golden thread, ready to knit his wounds back together.

At first it merely glowed warm in my palms. Then, as sweat broke out on my forehead, I felt the golden filament begin to heal the scrapes and minor burns on my hands. Yet the energy seemed reluctant to move out of my body. *Be master of your emotions*, I thought, squeezing my eyes shut and pounding my focus into one single, unified idea: *Heal Yarrow!*

It was like forcing a frayed thread through the eye of a needle, and I felt I had been sitting in the mud for hours before I sensed it obeying me at last. Unlike firing bursts of sunlight, however, this energy did not disconnect from me when it seeped into Yarrow; rather it seemed to tie me to him.

I faltered as my consciousness followed the light into his wound. There was much more damage than I had counted on, and I could feel my sunlight draining quickly. I didn't dare break focus to reach for more, though, and I could feel myself shaking with the effort of holding on. But I could also feel tiny, incremental changes in Yarrow's wounds. Only a little longer . . .

Just when I thought I might faint from the effort, I felt the most critical part of the injury heal. I drew my attention to the entry wound, knitted the skin together, and slumped back, trembling with exhaustion. The work was barely started, but this would at least keep him from bleeding to death while I replenished my sun energy.

"Elegy, look," I croaked, fumbling for Yarrow's wrist to see if his heartbeat was any stronger. I was so weak I could barely grip his arm. "Feel his pulse now."

She did, and then stared at me in disbelief.

"Can you go find help? Bring back any other survivors? Yarrow won't be well for a while yet, and we'll need help if we're going to try to rescue the others." *Linden*, I thought with another seizure of dread. *Eamon*.

Her eyes grew round, but she nodded before turning and running into the wrecked village. I reached up through the late afternoon Darkness again, and energy poured into me, as welcome as water to a dry throat. I let it fill me past full until it poured out of my skin in golden, smoke-like tendrils, shimmering on the air, then I drew it back in and placed my hands on Yarrow's stomach once more.

It was agonizingly slow work, and I had to stop and refill my energy so many times I lost count. At last the sun sank beyond my reach, and I could do no more. When I removed my hands, the yellow tinge had left his skin and his heart-beat was strong and regular, though he did not wake.

I sagged back onto my heels. Although the air was cool, sweat trickled down my neck and over my temples. I was utterly spent, and weak with relief and hope. But I felt something else as well.

Before, when I had taken ownership of my power, it had been from a desire to be brave, and to defend my people. I had never felt proud of it before. Even the day I had saved Elegy, what pride I'd felt had been for my hard-won courage, not for anything my power could do.

Yet now I saw my gift could be used for truly *good* things. It could save lives. For a while I sat beside Yarrow, simply watching his chest move up and down.

I was just thinking of getting up and rummaging for something to eat when I heard a sound that made me freeze, the hairs on my arms and the back of my neck lifting.

Hooves. Someone on horseback was approaching.

49

CHAPTER

Scrambling to my feet, I hurtled into the shelter of the trees, seized a low limb, and swung myself into the branches. I had climbed only a few feet before weakness and exhaustion made me stop, and I clung to the trunk, praying Yarrow would stay unconscious a little longer.

Had the soldiers sent scouts back to find me? Had they, perhaps, not all left yet? What if they found Elegy?

The deepening twilight made it difficult to see beyond the trees, but as the horses drew nearer, I could make out shifting, muscular flanks, a straggly mane, a man's boot. The horses stopped, pawing at the ground and whuffling, as if their riders knew I was close.

"Siria?"

It was Elegy's voice. They had captured her, then. I closed my eyes, thinking hard . . .

And then a second voice: "Siria, are you here?"

I started, utterly bewildered. It was a woman's worried voice, not a gruff, demanding soldier. And . . . I frowned . . . Wasn't there something familiar about it?

"Siria?" cried Elegy again, sounding tearful. "Oh, what if something's happened to her?"

This was definitely not something she would say to an Umbraz soldier. I clambered back down and stepped out from the trees to gape at the two people on horseback.

It was Bronya and Roark Dell.

"Oh, Siria!" cried Bronya, as if the remarkable thing about this encounter was that I was alive, not that we had met in a burned-out patch of the Northern Wilds, strewn with massacred rebel bodies. "You're all right! We were so worried."

Her husband swung off his horse and went to give Bronya a hand down, and Elegy ran at me, throwing her skinny arms around my waist.

"Elegy says Yarrow was badly injured," said Bronya, coming forward to hug me too. Her deep-brown face showed confusion and pain, and I remembered the strange tension between Yarrow and the Dells. "She said you may be able to heal him."

"I have. Or at least, I've started to."

She looked overwhelmed. "W-where is he?"

I led them to the place where Yarrow still lay in the mud, half-obscured by his cloak. Bronya and Roark crouched down to examine him, and though Bronya's expression was conflicted when she turned back to me, relief showed most prominently.

"He seems stable," she said in amazement. "Your powers, Siria . . . I'm not sure, but I think they're more than anyone could have hoped for. This kind of healing is . . . rare." She turned to her husband. "Let's move him, Roark. Get him out of the mud."

Roark gripped Yarrow beneath the armpits and Bronya took his feet, and as Elegy led them into one of the abandoned rebel houses, Bronya began to explain why they had come.

"About a week ago an Umbraz battalion rode by our farm, heading north," she said. "Roark and I were sure it had something to do with you." She readjusted her grip on Yarrow's feet and glanced fleetingly at her husband. "He decided we should follow them."

I raised my eyebrows at Roark.

"We didn't know what help we would be—if any," Bronya continued as Roark guided Yarrow's shoulders through someone's front door, "but we thought we might be able to offer some small aid if we followed the soldiers. The troops were so vast, we were able to follow at a distance without attracting notice. The only time we came close to being caught was when they all stopped just below the mountains, to build a bridge over the pass that could accommodate horses. I'm amazed to find you here and alive, Siria. The sheer number of them . . ."

"I'd be dead if not for Yarrow," I said, and quickly explained what had happened, including what I had deduced from the invitation in Yarrow's hand.

When I had finished, we were seated in the dark, cramped den of a house that had been built around the trunk of a huge oak, and Yarrow was lying on a straw mattress we had moved downstairs.

Bronya and Roark stared, horrified, at the green parchment invitation I had passed them, and seemed unable to articulate any reply. Elegy was curled like a gray cat in an armchair by the cold hearth, already asleep, and as I watched her side rising steadily up and down, I considered what Bronya had said. If the soldiers had been traveling for over a week, they must have left Umbraz a few days before I found Linden in Polter, then met up with the scout we had let escape, who had led them to the pass . . .

"Weedy?"

The other three started, but I jumped up so fast I banged my head on a low-hanging lamp. I hurried to kneel beside Yarrow's mattress. His eyes were open, but they were bloodshot and glazed. "How are you feeling?" I asked, tugging the blanket slightly higher over his chest.

"Weedy . . . where in the bloody Chasm am I?" His voice was a thick, weak version of its usual growl. "What happened?"

"Don't talk too much. You were . . . injured." I swallowed, trying to clear the sudden obstruction in my throat. "But I fixed the worst of it, I think. We're in one of the abandoned rebel houses. The soldiers have all gone. They took . . ."

I couldn't finish.

"The others," he said heavily. "Yes, I remember that. All except Elegy." He squinted at me, and then frowned and shut his eyes. "Are you all right?"

But I looked behind me, to where the other three sat in their chairs watching. Bronya got up and walked toward us.

"Yarrow," I said, "you'll never believe it. Elegy went looking for help, and she found—"

But I broke off, because Yarrow had gone completely still as he caught sight of Bronya behind me. His gray eyes filled with tears and his hands trembled beneath the blankets.

"Hello, Yarrow," said Bronya gently. "It's been a long time."

His mouth moved, but he seemed unable to speak. And then he croaked, "Ilona?"

I stared at Yarrow, then at Bronya, whose face crumpled in sudden, inexplicable grief as she shook her head.

"No, Yarrow," she said in a choked voice. "It's Bronya. Not Ilona."

Yarrow's wrinkled face closed like a trap, and angry

color flooded his cheeks. Before I could stop him, he had flung off his blankets and pushed himself up from the mattress, limping across the small room to the door.

"Yarrow!" I cried, scrambling to my feet.

I turned to Bronya as the door swung shut, hoping for some explanation, but she merely said, "Damn him!" and hurried after him with tears on her cheeks.

Roark seized a lit lantern, and Elegy and I followed. It was fully dark outside now, and Yarrow was making less impressive progress down the charred, rubble-scattered lane. He appeared to be losing strength, as he kept landing heavily on his right foot and lurching out for branches and saplings. Bronya had almost caught up to him, though her legs were much shorter than his.

"Yarrow Ash!" she said. She seemed to have regained control of herself, for there was no more tremor in her voice. In two more strides she had moved to stand in front of him. "Stop this nonsense and talk to me."

Yarrow made a noise somewhere between a grunt and a snarl and sidestepped her, stumping off into the woods.

Bronya followed, Roark, Elegy, and me trailing after her with the lantern. A short distance into the trees, she stopped, batting branches away from her face as she looked down.

Yarrow was crouched in the underbrush, hands busy near the ground with something I could not see. He did not turn when we approached.

"You're going to hear me out, whether you like it or not," Bronya said to his back. "You've been running from this for too many years."

Showing no sign he had heard her, Yarrow continued what I now recognized as the assembly of a small snare. I almost laughed at the absurdity of it: Bronya had pursued him to the edge of doom to say whatever it was she needed to say, and Yarrow was trying to catch rabbits.

"I'm sorry," Bronya said. "I'm sorry for all of it. But I can't help what happened any more than you can, and if our decision was different from yours, you can't judge us for that."

Yarrow stood up a little unsteadily and fished inside a pocket for more twine before stomping off again.

"We want to help you, Yarrow," Roark called as we all followed. "Put the past aside, man, and let us!"

"What past?" I asked, tripping over a fallen log. "Yarrow, what's going on?"

He grunted but made no reply. Bronya said shrilly, "What's going on, Siria, is that he won't forgive us for leaving the rebels. He thinks that if *he* could carry on after all that happened to him—"

"Bronya," Yarrow snarled, twisting around to face her. It was the first time he had spoken her name, and his voice was so tight with fury it startled me.

But Bronya plunged on, voice wild. "He doesn't understand that some people take longer to heal than others, and other people don't heal at all—they just run from the past and try to forget it by throwing themselves into new tasks they hope will erase the wounds over—"

"*Bronya Dell, I forbid you to say another word!*" Yarrow was on his feet now, and with his bloodstained clothes, his muddy skin, and the mess of twine swinging from his fist, he looked completely deranged.

"No!" Bronya shouted, seeming to match Yarrow's anger. "You *fool*, Yarrow. The time for secrets is over. This girl trusts you with her life. And if you'd stop being so proud, you might notice there are other people who've suffered too, and from the same wounds you have." Bronya was crying now. "Yarrow, my children are not my only loss. I miss Ilona too."

His face twisted—whether in fury or grief, I could not tell—and for a wild moment I thought he might run at Bronya. But then he turned and marched off through the trees again, back toward the rebel houses, branches snapping beneath his feet. Bronya slumped against a tree and sobbed.

I could not understand what had happened. Roark handed me the lantern so he could take Bronya in his arms, and I stood beside an equally bewildered Elegy, not even sure where to direct the light.

At last Bronya's sobs subsided, and she wiped at her cheeks while Roark smoothed back her hair. Dim suspicions had begun to form in my mind. I took a deep breath.

"Bronya," I said, "will you tell me how you met Yarrow?"

She gave me a bleak look. "He obviously would rather I didn't."

"If he wanted to stop you, he shouldn't have left."

She chewed her lip. After a long moment, she nodded. "Yarrow Ash," she said bleakly, "is my brother-in-law. My oldest sister was his wife."

His wife.

His wife?

Even though I had thought the answer must be something like this, hearing it spoken sent waves of shock through me. It was almost impossible to imagine Yarrow—gruff, solitary old Yarrow—with a wife.

"He resents our decision to leave the rebels because Iyzabel killed his family too—his three children as well as my sister. I think he wanted to forget them, forget his pain . . . but anyone could have told him that helping you was the wrong way to do that. You remind him more of Ilona than any other person alive could. It's part of why he loves you so much, I'm sure."

I swallowed, my heartbeat so loud in my ears it made my voice seem muffled and distant. "What do you mean, I remind him of her?" A thousand memories poured into my mind, moments when Yarrow had flinched or balked at the sight of me. Every single one of them since my transformation.

There could be only one answer.

Her lip trembled. "Because, dear heart," she said, a tear catching in her bottom lashes, "my sister Ilona was a sunchild."

50

CHAPTER

When we returned to our adopted tree house, we found Yarrow collapsed on the floor, and I suffered a moment of terror before we determined he had only passed out. After we lifted him back onto the mattress and I used more sun energy to ensure he was continuing to heal, we left him to sleep and went back out into the night.

Yarrow once had—and had lost—children, just like Bronya and Roark. But unlike them, he'd also lost his spouse. He had in fact lost everything, and yet he still came south to find me, to raise and protect me. Maybe he should have faced his grief in the ways Bronya said, but I admired him all the more now that I understood what he had done. Not only had he refused to give up, he also let himself love Linden like a son, me like a daughter. Me, a sunchild, a constant reminder of his dead wife. And though he'd been a little prickly at times, and had struggled to look me in the face after I had transformed, he had never pushed me away.

If Yarrow could be that strong after losing everything, I could do what had to be done now.

"Right," I said as soon as the door shut behind us, and was surprised to find Bronya, Roark, and Elegy looking at me in expectation, as though they had been waiting to hear my thoughts. I blinked in the lantern light, trying muster my courage. "I don't have much time, and we really must tend to—to the dead." I paused to steady myself. "But then I think our paths must split. Can your horses bear two riders?"

Roark frowned. "At least long enough to get us to new mounts. I know a man below the pass who would loan us horses."

"Good. Then I want you to take Yarrow home with you to your farm, and see that he's nursed back to health. Elegy— " I looked at the banshee, who was already wide-eyed and shaking her head. "You're free to go. Stay with Yarrow and the Dells if you want, or go where you like, but I won't put you in any more danger."

"No—" began Elegy, but Bronya spoke over her.

"What will *you* do?"

I sucked in a breath. "I have five days until the equinox, at which point I must be in Umbraz, or Iyzabel will kill my brother, and probably Linden and Merrall as well. And if I'm to have any chance of saving them, I need to see the sun. I'll go north, to where the Darkness ends, and then fly above it to Umbraz."

This bald synopsis of my plan sounded even worse spoken aloud than it did inside my head, but Bronya looked unfazed. "I thought so," she said. "You're like Elysia. But this won't be easy, Siria."

"I don't have much choice."

She nodded. "I know. We can do it, though—the four of us. If we keep switching horses and ride hard, I think we can be in Umbraz in time."

"What?" I said, startled. "No, Bronya, that's not what I meant—"

"You can't think we'd let you go alone," said Elegy, looking profoundly relieved. "We're going to help you, Siria. This matters to us too."

"Elegy, it's too dangerous. Bronya, Roark, please . . . Yarrow's not even conscious."

"But he will be," said Roark with a wry smile. "And can you imagine what he'd do if he woke up and discovered we'd let you run off to Umbraz alone?"

I pressed my lips together. He was right, of course, and I couldn't deny that the offer of help in this mad endeavor was tempting. But I couldn't risk their lives.

"You can't do this alone," said Bronya frankly. "You'll die, and so will the others. If we help you, it's possible you'll stand a chance."

Her expression seemed to finish her thought for her: *Not much of a chance, but a small one nonetheless.*

I bit my lip, thinking hard. Now that they knew my intentions, I doubted I could keep them from going to Umbraz. It would be better to plan with that in mind.

"Fine," I said, rubbing my eyelids. "But listen, then, because time is short." I took a deep breath. "Iyzabel has this urn—a shiny black one—that she keeps with her on special occasions. I saw it the night I transformed. Yarrow thinks it's linked to her power somehow, so if we destroy it, she might be easier to defeat. We also need to find Linden and Eamon and Merrall when we arrive, so I think the best chance will be for you four to split up and enter the Black Castle in disguise. Elegy and Yarrow will have to use his magic and stay hidden, but I think you two"—I nodded to Bronya and Roark—"shouldn't have much trouble getting into the ball if you wear the right clothes and take that invitation."

Bronya nodded. "We can manage that. And I suppose if Iyzabel is in her ballroom, that's where the urn will be?"

"I think so," I said. "So if Elegy and Yarrow work on finding Merrall and Linden—because I think Eamon will be in the ballroom too—then when I come, I can hopefully cause enough of a scene to give you a shot at the urn. And if I have Iyzabel's attention, the rest of you can try to free the others. Elegy, if you sing, you might be able to cause enough panic to get them all out before anyone notices."

She nodded eagerly.

I met Bronya's eyes and saw in her face a mirror of my own feelings: trepidation, doubt, and fear, mixed with fierce determination. It was a weak plan, riddled with holes, but we still had to try.

"Let's pile the bodies," said Roark. "A pyre is less than they deserve, but it's all we have time for."

Even Elegy helped, and we worked through the night, aided by those rebels who had survived and were still too shocked or angry to grieve. I didn't ask any of them to join our suicide mission, but as dawn crept closer to the horizon, two of them volunteered.

"You'll be going after him, won't you?"

I looked around at the sound of the deep, hoarse voice. It was Sedge, accompanied by the elf woman who had loaned us her house, Freda. Like me, they were filthy, covered in dirt, ash, and blood. Freda's wrinkled face bore burns and cuts, and Sedge was limping; a bloody gash in his right thigh had stained his entire trouser leg.

"Briar's dead," he said harshly. "Along with most everyone else who led these people. But that witch took our prince, and I have a sworn duty to help him. If you're going south, I'm coming with you."

Freda said nothing, but her gaze was steely in the light of her lantern, and I remembered what she'd said the night we arrived.

I nodded.

By the time we had finished piling all the bodies we could find into a half dozen pyres, the night was nearly spent. I went from pyre to pyre, setting them alight with fire from my own hands, and the rebels who stood by to mourn choked out thanks, or bowed to me and called me Highness. I wished they wouldn't. With every maimed corpse I had dragged onto those piles, I felt more heavily the weight of my responsibility for their deaths. Regardless of the rebels' failure to reinforce their borders, it had still been my presence that had led the soldiers here. The horror and grief were almost smothering.

Yet I did not have time to dwell on it.

"He's awake," said Elegy as I came, weary and filthy, toward the house where we had left Yarrow.

"Thank you," I said with a smile I didn't feel. "Will you find Bronya and Roark? It's time to get going."

She nodded and ran off, and I went into the house.

"The banshee told me what you're doing," croaked Yarrow from the mattress.

I crossed to sit on the edge of his bed. "I suppose you're going to tell me not to go?"

He gave a dark, wheezy chuckle. "What could I do about it? No, Weedy, I'm not going to try to stop you. As a matter of fact, I think you're doing the right thing."

I nodded, but the pride in his flinty eyes was making my throat tighten again. I let out a long breath and bent forward, putting my face in my hands.

"Oh, my girl," murmured Yarrow, laying a hand on my

back and rubbing slowly up and down. "My brave, hard-headed lass."

"Yarrow, what if I can't save them?" The words came out in a choked squeak as I struggled to hold back my tears.

"You may not be able to," he said. "You may not even be able to save yourself. But we're past the luxury of options, aren't we? You're the last hope of this kingdom, Siria, my dear, and the equinox is the best chance you've got. Use it."

"No matter the cost?" I raised my head to look at him.

His expression was bleak. "If you can kill Iyzabel, banish this Darkness, and ignite the sun? What do you think?"

"I think some costs will always be too steep."

He smiled sadly. "You do remind me of her." I realized that for the first time since I had transformed, he was looking me full in the face, taking in every detail. "Same loyalty. Same passion."

"Someday, will you tell me about her?" I said. "And your children?"

"Someday," he said, though I knew by his tone that he didn't believe that day would ever come.

I stood up and bent down to put my hands on his belly again, sending my sun energy down into the wound to check its progress. It was mending very well, but I did what I could to strengthen him for the journey ahead.

"You could stay here," I said, even though I knew it was pointless to try and convince him. "Safe. Away from Umbraz."

He laughed. "Oh, my dear girl. No, I am with you. Unto death, my little Starthistle."

I leaned to kiss his forehead. "Please," I said. "Call me Weedy."

"Take care of Yarrow." I lifted my satchel, which Elegy had recovered after the fire, and slung it over my shoulder. "And yourselves."

Bronya and Roark, who had been discussing lodging, timing, and distance with Sedge and Freda, broke off their discussion, looking solemn. Elegy hurried forward for a hug, and I felt suddenly—embarrassingly—close to tears again. I squatted down and pulled her into my arms, stroking her head. "Be safe," I whispered, "and do what Bronya tells you."

She nodded against my neck, and I could feel her hot tears on my skin.

"Siria," said Bronya, looking me in the eye. "Be careful." She handed me the lantern she was holding in the waning dark. "We need you, you understand?"

I did. That was what terrified me most.

Roark hugged me, then Bronya did, with a fierce, tight grip. I nodded briefly to Sedge and Freda, then turned away before my nerve could fail, gripping the lantern handle so hard my knuckles ached, and holding back my tears with all my might. But by the time I had walked all the way through the ghostly, charred camp to its northern borders, where the fire seemed not to have reached, I found that I no longer wanted to cry.

I set off into the trees to the north, determination pulsing in my chest as a softer accompaniment to the anticipation now crashing through me like a drumbeat, quickening my steps and stealing my breath.

I let myself feel it fully now, that tug at the center of me, which had been present since I arrived in the Northern Wilds.

At long, *long* last, I was going home.

To the sun.

PART FIVE

"Into the darkness they go,
the wise and the lovely."

EDNA ST. VINCENT MILLAY,
"DIRGE WITHOUT MUSIC"

51

CHAPTER

My energy was spent, so I hiked the ever-steepening woodlands toward the northern peak rather than trying to fly. When dawn came, I would have access to more sun—and when dawn came, I planned to be waiting at the pinnacle.

I considered Yarrow's instructions in a new light now, knowing they were founded on firsthand knowledge of his wife. I wondered what she had been like, how they had met, how old they had been when they married. It seemed plain enough that Yarrow had at least been present through her training.

He had told me that a sunchild's powers were not complete until they stood in the direct light of the sun. But would it be enough? Would my power be strong enough to compete with Iyzabel's Darkness, or Iyzabel herself, once I arrived in Umbraz? Or would she kill me before I even had the chance to try? I had only spent two days using my practical skills, and she'd had a lifetime to perfect her own.

The night began to soften, turning the sky a rich cobalt beyond the evergreens above me. The forest was tranquil, its colors a soothing balm, and I took steadying breaths as I walked.

I was willingly going into a trap.

I raised a hand to the jasmine and honeysuckle wreath still tangled in my hair and felt my chest contract. What was happening to Linden now? Would he try to escape the soldiers, or would he hope for rescue? And what would Iyzabel do to him and the others once they reached Umbraz?

I took another deep breath and thought about the color of the sky. It was becoming more purple than blue. A gentle indigo. I walked faster, my clothes catching on briars and thorns.

I wondered what Yarrow and Ilona's children had been named, how old they had been, before Iyzabel murdered them. Would my name—and Linden's, and Eamon's—soon join that endless list of the dead; those countless names the Darkness had blotted from memory?

The sky was deep periwinkle now, and beyond the pine needle canopy I could see a pack of fluffy clouds in the east tinged with pink. The sun was very near the horizon. I increased my pace.

What would I do now if I knew for certain I would soon be dead? If I knew I had nothing left to lose?

To the east, I could feel the sun's steady presence rising, a low glow beneath the edge of sight. I started to run.

The break in the trees was abrupt, and I stopped on an outcropping of white rock, which wound farther up to the mountain peak to the right and dropped off to the left as a sheer, bare cliff above the roaring sea. Here at last the edge of the Darkness showed itself: to the south, a frayed, hulking dark thing far overhead, whose fingers reached but failed to grasp this last patch of Volatian sky. The place was so remote, I supposed Iyzabel hadn't bothered to push her enchantment over it at the beginning of her reign.

But that was her mistake.

The pink northern sky was exposed, obscured neither by tree branch nor enchantment, and I stared out at it with an awe that prickled my whole body. It was so vast. Bigger than trees, bigger than mountains, and as I gazed up at it—this infinity of glowing color and fathomless space—I saw with sudden clarity that I was a mere speck on the endless scroll of time. The idea was bizarrely comforting. Iyzabel could cover up this majesty, she could starve an entire kingdom of its presence, but in the end she was a speck just like me, and she could no more destroy the Light of the heavens than swallow up the ocean.

Pushing through a patch of heather, I clambered up a rocky rise and stood upon a bleached white boulder. *I am here*, I thought, feeling the sun's searing presence rising inexorably to my right, approaching the skyline and lightening the eastern sky.

The scudding clouds turned a vivid orange, shot through with a color like leaping salmon, and a gold so yellow it made my eyes stream. Never had I seen colors like these: colors that breathed, danced, sang. Burned. And now the gray of the west over the sea was blushing, and the pinks and violets were spreading, casting arms out across it, reaching to lighten the earth . . .

I turned upon the bleached cliff that stood like the last sentinel of the world, overlooking sea, wood, and mountain, and stood as straight as I could, raising my face eastward, and holding my arms out, palms stretched open.

"I am here!" I said, and the first true ray of morning burned red over the rim of the world and fell upon me like a flame.

52

CHAPTER

The sunlight ignited my blood and swept through me like brush fire, burning so hot it was almost as excruciating as my initial transformation in the Black Castle. I gritted my teeth and made myself bear it, knowing it was necessary to complete the process my body had begun nearly two months ago.

But unlike that day, when I had not wanted or understood the change, I was ready for this. I *yearned* for it. It did not feel like becoming a stranger now; it felt like becoming myself.

So I stood still on the white cliff, my back to the sea, and let the sunlight pour through me from the crown of my head to the soles of my feet, through my arms and legs and fingers and toes, through every wild hair follicle, behind my eyes, and into the sunspot in my chest, like water filling a pitcher. The sunlight pushed away my fear, and as it made its way through me, finishing the work it had begun on my birthday, I felt a whole new set of instincts—hazy and half-formed before now—solidifying within me. The skills I had worked on over the last months sharpened like new blades, and I knew I would now have no problem controlling my energy, healing, or even flying. But that wasn't all: I now understood Yarrow's practical training on a more fundamental level, and saw how my sun energy could be used for all kinds of tasks, even beyond what he'd shown me. I was conscious of my powers in a way I had never been before, as if I had been half asleep since my transformation, and now, suddenly, jolted fully awake. I understood, too, that as long as I remained in view of the sun, I would not weary from use of my power; its current running through me was a fathomless, endless source.

Turning my focus outward again, I found myself several inches above the rocky ground, my body hovering as if weightless. Just as Yarrow had said, it was now difficult to make myself return to the ground. I laughed in delight.

When I had planted my feet once again, I crouched to retrieve my abandoned lantern and blew out its flame—now barely visible in the light of the morning sun. Then I rummaged in my satchel until I found the only clean item it contained: the white-and-gold dress the rebels had given me.

White and gold, Linden had reminded me, were Luminor's colors. I shook out the dress and folded it on top of my satchel, then disentangled Linden's crown from my hair, placing it carefully on the folded dress. Then I began to strip off my filthy clothing.

When I was completely naked, I faced the sun once more and let it fill me until the glowing energy seeped in and out of my bare skin as if my body were made of light. Then I stepped to the edge of the cliff and looked down at the whitecapped waves far below.

It was strange to gaze from such a height, to prepare myself to leap, and feel no fear. Indeed, it was strange to do *anything* and feel no fear. But the sun had at last finished my transformation, and I knew myself now. I knew what I could do, and diving three hundred feet into the ocean without hitting any of the craggy boulders jutting up between the waves seemed not only possible, but *easy.*

Sun energy cushioned my impact as I sliced into the water. The air was cold, and the water colder, but warmth encased me as I kicked farther down into the cerulean depths, scrubbing myself clean and letting the seawater carry away the blood, dirt, and sweat that coated my skin and hair. I felt a pang for Merrall when I broke the surface, spraying salty droplets through cracked lips. She would love to be here. Thoughts of the naiad pounded my focus to a sharp point, and I clambered onto a slimy boulder and shook out my hair—curling madly with the salt water—then kicked off into the air.

By the time I reached the top of the cliff again, the sun's warmth—inside and around me—had dried me completely. My bruised ribs and sternum, I realized, were completely mended.

Linden's garland went back on my head, woven into the curls that now glowed with burning light, and I slipped into the dress, which was flexible and had good range of motion. If there was a piece of clothing more likely to cause a wild uproar in Umbraz than this blatantly Luminorian attire, I couldn't imagine it. I laced on Linden's old boots, then dug out my citrine dagger and belted it to my hip beneath the dress, accessible through a slit I cut in the folds. Then I emptied my satchel of everything but the food and water skins I had brought from the rebel camp. My filthy clothes and the extinguished lantern I tucked into a nook between two rocks.

If I lived, I could come and retrieve them. If I didn't, well . . . I certainly wouldn't need them anymore.

Straightening up, I walked to the edge of the cliff and faced not the risen sun but the boiling black presence that swelled like a coming storm above the southern landscape. I would have to fly above the Darkness, where the sun could still reach me, and I would likely have to fly continuously, since I didn't yet know what would happen if I touched the Darkness itself. I hoped that when the time came to break through, the citrine dagger would prove useful. But I wouldn't know until I tried, and the longer I waited, the less time I would have to work out alternate solutions if that one failed.

"Right," I said aloud, squaring my shoulders. "Rise and shine, Weedy."

And as the energy expanded inside me, and light burst from my skin like glittering smoke, I flung myself once more over the side of the cliff and soared upward, toward the malevolent dark crust that had loomed above me for as long as I could remember.

53

CHAPTER

Yarrow had said once that flying was, to a sunchild, more like levitating. *When sunlight hits you*, I could hear him saying, *it draws you upward, like a flower or a tree. Only you don't have roots, so you leave the ground.*

He almost had it right. It was certainly not flying in the sense I had always thought of it: the way pixies or wood sirens or wyrms flew. They had wings and could propel themselves through the air.

It was not so with me.

It was like swimming—the way the water holds you suspended, and yet you can move through it—but even that comparison fell short. The difference was that swimming was an act of immersing yourself in something foreign, disparate from yourself, whereas this union of body and sunlight was like becoming *more* me. I had only to intend a movement or direction, and my body complied.

Soaring above the landscape of pitted, black sorcery that served as Terra-Volat's ceiling with nothing to separate my body from the sun except thin, clear air and wisps of cloud, I could finally appreciate what it must have been like for sunchildren who had lived before Iyzabel's Darkness arrived.

It was sheer, undiluted pleasure.

The idea of going back down beneath the Darkness, separating myself from this power, was unbearable.

But Linden was down there, and Eamon, and Yarrow and Merrall.

I thought of speed, and the endless black beneath me blurred into a smear of shadow.

By the time the sun began its slow arc toward the west, some of my euphoria had worn off, and I was beginning to think practically about my situation again. I had no way of guessing how far I had flown, but the Darkness was still somewhat thin, which meant I was probably only about a fifth of the way to Umbraz. It was an impressive distance to fly in one day, but not nearly far enough. Noon in four days was my focus, when Iyzabel's invitation declared she would kill Eamon, and I needed to be in Umbraz before that.

Beneath me, the Darkness stretched out in all directions like an endless landscape of volcanic rock. It looked more solid than I had expected. From far below, it had appeared to be a cloudy, wispy presence, able to admit rain and snow, though I knew that when I tried to force light through it, I would find it stronger and more substantial than stone. It was relatively easy to keep flying now, even for hours on end, but what would happen when the sun set and its light could no longer hold me up?

I could, of course, try to break through the Darkness now—practice on a weaker point than over Umbraz, and spend the night on land—but if it closed over my head again once I was separated from the sun . . . I couldn't risk that.

Through the remaining hours of daylight, I pushed myself harder, trying to cover as much distance as I could. When the sun finally slipped below the horizon, leaving behind a sky covered in soft, purple clouds, I was as full of sun energy as I had ever been. I wished I could stop myself from glowing to retain the excess energy, but I had to admit the light was welcome company as night fell.

When my light eventually receded and it was full dark, it became much harder to tell where I was heading, and I worried I was flying off course. I fought to ration my sun energy, but that too proved difficult, and soon I was dipping closer to the Darkness than I wished to. I flew slower, more carefully. Every ounce of energy spent felt like something precious slipping through my fingers.

Soon the sky was so black I could not tell the difference between the night and the Darkness. After nearly an hour of slow, blind drifting, my hand brushed something—at first almost solid, then cloying like sap to the touch—which burned so cold I cried aloud, and did not stop burning even as I soared up, away from what I knew had been the Darkness itself. Shaking with the effort to control my sun energy, I sent just enough to my hand to heal it. As it glowed, I glimpsed the skin before it turned back to normal—burned and scaly as charred bread.

I hovered, trying to master my terror. I had assumed I should not touch the enchantment, but I had never imagined that a single brush of the hand would do so much damage. What if the dagger could not break it? And how could I stay away from it if I could not see where it was?

As if in answer to my question, the clouds, which had blanketed the entire sky at sunset, drifted apart to reveal a scattering of silver pinpricks in the dark. As light strengthened and blazed from the bright dots, I realized what I was seeing: the clouds had been hiding the *stars*.

I had once thought stars were just another fairy tale,

like the sun. And the moon too—but there it was, off to the east, rising in a halo of the silver specks that now shone pearly light down onto the surface of the Darkness, making it look strangely and unexpectedly beautiful.

I gazed around in wonder, tears prickling in my eyes. I could see perfectly now, and would be able to carry on all night without trouble if my energy lasted. I tried not to think about how tired I was as I readjusted my course, focusing instead on the starlight, memorizing it so I could describe it to Linden after I rescued him.

When dawn finally reached the eastern horizon, I was so emptied of light that I could no longer fly at all. I hovered a foot above the Darkness, measuring out my strength in determined droplets to keep myself from falling onto the black surface, and clenched my teeth with such force it was giving me a headache.

The stars had faded, and the moon was a pale shadow in the west. The sky was silvery blue, lightening minute by minute, bringing the sun ever closer—yet I wanted to scream for it to hurry up. My arms ached from being clamped to my sides.

"*Come on!*" I bellowed.

My eyes were fixed on the Darkness, along with all my hatred, but in the periphery of my vision I could see the sky turning pink again. "You're not having me today," I snarled down at the pitted surface.

And then, just when I thought I must fall, the first beam of light broke the horizon. I shot up, into the infinite, deep blue, pulling the new rays into myself as I went. "Where have *you* been?" I demanded of the rising sun, which merely beamed at me. "We have work to do!"

The sun made no reply, but even the inky Darkness glowed molten gold as the brilliant rim crested the lip of sight and spread its rays across the infinite sky. I breathed deeply, gathering my wits, and carefully slipped my satchel around to my chest so I could reach a bit of food and water. Who needed sleep? I was a sunchild, and in four days the vernal equinox would give me all the strength I needed.

CHAPTER

54

Yet they were the longest four days of my life. The daylight hours remained intoxicating with their light, and the night brought moon and stars, but lack of sleep took its toll. I began to dread the nightly return to darkness. I focused with obsessive intensity on the enchantment below me, marking its changes to determine how close to Umbraz I had come. It was like following the landscape of some enormous, gruesome wound: the closer I came to the Royal City, the more the Darkness seemed to fester and boil.

But at last, on the morning of the equinox, I arrived.

While the sun climbed toward its zenith, the Darkness thickened and curdled below me, roiling up noxious, green-tinged clouds from its craggy surface, as if the enchantment here were boiling beneath a cauldron fire. I steered myself into this thickening fog, though it made me choke and gag, and found all the proof I needed: at the spot where the agitation seemed most intense—the Darkness shifting and swirling, sometimes appearing solid, other times like melted onyx—a dark terror curled into my chest, wrapping like a cloak around the place where my sun energy dwelt. It was a familiar anxiety—the fear that had nagged me my entire life beneath the Darkness.

Except now I had an antidote.

I closed my eyes and turned my focus toward the sun, still on the eastern side of its slow ascent, a little over an hour from midday. One hour from the equinox.

Drawing the citrine dagger, I let the sun fill me as completely as I could, trying not to think about Linden or Merrall, or what exact time Iyzabel planned to murder my brother. Instead I tried to remember what Yarrow had said about the equinox. He'd said there had been festivals on this day, and that sunchildren would join to send their light into the reaches of the sky as a symbol of peace. At noon they became as bright as the sun itself, soaring above the people like beacons of hope.

Hope. It rose within me, swelling in a great bubble that pressed painfully against my heart, containing the names of the people I loved most in the world: Eamon, Yarrow, Bronya and Roark, Merrall, Elegy.

Linden.

If they were not reasons to hope, I did not know what was.

I turned my face up and the sun pressed red, fiery light against my closed eyelids. I lifted the dagger and invited it in.

A rushing, roaring sound filled my ears. I opened my eyes. Sunlight poured into me, filled me, burned me, so I knew I was but a small star beneath the brilliant orb. The sun and I hung above the Darkness like a pair of challengers before a city gate. I turned my burning eyes toward the enchantment, the disease that hulked resolutely black above my kingdom, and fury stirred in my heart.

My kingdom. Not Iyzabel's.

My people suffering beneath.

The sun's energy rushed through me, out of me, down toward the Darkness as the endless light flowed into my body like an ewer pouring into an overflowing glass. Only now we were both infinite, the brilliant morning sun and I, and I was the conduit that sent the sun's energy speeding down into the curse that had been built to contain it.

The Darkness seethed and heaved at the point the light touched it, wisps of smoke coming away with a smell like burning pitch, while sunlight rushed toward it in a scorching cataract. My body shuddered with the strain as the Darkness resisted, churning against the light. I hoped I would not shatter before the Darkness did.

I gripped the citrine dagger. With a wrenching effort, I forced as much energy as I could through my own body, down the blade, and into the pillar battering the Darkness. I gritted my teeth at the heat and screamed until my throat tore.

From below, I heard a deafening *crack*. Plumes of smoke issued from the black surface, curling long fingers from a spot far below me where the sun had pierced it. Though my body shook, I redoubled my efforts toward the weak point. There was a screeching sound and a jagged fissure opened, revealing the capital city far below in a blur of smoky gray and green. Another deafening screech, and the crack widened to a gaping hole.

Brimming with sunlight, I gave the sun one last look.

"*Luminor*," I whispered, and flung myself into the fissure.

CHAPTER

55

I landed in the cobbled courtyard of the Black Castle amid a cacophony of screams. The hole in the Darkness was blinding against the black, a wall of sunlight cascading from one end of the courtyard to the other. I could hear people running, screaming, desperate to escape the light—or perhaps me. And while I understood their terror, there was nothing I could do now to assuage it.

I could still feel the pull of the sun, feel it warming my head and filling my chest, but the green light, cobbled streets, and familiar sounds of Umbraz brought back a wave of my old fear. As I stepped out of the wall of light, I could sense the sun retreating, giving in to the Darkness. The fissure did not snap shut, but it was only a few seconds before the Darkness had shrouded the light, and less than a minute before it sealed itself and covered the sky as if the sun had never been there at all.

I was alone.

I did not release my light, though. The plan was to attract attention. Slipping my hand into my skirt to make sure my dagger was ready, I let the sunlight drift around me in a shimmering cloud of gold, and walked, straight-backed and swift, toward the steps of the Black Castle.

The green lamps seemed weak and sickly beside my light, and in their shadow I almost didn't notice the glimmer of silver as something shifted at the top of the stairs. I stopped halfway to the top.

A group of soldiers stepped forward and stood in a phalanx of armored bodies above me. They each held a drawn sword.

"The queen will see you, sunchild," said a man in the middle.

"I assumed as much," I said. I hoped my friends had managed to accomplish some of our goals, but the equinox was close now and I could not delay. I started up the steps again.

"You must submit to being bound," said the soldier, holding something out. It was black, and gleamed when the light hit it. An obsidian band.

I stopped dead, raising my hands in warning. "If your queen wants to talk to me, she's going to do it without that thing."

The soldier nodded to one of his comrades, and the wall of silver armor parted as a tall, dark-haired man was shoved through. I would have known his face anywhere, which was the only reason I recognized him.

Linden's wild hair had been cut short and combed neatly back, his stubbly jaw shaved, his well-worn jacket, cloak, and deerskin trousers swapped for a dapper black tailcoat and breeches. A silk cravat had been tied around his neck, and his boots replaced with a pair of fine, black leather ballroom shoes.

He should have been brutally handsome. Instead he looked like a marionette.

The only thing about his attire that was not in strictest keeping with the current fashion was his left sleeve, which had been cut away at the shoulder to reveal his bare, wiry arm, ending in a clenched fist. His skin was unadorned, except for the black, obsidian band that had been fitted around his upper arm. As his chest thrust forward in response to someone's prod to the back, he grimaced down at me, green eyes bright and agitated. He seemed to be shaking his head very slightly.

"You will submit," said the soldier again, raising his sword toward Linden's neck, "or your friend here—"

I didn't let him finish. Snarling, I sent a bolt of sun energy smashing into his chest, and he staggered back with a scream, clawing at his armor as I had seen the man in the forest do. But in his place, more soldiers swarmed down the steps toward me, and I almost tripped in my haste to keep them in front of me as I shot sunlight from both palms, blasting as many as I could while their numbers continued to swell. I had brought a dozen of them down before another voice bellowed, "Stop, or they all die!"

My head jerked up. At the top of the steps, bound and gagged, each one with a sword against their throat, stood Yarrow, Merrall, Elegy, Bronya, Roark, Freda, and Sedge, all dressed in Umbraz fashion. The sight of them hit me like a physical blow, and I swayed a moment, fighting to regain my breath.

I scanned the soldiers, but even at a glance I knew there were far too many. I could not take them all down before at least one of my friends died. And Eamon was still trapped in the castle with Iyzabel.

I had to get inside.

"I'll bargain for their lives." I lifted my hands in surrender.

"If you'll release them, and take off their bands, I will let you bind me. You can set up a magical barrier to keep them out of the castle if you like, but I want them escorted safely away and freed before I will allow you to touch me."

Yarrow's eyes flashed like flint sparking flame, and he and Merrall both shook their heads wildly. Their guards jabbed and jostled them, and I started forward again, flames blazing up in my hands. The swords moved to press harder against all of their throats, and I stopped.

"Do we have a deal?" I demanded.

Two of the soldiers were conferring, but after a moment, one of them nodded. "If you move so much as a hair before the prisoners reach the gates, sunchild, we will kill them all. Do you understand?"

Beyond the heavy Darkness, I could feel the sun climbing toward midday. "Yes."

They led my friends away. When the entourage stopped just beyond the gates to the courtyard, they stepped apart so that I could see, through the gloom, the black bands removed from Linden's, Elegy's, Merrall's, and Freda's arms. No band was needed for Yarrow, of course, if they had taken his Runepiece. I half hoped they would fight, half prayed they wouldn't. Then a greenish light flickered, and my friends disappeared from view. The shield was in place.

As I watched the pack of soldiers march back across the courtyard toward us, trying to think what in dark night to do, I felt someone grasp my sleeve and yank. I whirled as the white fabric ripped, but something had already clamped around my upper arm, constricting it in a solid, inexorable grip.

I looked down at the obsidian band in horror even as I felt its power seep through my chest to the sunspot in my core and imprison it within a dark, impermeable shadow. The sunlight on my skin blinked out, and I felt my whole body weaken.

I raised my head.

Queen Iyzabel released my arm, her midnight-blue eyes glittering beneath kohl-painted lids as she smiled. "Welcome back to Umbraz, sunchild."

56

CHAPTER

She didn't even need to touch me to compel me forward; she merely twitched her obsidian-hilted dagger and I drifted after her as if on wheels. It felt as though someone had swapped my brains for wool. Why had it never once occurred that she might actually rob me of my powers? Now that she had, I couldn't think of a single thing to do. I would be more useless than Eamon when the equinox hit.

Unless . . . Could the equinox possibly help me break free? It was the only hope I had left.

Just as I had once followed Madam Pearl through the great, ebony front doors of the Black Castle, a lifetime ago at least, I now followed the Witch Queen, my feet skimming the marble floor and my hands clamped to my sides as her soldiers flanked us into the cavernous entry hall.

"Meet us downstairs," she said to one of the soldiers.

Then she raised her silver knife and used it to draw a large green circle in the air, which she flicked at me. The circle floated like a smoke ring and dropped over my head, falling past my shoulders, my hips, my knees, to settle on the stone floor around my feet so that I stood within it.

The floor beneath me disappeared. I plummeted through

empty space, and I couldn't breathe enough even to scream. Iyzabel, the entry hall, the green light—everything—had vanished, and all I could see flying past me was a whirl of shadow, as if I were passing through solid matter transfigured into smoke.

Suddenly the ground rose at me in a moment of clawing horror, and then—

Solid stone broke me apart like cliffs wrecking a ship, and for a moment all I knew was blinding, shattering pain. I gasped where I lay, robbed of air; and when it returned, garbled cries poured out of my mouth beyond my heed or control. Both my legs had broken below the knees.

I scrabbled helplessly with my hands, lying on my side without even the strength to raise my head, and my screams become a hideous, guttural sobbing. Nothing, not even the arrow through my arm, had ever hurt as much as this.

"Shut up," said the witch above me in disgust, and my voice broke off as if someone had stolen it.

Her sharp footsteps receded, and though tears continued to course down my face and pool in my hair, the enforced silence had awakened me to reality. *Eamon. The equinox.* With a tremendous effort, I wrenched my thoughts away from my legs and strained to peer around. We had arrived inside some kind of crypt; it was dark, damp, and cold, and green torches shone rather than lamps. The floor and walls were stone. On one side, they recessed into a narrow staircase, and on the opposite end a range of iron bars separated shadowy catacombs from what appeared to be an embalming chamber.

A shiver ran the length of my body as I caught sight of the shelves and tables along a third wall, cluttered with glittering vials and evil-looking tools . . .

And the raised marble slab, upon which lay an utterly motionless, black-haired young man.

Eamon.

His eyes were closed—one of them seemed to be bruised and swollen shut—and his hands and feet had been bound with the straps anchored to the slab. There was no reason to tie up a dead man, I thought with a small burst of relief; and sure enough, I could see the slight rise and fall of his chest. It wasn't too late.

"Ten minutes to the equinox," barked Iyzabel to the aproned and bespectacled men bustling around the tables. "Get the other slab in place and move the girl."

"No!" cried a voice from somewhere beyond Iyzabel, and while it was a voice I knew well, I couldn't understand how it could be here. "No, you haven't—you can't have—" Linden's yells were wild, hysterical, senseless, and I could see his long hands gripping the bars of the shadowed catacombs.

I gaped. How had he gotten here? I had *watched* the soldiers escort him—

"Hush, boy," growled another voice I knew, and my thoughts spun into freefall. Yarrow too?

It was impossible. They were safe, I was sure—

But as I squinted to see beyond the bars, I caught sight of Linden's shadowed face—filthy, thick with stubble, hair still wild and overgrown—and the truth hit me like a blow to the head. The people I had seen escorted to safety in the courtyard had not been my friends. They had been . . . illusions, I supposed, or strangers disguised by enchantments to look like them. And all along, the people I loved had been locked in this dungeon . . .

"Siria? Is that Siria you've brought here, Your Highness?"

This time the voice was a woman's; familiar, but not

Merrall's throaty tones, or Bronya's or Elegy's voices. I could see nothing behind the bars but another shadowy figure, but the voice was hopeful, refined, sycophantic. And as I recognized it, the bottom of my stomach fell away.

It was Milla Nightingale.

Iyzabel ignored her, focused on something her spectacled sages were doing.

"Siria!" Milla shrieked, a pale, clawlike hand shooting through the bars of the catacombs to grasp at empty air. "Tell her we're innocent! Tell her we didn't know what you were! *Tell her!* You know we don't deserve this! We have always, *always* been loyal to the queen!"

Iyzabel flicked her silver knife once more, but this time the jet of light flew toward the catacombs, and Milla fell abruptly silent. Despite the sting of her words, I hoped Iyzabel had merely silenced instead of killed her. How long had Milla been in this dungeon? Had she been tortured in an effort to gain information about me? The thought made me sick.

But I didn't have long to brood on it, because Iyzabel's soldier thugs came for me then, one of them scooping me so carelessly off the ground that, had I been allowed my voice, I would have filled the crypt with my screams again. Every slight movement sent fresh waves of agony through my legs. When he set me down, it was another few minutes before I came to my senses enough to look around once more.

I had been given my own slab, right beside Eamon's. I lay gazing at him for a moment, trying to guess the extent of his injuries, but then something behind him drew my eyes. Sitting amid all the cruel-looking instruments and strange vials on the table near the catacombs was a large, shiny black urn. The same one I had seen beside Iyzabel the night of the Choosing Ball.

Could I get to it somehow? My mind spun like a stormy whirlpool.

Apart from the obsidian band, I had been left unbound, presumably because Iyzabel thought I would be helpless on a pair of freshly broken legs. I was inclined to agree, but perhaps she would bring the urn closer. I closed my eyes and lay limp, hoping they would think I had fainted, but my thoughts galloped at a breakneck pace. The obsidian band blocked my connection to the sun so thoroughly that I could no longer detect how close it was to its peak, which meant I would have to rely on Iyzabel's countdown to know when the moment came.

But why was she counting down at all?

She clearly hoped to use the equinox for something too . . .

Could I beat her to it?

"Five minutes, Majesty."

"I just need to link them," said Iyzabel from near my head. "Remember, we have only one minute when it starts, so work quickly."

Someone came with a rope and tied it around my middle, pinning my arms to my sides. Then, nearly shocking me out of my feigned swoon, Iyzabel drew a long, icy-cold line below my collarbone—with that familiar tingle of magic— and something jolted my insides from head to foot—sharp, tingling, and slightly painful. It was like a splinter that went through my whole body, as if something huge and new had been added to the very fabric of my being.

Beside me, Eamon twitched and gave an almost inaudible gasp, and I realized what had changed . . . what Iyzabel had done. *I just need to link them*, she'd said. I couldn't fathom why, but I was sure that if I opened my eyes, I would see a thread of magic binding our two bodies together.

It was as if my brother's body, soul, and mind had been shoved in like an extra layer on top of mine. I was aware of every part of him—every bruise, wound, thought, heartbeat, and fear—just as I was aware of mine.

But that wasn't the most shocking thing.

I was also now aware that Eamon was very much awake.

Don't look at me, I felt him think, urgently. *She cannot know . . .*

I knew exactly what he meant, and as I thought it, I felt him feel me think it—and the bizarreness of it all nearly threw off my focus.

Eamon, I'm going to try and use the equinox.

He knew already. Of course.

The urn, he or I thought.

I'll smash it, said Eamon.

"One minute!" Iyzabel's voice was ragged and hungry.

By tiny degrees, I inched my hand into the slit in my dress.

"Forty seconds!"

Eamon was tensed like a cat ready to spring.

"Twenty-five . . . Twenty . . . Ten . . ."

I tried to keep my breathing slow and level, my eyes softly closed. In the folds of my skirt, I found the hilt of my dagger and wrapped my fingers around it.

"Five!" Her voice was very near now, and I suspected I would find her knife raised over Eamon or myself if I opened my eyes.

"Two!"

"ONE!" I bellowed, and ripped the citrine dagger free of its sheath, pouring all my thought, strength, and hope into that yellow jewel in the hilt as I twisted my wrist up and pointed the blade toward the sun.

57

CHAPTER

The sun answered.

Light exploded through me in a roar of sound and brilliant gold, and I hauled myself to sitting as the obsidian band clattered to the floor and my ropes fell away in smoking ruins. My connection with Eamon broke.

Without pausing to think, I raised my hand and sent a torrent of sunlight smashing into Iyzabel's chest. She shrieked and fell back, but I did not wait to see how she fared. I flung up a sunshield in front of Eamon and myself with the dagger, and put my free hand to one leg, where I poured healing energy as fast and thick as I could. The power of the equinox surged through me like fire, and my legs were healed almost as soon as I touched them. Next moment, I swung sideways to slice through Eamon's bonds, and with a movement like a wildcat, he leapt off his slab and crossed the crypt at a run, scattering sages and glass bottles alike as he lurched for the urn. In one swift movement, he lifted it above his head and hurled it at the stone wall.

I watched, transfixed, as it soared through the dark crypt, its gleaming surface flashing in the light of the green-flamed torches, and then—

The urn exploded with a sound like lightning striking, and fine white powder shot up the wall and across the floor in a dusty cloud. Iyzabel, who had only just managed to overcome my attack, whirled around to stare at the wreckage, and for a moment the crypt went entirely, eerily still. Then she turned toward Eamon, and the sound she made was anguished, furious, and hopeless at once. She seemed for a moment to forget even about her magic as she lunged for him, apparently thinking to tear him apart with her bare hands. I blasted her back with a burst from my palm, and she fell with another shriek of agony, face contorted, and fingernails raking at the stone floor like a wild animal.

"Lomac!" she screamed. "*Lomac!*"

Lomac?

"This is your fault!" she shrieked at me, pointing a shaking finger and scrabbling at the floor for her dagger. "Your fault, and my wretched sister's! No one should have magic except me! No one else can be trusted with it!"

The unbounded current of the sun's power ebbed away, and I was left with just my full sunspot once again. The equinox's moment had gone, and now I was disconnected from the sun. Iyzabel, however, still had full access to the Darkness.

I darted forward to try and snatch her dagger off the floor, but she got there first, and her streak of black lightning hit me so hard I crashed into the table Eamon had just vacated. But the blast did more—and it seemed to be more than even Iyzabel anticipated. The binding thread of magic she had used to connect me to Eamon still clung to my chest like a glittering purple cobweb, and it rose to answer the blade that had made it. Before I knew what was happening, the purple thread uncoiled and shot toward

Iyzabel—and then for a moment we were joined just as Eamon and I had been.

Raw, desperate fury coursed through me—through us—but just as strong was the surge of agonizing grief that throbbed like a wound that wouldn't heal. Flashes of memory beat into my mind, each crashing and breaking like a wave against a cliff, there and gone with relentless speed: *Serving beer to rowdy men in a dark, crowded pub, and across the room, a tall young man appeared with fathomless black eyes and pale skin that flushed occasionally deepest, stormy blue. He glanced at me, and a delicious shiver ran down my spine. Sitting in a bright cottage parlor filled with laughter and chattering female voices. My head splitting with pain at the presence of so much light. A woman shouting at me to make myself useful and start cleaning fish for the supper, while a rosy-cheeked, freckled girl with orange hair smirked at me from her chaise lounge by the window. My beloved fisherman father, glassy-eyed and dead in a casket, and me, alone. A night of blessed, true darkness, skin against skin and exquisite sensation with the tall young man from the pub. Standing tall and furious on the banks of the Elderwind River, obsidian dagger in hand while Darkness churned overhead and Lomac took water from the river and made it seethe with hurricane vengeance. Then a man, middle-aged, grim-faced and silver-eyed, who walked ahead of the advancing army to meet us, a Runepiece raised in his hand. Lomac, dead in a pool of his own cold water while the mage stood over him. Storing ashes in an urn while tears burned hot streaks down my cheeks. Months turning into years of searching books for ways I might bring him back, lessen this desperate, empty loneliness.*

Iyzabel burned with cold, raging urgency, as did I, trapped alongside her, and I felt her awareness of me triple her wrath. And then, even as she tried to keep it hidden from me, I became aware that her idea had been to use my raw magic and Eamon's body to resurrect this Lomac, this witch she had loved, in an effort to alleviate the terrible loneliness that haunted her. Then to take vengeance on Yarrow, to eliminate the last threats to her Darkness, and finally to live secure in her kingdom of Darkness. Happily ever after, worshiped, indulged, like she deserved.

Iyzabel screamed and shoved me out of her head with another bolt of black lightning, disintegrating the linking thread. I staggered, but before she could do anything more, I flung out a hand and sent a sunburst at the pile of ashes across the crypt.

There was a crack as it hit, and the dusty pile burst into flame.

58

CHAPTER

Iyzabel's scream was inhuman. A blast of green light sent me sprawling backward again with a cold burning in my shoulder, and I landed hard. I blinked, and for the first time since I had arrived in the crypt, I found my gaze directed toward the vaulted ceilings.

For a split second, I froze.

High on the damp stone walls, a collection of mounted heads gleamed in the torchlight—but they were not animal heads, like I had sometimes seen in pubs and inns. Everywhere I looked, the blank, dead eyes of some magical being gazed back at me: satyrs and she-fauns, naiads, elves, pixies, dwarves . . .

With a sick jolt, I recognized one of them: Beq, the dwarf woman who had sheltered us in her home before betraying us for the sake of her son. Her eyes looked sad, even as empty, marble orbs.

I barely saw Iyzabel move—perhaps she could become shadow herself—before she knocked me onto the floor yet again, and I just got my hands up in time to save my throat from her dagger. I lay beneath her, the blade cutting into my palms as I held it back, while an acrid, cloying smoke curled from the silver where it touched my flesh. Iyzabel looked like she had transcended fury and landed in some distant realm where mere anger was a charitable virtue. Somewhere, I could hear Eamon bellowing as he fought her men, and beyond that, the shouts of my friends in the catacombs.

"Do you like my collection?" Iyzabel hissed. Her knife moved a fraction of an inch closer to my neck. "It's taken me years to assemble them all. I have one of every species."

I gritted my teeth, knowing she meant people, not animals. My arms trembled, and the light burning inside my skin made it look like thin, speckled paper. With yet another plunge in my stomach, I understood how Iyzabel learned we were heading north for the equinox. Hadn't Beq's house been the first place Yarrow attempted to explain our plan?

"Did you hear me, sunchild? I said I have one of *every* species."

My eyes were locked on hers, and I refused to move them an inch. I didn't want to see what she was gesturing at, because I already knew what it would be. The knife edge grazed my neck, cool and sharp, and dug still farther into the flesh of my palms. I could feel hot blood beginning to run in rivulets down the sides of my arms.

"Siria, look," said Iyzabel, and I was so startled by her use of my name that I did look.

The real thing was even worse than I had imagined. I didn't know whether it was Yarrow's wife or some other poor sunchild Iyzabel had killed during the overthrow, but she was waxy and pale on the wall, in spite of her deep-russet skin, freckles, and vivid curls. Unlike the coppery red that dominated my own hair, this sunchild had shocking yellow hair, like gold caught in bright firelight.

In another moment, I knew, my head would be well suited to join hers on the wall.

I looked back into Iyzabel's eyes, dark blue with a neb-ulous black shadow drifting over the irises, and knew that whatever motives she still had for keeping us all here, my desire to get us out was stronger.

"What have you got, you mad old witch?" I gasped. "Manipulation? Power?" I did my best to sneer. "*Darkness?*" I heaved sunlight into my arms and felt the blade lift slightly. "Those things may be enough to take a kingdom, *Your Majesty*, but they aren't enough to keep it."

"What do you know about it?" she hissed, redoubling her efforts on the dagger even as it sparked and smoked, a churning cloud veined with gold. "You're just a child."

"Maybe," I said, my voice growing stronger as the light around us swelled. I pushed her farther back. "But I've lit enough candles in my short life to have learned the most important thing."

"Oh really?" Iyzabel tried to look scornful, but I saw her eyes dart from the growing light around me to the roiling smoke coming off her knife as I gripped it. "And what's that?"

I smiled at her. "Light beats darkness. Every time."

With a tremendous, bone-rending effort, I sent all the sunlight I could into my hands. There was a deafening crack, and the blade of the obsidian dagger poured through my fingers in a fine, silver powder. Iyzabel toppled sideways off me, eyes huge, mouth open in silent horror as she gripped the useless hilt.

"Soldiers, to me!" she shrieked, scrambling to her feet.

But I drew my own dagger and flung a blast of sunlight straight at her chest, where it collided with a blinding flash. Smoke poured thick and fast from the spot, enshrouding her as she fell to the stone floor.

"Eamon," I shouted. "Get the others out!"

I had counted almost thirty of Iyzabel's soldiers, and all of them were now running toward either their queen or me. With all the sun energy I had left, I raised a shield to split the embalming chamber, trapping the soldiers on Iyzabel's side in front of the stairs.

I heard the clang of metal behind me and glanced over my shoulder. Eamon had found a hammer and was swinging it at the catacombs' padlock. Yet even as I stood, pouring strength into the sunshield, I could feel it weakening.

"Hurry!" I shouted.

Eamon grunted, and I heard the padlock break.

A moment later a hand squeezed my shoulder, and I looked back to see Linden, grubby and bruised, giving me a proud, bracing look. Yarrow appeared at my other side, face set. I nodded at him. Robbed of his Runepiece, he lifted a discarded sword, and Linden raised a pair of mace-like clubs that had been lying on the table with the urn. Behind us I could hear the others arming themselves too.

"This is the last of it," I muttered to Yarrow, nodding at my sunshield.

"Then you move to the back with Elegy and focus on getting more. We'll guard you until you do."

I nodded. "On my signal, then."

But another hand forestalled me.

"Siria," said Merrall's voice from behind me, and I turned to find her at my shoulder, a look of fierce approval on her cut and bruised face. "It is an honor to fight beside you."

A lump grew in my throat. "The honor's mine, Merrall."

Something collided with my sunshield before I could turn, and I felt it blink out.

"Now!" I screamed, and stumbled backward as my friends rushed into the wall of soldiers.

59

CHAPTER

Elegy slipped her hand inside mine, but I could not spare her any attention as we pounded after the others—all but Phipps and Milla, who trotted along behind us in mute terror. Harder than I had ever done before, I concentrated on pushing my mind upward, through the Darkness, toward the sun. In the farmlands, it had felt like slipping my hand through the holes of a shifting net, but here it was like trying to push my fingers into a brick wall.

I would never reach the sun without my dagger. I fumbled for it, but Elegy's hand slid out of mine, and I looked back to find that she had stopped where she stood, strangely rigid. The next moment I collided with someone in front of me, and made a wild grab for my knife—only to find that it was Merrall.

I seized her shoulders to steady us both, but she barely seemed to notice. She was staring up at a high wall with a frozen expression. I followed her gaze, to where the countless mounted heads encircled the room like ghastly spectators, and felt as if cold fingers were closing around my heart.

I knew right away which one had caught her attention. He was a young man with a rugged, kind face: handsome, pleasant-looking. Even from a distance, I thought I could detect laugh lines around his eyes and mouth. A fishing net had been draped artfully around his plaque, and his deadened marble eyes stared down into the crypt, blind to the aqua eyes now staring back.

I remembered what Merrall had told me that day at the stream: how she had lost the young fisherman she loved and had been looking for him—waiting for him—for so many years. How despite everything, she had never lost hope of finding him.

My fingers tightened on her shoulders. "The obsidian band!" I hissed, but it was no use. She twisted out of my grip and flung herself forward with a tearing scream, right into a pack of soldiers standing guard around the Witch Queen.

Unlikely though I knew it was, I had dared to hope Iyzabel might die from the last wound I dealt her. Now, however, I saw her standing erect and furious behind her soldiers, black smoke swirling about her fists in currents of raw, undirected power. She had also acquired a sword. With helpless dread, I watched the naiad duck between two surprised-looking soldiers and throw herself on the witch.

"Weedy!"

Linden had come back and was trying to pull me on, but I could not leave Merrall. I tried to tell him this—but as I caught sight of Elegy, just a few paces behind me, the words died on my tongue.

The banshee was bent double, jerking and convulsing as if she were having some kind of seizure, fingers gripping her throat. Her eyes were like violet coins, huge and round, and her mouth opened and closed as if she might be sick.

"No," I whispered.

Elegy gave one last shudder, then released her throat and straightened up again. She no longer looked like herself as she drifted a few inches off the floor: Her eyes were misty white, her face cold and expressionless as marble, her posture stiff. As on the day we had met her, she was glowing with silvery light. And when she opened her mouth, the sound that poured forth to fill the crypt was nothing like the music I had heard her sing before.

It was cold and terrible, like the chill that creeps into your heart when you think too much about the long dark of death, and it sent shivers running down my spine and over the skin of my legs. Despair crowded the hope burning in my heart and extinguished it.

I spun around, but three soldiers were already running across the crypt toward their queen, who bore a long gash across her cheek from the surgical knife Merrall was wielding. Before I could so much as lift my hands, one of the soldiers lunged forward—and Merrall buckled with his blade in her back.

The floor tilted. Something inside me was crashing down, and I had to shout to hear myself over the roaring in my brain. I was only vaguely aware of what I said: "Linden, get everyone into the stairwell!"

"Siria—"

"Now!" I screamed, my voice cracking. "Take Elegy!"

He darted around me to pull Elegy, Phipps, and Milla after him. Through a brief gap in the scrum of soldiers—many of whom were running for the stairs out of terror of Elegy—I glimpsed Merrall's still form on the floor, blood pooling over the stones around her. I felt a desperate desire to heal her, even though I knew I would die before I made it halfway to her body, and I remembered as if from another lifetime the group of blonde and redheaded girls left on the platform the day of my transformation. I had not been able to save them either.

Everything inside me was crumbling, and I could barely hold myself upright.

Crumbling.

I threw a wild glance at the ceiling. Maybe I could not save Merrall, but I could at least give her a proper burial with her love. I could keep her from becoming another head on a plaque for Iyzabel's collection.

With a massive effort, I put aside my grief, dodged a whistling sword, and ran after the people I could still save. I stopped just before the arched stairway where my friends had disappeared and wheeled about to face the soldiers who had not already fled. The sunchild head on the wall seemed to watch me with a touch of a smile as I lifted my arms to point the citrine dagger at the ceiling.

One of the lead soldiers shouted something, but I barely heard him. I closed my eyes and focused upward.

The dagger became an extension of my reach, and I strained up, up through the stone ceiling, through floors of decadent parlors and marble ballrooms, and out of the Black Castle, through empty space, toward the malevolent crust of the Darkness itself. Then I paused a moment to search for the thing all my hope now rested on.

The crack I had made when I arrived.

I sucked in a breath as I found it, my arms shaking as I gripped the hilt of the dagger and pulled with all my strength.

"Stop her!" Iyzabel shrieked, but it was too late.

The first cascade of light came like a stream of dazzling gold, passing through the ceiling and into the crypt with a brightness that made the soldiers shriek. It sped down the dagger and into my arms, so that to create a sunshield I had only to open my eyes and look at the spot where I wanted it to appear. It did, and the first soldier's desperate, blind swing of his sword slipped off like a foot on ice as it met the illuminated surface.

My stomach clenched with grim resolution as I gathered the energy between my hands.

The dagger hilt shook in my grip as the citrine increased the already thrumming power. When it was as full as I could bear to make it, I flung the energy up the blade, and it soared through the crypt with a sound like crackling flames. The noise when it met the ceiling was like nothing I had ever heard—a massive crack, followed by grinding and groaning—and the sunburst ripped a hole in the ceiling as big as a carriage wheel. Chunks of stone fell almost gracefully from it, landing with thunderous crashes on the flagstone floor, which cracked beneath them. But where they struck my domed sunshield, they merely glanced away.

Iyzabel's soldiers were bellowing like bulls, trying to flee to safety, and two leapt right into the path of a falling slab. The queen herself was electric with rage, but without the silver knife, her magic had no control, and it ricocheted off the walls, blasting stone and mounted heads alike. She advanced as close to the shield as she could, teeth bared and eyes blazing as she stalked in front of it, looking for a way in.

Above me, the sunburst was still passing through floors of the palace like a boulder flung from a trebuchet, smashing it apart as it sped, comet-like, toward the sun. The Black Castle trembled from foundation to ceiling, but that was as nothing to what was coming next. I looked Iyzabel in the eyes to make sure she knew, and the hatred I saw in them was all the confirmation I needed.

I turned my head to where the others now stood behind me, grouped on the stairs with various expressions of grief, awe, and terror. "Run," I told them.

The sound that came when the sunburst began its return journey shook the stones beneath my feet. I closed my eyes, and in my mind I saw it: the great, burning sphere, swollen and wreathed in fire from contact with the sun, crashing through the crust of the Darkness and speeding back down the stream of light toward the castle.

Toward the citrine lodestone that was guiding it, held aloft in my hands.

60

CHAPTER

When it struck the top of the castle, the sound was like mountains breaking apart, and the floor pitched so violently I almost fell. The subsequent crashes as the sunburst smashed through countless floors above us were no less violent, and I could hear an eerie moaning from the stone as it strained to hold itself up.

Many of Iyzabel's men were now running for the catacombs, but the queen stood like a pillar of ivory and onyx in the middle of the floor, gazing up at the ceiling. When the next crash came—the loudest one yet—she bared her teeth like a cat hissing.

I braced myself to hold on, to draw the burst of energy all the way to its destination. Light blazed beyond the hole of the ceiling.

And then arms closed around my waist and hauled me back, just as the sunburst ripped the ceiling apart and plummeted like a falling star into the crypt. My sunshield flickered away. Linden's heartbeat pounded against my back as he dragged me beneath the arch of the stairwell, and then there was an earth-rending explosion and a glare of diamond-bright light.

For a frozen moment in the sea of blinding gold, I saw Iyzabel's mouth open in a scream of agony, her veins stark beneath her porcelain skin, thick smoke pouring from her limbs.

And then all sound was sucked from the world as the sunburst buried itself in the flagstone floor exactly where she was standing, opening a great chasm that split the crypt from end to end. The world rocked beneath us, and Linden and I toppled back onto the stairs as a piece of ceiling fell onto the bottom step, crushing the archway and sealing us out of the crypt.

The whole castle was coming down.

I scrambled up and pulled Linden to his feet, and we leapt two stairs at a time, hands grasped tight. About half-way, I felt something strike my hand, and realized Linden's obsidian band had fallen off. Yarrow was waiting for us at the top, pale as death, and I glimpsed Roark disappearing through a door at the end of the room. We fled after him.

I could hear only the deafening smashing of stone and the groans of the walls as the structure swayed. The castle was full of people escaping, mouths open in screams I could not hear over the roar of the toppling building, and I saw soldiers and courtiers alike. I remembered the nymph servants Linden and I had met in the kitchens so long ago, and hoped they would have time to escape.

I counted my companions constantly, mentally stumbling each time I remembered Merrall was gone, and fighting down a searing pain as I saw her motionless form in my mind, harpooned in a bloody pool on the flagstones. Then at last, through an opened door ahead that was crowded with terrified people, I glimpsed a patch of dark sky.

It was a small, wooden door in a part of the castle I guessed only the servants used, and we all scrambled through it, clambering over rubble and bits of fallen ceiling into the smoking, churning air of the wounded Darkness. Outside, we did not stop. The towering onyx structure moaned, and all around the sounds of smashing rock crashed like thunder, sending tremors through the cobbled courtyard.

Eamon seemed to have used most of his strength in the crypt, and Sedge and Roark now supported him as we ran. Phipps and Milla still sprinted alongside us, apparently so focused on surviving that they had not yet thought to go their own way. We didn't stop until we had put several city streets between ourselves and the castle—though even then the ground shook with every distant boom.

It felt unreal to be here, in these same Umbraz streets where I had been hunted, and know the Witch Queen who had caused all my suffering now lay defeated in the bowels of her ruined castle. As we stood and caught our breath, Phipps and Milla seemed to realize the sort of company they were keeping, and shot furtive looks down the empty street beyond. But they darted glances at me too, plainly afraid I might roast them alive if they tried to leave.

"I won't hurt you," I said wearily. "And I've let go of the past." As I spoke the words, I realized they were perfectly true. I now felt only pity for these people whose home, life, and name I had shared, both for their years of emotional enslavement to Iyzabel and the selfishness that had driven them so easily into her net. They had neglected me and failed to love me, but I was lucky enough to have had Yarrow and Linden at hand, ready to counter my feelings of unworthiness with their own stalwart faithfulness. To my astonishment, I felt a tired smile lift the corners of my mouth as I gestured around at them and the others. "I've found my real family."

They nodded, still looking terrified, and turned away. But a moment later, Milla faltered and looked back. "We never wanted to betray you," she said very quietly. Her eyes were clouded with confusion and pain, and I wondered what would happen to her now that Iyzabel's sway had been broken. What would she be like without it? Before I could reply, though, they scuttled away down the street and out of sight, and I watched them go, the last remnants of something tight and frayed crumbling away inside of me.

I took a deep breath, then turned to Yarrow for instruction, only to realize that he and the others were watching me.

"What now, Siria?" asked Sedge.

I looked at each one of them in turn—Linden, standing tall and ready despite his many injuries; Eamon, watching me blearily through one eye as he leaned on Sedge; Elegy, still crying thick, silent tears for Merrall; Bronya and Roark in their opulent Umbraz disguises; and Yarrow, exhaustion in every line of his face, but brimming with pride as he leaned on his stolen sword and regarded me—and then turned back to peer up at the churning black sky above the ruined castle. The new hole I had opened in the Darkness had not closed, but sagged apart like a fatal wound, pouring sunlight in a narrow column down onto the cobblestones.

"This city will be in chaos for some time," I said slowly, "but Iyzabel's manipulation should lift, which will make the transition easier. The critical thing now will be for me to break the Darkness apart more thoroughly and speed up the decay of the enchantment so we can convince people she's really gone. Then we can get Eamon back on the throne."

Everyone nodded solemnly except Eamon, who gave a weak chuckle. "Take your time."

"Obviously, a place to rest and recover a bit is next on the list," I added. "And . . . and I'd like to hold a funeral for Merrall."

There was silence for a long moment, broken only by distant screams and continued, smaller crashes from the castle.

"There's an inn," said Yarrow, "just outside the city. Linden and I used to go occasionally for news. They should have room for us."

Roark nodded. "I'll see if I can find a horse or two."

"And I'll be right back," I said.

A few minutes later I stood once again in the courtyard before the Black Castle, which now lay in a vast, mountainous heap across the once-splendid square. Dust hung like dense fog, eerily lit by green lamps and that single shaft of sunlight, and people wandered, stunned and aimless, amid the wreckage. I hoped there had been enough time for most of the castle's inhabitants to escape before the place collapsed, though it was some small consolation to think there had been no ball underway during the calamity. If *we* had made it out, I thought the servants at least had good odds, if not the soldiers in the crypt. Even so, my heart ached for the deaths I had caused—innocent or not.

I turned my attention to the sky and raised both dagger and palm to the Darkness. It was easier now that Iyzabel's power was broken, and the hulking crust above the city seemed to thin as I drew sunlight through it, pulling apart in places like something weak and fibrous. After a while the sky was full of strange, floating chunks, which seemed to wither as the late afternoon sun glowed down from behind them, casting odd shadows over the Royal City. Fresher air swept in to mingle with the cloying warmth of the Darkness, scattering it like mold on the breeze.

It was a good start.

I turned to leave, and saw the courtyard had filled with timid watchers, all shielding their eyes from the sun they had not seen in fifteen years.

As I crossed the cobbled courtyard, I stopped at the base of the carriage drive, where the large crest of Umbraz had been worked into the street as a mosaic. Pointing my citrine dagger carefully down, I drew a slow, crackling circle of sunlight right in the middle of it, the fiery heat melting right through the stone. Then I added a dozen lines, branching out from all around the circle. I stepped back from it and walked away, knowing it would say as much about the return of Luminor as any crown prince could ever hope to do.

Linden was waiting for me at the gates. He pulled me into a silent hug as I reached him and held me for what felt like a long time. I was ready for food, ready to sit in the inn's common room and drink to Merrall, ready above all else to sleep. But before I did, I wanted to stand and hold on to Linden for just a little while longer.

Eventually we drew apart, and he raised a hand to lift the jasmine and honeysuckle circlet from my head. It was slightly wilted, but still alive; Linden had done his work well. Silently, he took my hand and led me just outside the huge iron gates, where he knelt down and began digging with his bare hands in the hard-packed dirt beside them. Then he took my circlet and broke it apart, planting its ends in the barren soil. His skin glowed with brown whorls for a few moments, then he stood up again and moved aside.

The vines had grown, twisting in and out of each other, across the dirt, up the side of the gate, and into its twisted ironwork, so that the huge metal *U* was totally disfigured by yellow and white flowers.

Linden's hair glowed in the sunlight as he smiled at me. "Welcome back to Luminor, Siria."

I took his hand, and together we walked out into the city, the sun warm on our backs as it sank toward the horizon.

ACKNOWLEDGMENTS

This book has been on a long road—a decade, in total!—and I am therefore indebted to more people than I have space here to thank. But if you ever read a version of the book once called "Sunchild," and gave me feedback, I thank you from the bottom of my heart. You helped this story find itself. Chief among those who read early versions are: my dear friend and critique partner, Amie McCracken; my soul-sister and INFP commiserate, Joanna Ruth Meyer; book-brother, Peter Myers; and fiercest and most loyal encourager, Jaclyn Metcalf. Thank you all for lending your eyeballs and your brains to help me through countless swamps, and for doing it more than once.

I am also immeasurably grateful to my warrior queen of an agent, Jenny Bent, who put me through several mental Olympics with her edits, and helped this book shed its excess and become so much more itself—all before doing the incredible work of finding the book its home. You're a rock star.

To the team at Blink, who have worked so hard to

transform this story from a Word document into the gorgeous tome you hold in your hands, and especially to Hannah VanVels, who fell in love with Siria and her friends first, and to Jacque Alberta, who guided them through the subsequent stages of edits with love and enthusiasm. Thank you! (Mad props for finishing up the production of this book during a global pandemic!)

So much thanks and love to my brothers: Jordan, who wrote "Sweet Sadie of the Glen" for me when I needed a poem about a sunchild, and Adam, the Charles Wallace to the Meg Murray; to my mother, Sandy, always ready with hugs and delicious food when the writing life got hard; to my sister in-law Kelsey, who championed this book from day one; and to my Hutchinson family—Ted, Jane, Heather, Ian, and Cheryl—who cheered me on as readily as they welcomed me into their midst. Your encouragement has meant toe world to me. Also my beloved grandmother, Libby, who wanted to live to see this book in print but missed it by a mere five months. And to my dad, Jerry. Nothing less than death itself could have dragged him out of my corner, and even cancer had to fight tooth and nail to best him. His dogged encouragement and belief in creative passions as God-given fuels me even when every road seemed to end in failure.

To Ashley Sullivan, Emily Persson, Libby Keenan, Bethany Shorey-Fennell, Laurel Baird, and Megan Brown, and Ashley Ford: thank you for cheering me for so long. To my teenagers: thank you for always keeping me up to date on what the kids are saying/doing/dancing these days. You all are the worst, and I love you so much.

To my husband, Daniel, the love of my life, and the Beren to my Luthien: My heart is infinitely richer for the love you give day in and day out to me, to our strange animals, and now to Edmund. I love you more than the Doctor, Harry, Aragorn, and Jamie Fraser combined, and I would totally rescue you from Sauron's fortress if he imprisoned you. Together or not at all.

And finally, to my Lord and my God, without whose grace I am dust and ashes, words without form, and story without substance. Thou, my best thought by day or by night; Waking or sleeping, Thy presence my Light.